HOME BOYS

ALEX WHEATLE

HOME
BOYS

ARCADIA BOOKS
LONDON

First published in Great Britain under the title *The Seven Sisters* in 2002 by Fourth Estate
This revised edition first published in 2018 by Arcadia Books
This paperback edition published in 2022 by

Arcadia Books
An imprint of Quercus Editions Limited
Carmelite House
50 Victoria Embankment
London EC4Y 0DZ

An Hachette UK company

A CIP catalogue record for this book is available
from the British Library.

ISBN (MMP) 978 1 52942 933 6
ISBN (Ebook) 978 1 91135 055 2

10 9 8 7 6 5 4 3 2 1

Printed and bound in Great Britain by Clays Ltd, Elcograf S.p.A.

MIX
Paper from
responsible sources
FSC® C104740

Papers used by Quercus Books are from well-managed forests and other responsible sources.

ALEX WHEATLE MBE was born in South London in 1963 and is an accomplished and award-winning author of more than a dozen books, including children's and young adult novels. The story of his teenage years was the basis of Steve McQueen's "Alex Wheatle" in the *Small Axe* series (December 2020), and he has written and performed a play about his life titled *Uprising*. His novels for adults include the Windrush classic *Island Songs*, as well as *Brixton Rock*, *Brenton Brown*, *East of Acre Lane*, and *Home Boys*. His books have been adapted for theatre, radio and film.

PROLOGUE

Croydon, April 1985

It had been the third suicide of one of Curvis Butler's junior class-mates within five years. In 1980, Samantha Redding strangled the life out of her three-month-old baby, then, with the dead infant in the passenger seat, she drove at high speed, smashing head-on into a concrete pillar. During the summer of 1982, Mark Kelly had launched himself from a platform and met death under the steel wheels of a Northern line tube train. A few weeks ago, Elvin Walker had flung himself off a motorway bridge and died instantly beneath the hard rubber of a HGV truck. Following Samantha Redding's funeral, Curvis vowed never to attend another one. But shared memories tugged at him to pay his respects for Elvin.

A strange sense of apathy overtook Curvis as he approached the house. Flowers and cards showed how popular Elvin had been, but somehow, his friend's death left him numb. When he had heard of Elvin's fate, he couldn't summon any tears. He rebuked himself for becoming immune to the constant knock of death – a visitor that would never disappear.

Curvis swabbed his forehead dry of rainwater as he entered the lounge. Noting the teak-armed furniture, he wondered if he had remembered to wipe his feet on entry into the house. He surveyed the room and picked up a glass of apple juice from a table. The framed picture of a leopard in the African wild, hanging above the mantelpiece, caught his attention and he stood perfectly still, trapped in its gaze.

Elvin's wife, Michelle, who circulated the room, accepting hugs and kind words, noted the lines on Curvis's forehead. He had the eyes of a man who had witnessed bad things, she thought, yet there was a strange calm in his expression that bordered on indifference. She noticed the way he hung his head when he walked, almost staring at his feet. His goatish beard grew freely. He was of slim build but had a powerful presence, something between that of an 800-metre runner and a lightweight boxer. Dressed in an old mac and flared trousers that had been in fashion a decade ago, he was scanning the room as if he had to write an essay about it.

She approached him quietly and touched him on the shoulder. 'Why did Elvin kill himself, Curvis?' Michelle asked. He stiffened before recognising Elvin's wife. 'I know you weren't best friends with Elvin but you grew up with him in *that* home. You knew him better than most.'

Curvis fingered his brown, shoulder-length locks. The glass of apple juice shook in his other hand. He felt that Michelle deserved the truth. But he had been avoiding the truth, blocking it out of his everyday life since he was sixteen. For Curvis, only when death called did the truth return to invade his life. But he was sworn to life-long secrecy. He glanced at the framed wedding photos of Elvin and Michelle resting on the mantelpiece. He closed his eyes as an image of Elvin grew large inside his mind. 'It's … hard to explain what he went through in the home,' he finally answered.

'I thought he got over all that,' Michelle replied. 'The last three years were the happiest of his life. He had a decent job, good prospects and someone who loved him.'

'But all of that couldn't wipe away the memories,' Curvis replied, training his eyes on the leopard.

'What memories?' Michelle raised her voice. 'What happened to him in the home? Why can't you or anyone else tell me about it? I was his wife! Haven't I got the right to know?'

Curvis sipped his apple juice and met Michelle's eyes. If neither he nor any of his peers could handle the past, how then could a poor widow who could never understand or even begin to accept the unacceptable? 'He was picked on a lot, you know, beaten up by the people who were s'posed to look after him.'

Michelle led Curvis to the sofa and ushered him to sit down. Curvis hesitated before taking his seat. 'Go on,' she urged.

'That's basically it. That's all we know. Every now and again his housefather would pick on him.'

'Everyone gets a walloping from their mum and dad now and again,' Michelle said. 'There must've been something else.'

'Not that I know of.'

'Not that you know of? You're a liar! Just because people get picked on when they are kids doesn't mean they gotta kill themselves when they're adults!'

Michelle wiped her eyes as Curvis's discomfort spread through his body. He shifted in his seat and scratched the back of his head. 'Look, I'm doing more damage than good, maybe this wasn't a good idea.'

Michelle stood up. 'I didn't mean to…'

'It's alright,' Curvis reassured her. 'It's natural to try and understand why Elvin took his own life. What we go through in our childhood shapes our whole life. Sometimes it can be a blessing, sometimes it can destroy you, no matter how successful you are as an adult.'

Curvis got to his feet and prepared to leave.

Michelle watched him. 'What destroyed Elvin's life, Curvis?'

For a split second Michelle detected a glimmer of rage in Curvis's eyes. It went as quickly as it had come. 'Why didn't you come to Elvin's funeral?' she asked. 'A lot of your old Pinewood Oaks friends were there.'

'Because I want to remember Elvin as someone who was happy, not someone in a coffin.'

Michelle shook her head. 'You homes people are weird, different to everybody else.'

'That's cos we were treated different to everyone else. Look, like I said before, I'm gutted for what happened to Elvin. I would like to show how sorry I am but I don't know how.'

'You could try,' Michelle interrupted.

Curvis took in a breath. 'Elvin was alright, a good mate, but he wouldn't want you to look into his past.' He bade her farewell and left.

The rain had relented. Small puddles filled the potholes in the tarmac. Curvis debated whether he should have told Michelle the truth about what Elvin had suffered. But if Michelle learned the reality, she would remember Elvin as a victim, not as a husband, not as a best friend and not as a man who enjoyed adult life. Elvin wouldn't have wanted that, Curvis concluded.

As he trudged to the bus stop, images of his childhood in Pinewood Oaks flashed through his mind. He could see his friends, Bullet and Glenroy, wrestling on the grass. He saw Carlton, his best pal, speeding by on his bike. Elvin came to life, giggling and hiding behind a bush. Lastly, Curvis saw himself, adventuring into the Pinewood Hills, running up and down between the trees and the foliage.

Curvis boarded the bus. His mind refused to return to the present. '*Four, mighty are we,*' he muttered under his breath. He ran a quick check to see if there was anybody else on the top deck. There wasn't. A second later, he slammed his forehead against the Perspex glass.

A young man's head was tilted over the metal rail of the bed, his throat viced by taut fingers. The victim's eyes betrayed his fear as blood spilled out from his torn nostril, spotting the concrete floor.

'Don't *dare* tea-leaf my bacco again, *right?*'

A right fist connected with the thief's cheekbone, sounding like a cricket ball against a billboard. 'Do you hear me? You fucking tea-leaf. *Do* you hear me!'

A black guy entered the cell, chewing a matchstick like a stressed soccer manager grinding gum. For a moment, he was strangely fascinated by the victim's petrified eyes. He was about to turn around and leave the thief to his sorry fate when he noticed the flecks of blood on the cold floor. In a calm voice, he ordered, 'That's enough, Gravesey. I think you've persuaded him not to do it again.'

Gravesey released his grip, turned around and looked at the solid, coffin-shaped jaw moving up and down and reducing the matchstick to a pulp. 'You know I hate tea-leaves.'

'You're gonna have to get used to 'em here.'

Satisfied with the punishment inflicted, Gravesey left, wiping his bloodstained fingers on his denim prison overalls.

'Thanks, Carlton, you're a diamond,' the thief stuttered gratefully. 'A real mate.'

'And what makes you think I'm your mate?' Carlton replied. 'I just don't like to see someone who can't defend themselves getting the shit kicked out of them. You're new here, and you'd better learn rapid-like that bacco is like gold when you're doing bird.'

Before the man had a chance to say any more, Carlton about-turned and left. As he made his way to his own cell, he glanced down from the iron-railed balcony and surveyed his fellow inmates playing a variety of games: table tennis, cards and draughts. A trio of wardens patrolled the stone walkways, each bearing enough keys to open any treasure chest.

Carlton could always recognise the new arrivals. More often than not, they sat silently in isolation, their faces full of regret, pondering their crimes and missing their loved ones. They recoiled at the sound of metal doors slamming. Carlton liked to get to know the fresh intake. He knew that he would receive their respect and they would look up to him.

He found he had his cell to himself; his cellmate was gambling downstairs. The walls of his living quarters were partly decorated with pictures of topless women. The wardens thought this normal, but what they sniggered at were the pictures and cut-outs of trees that surrounded Carlton's bunk. Fellow inmates never questioned him, but during lights out, in whispered conversations he was referred to as the 'tree man of Wormwood Scrubs'.

Sellotaped to the wall, just above his pillow, was the only clue to Carlton's life before prison. A black-and-white photograph of a twelve-year-old boy sitting on his bike, flanked by his friends: one with a spanner in his hand, another eating a chocolate bar and a boy with a comic war magazine jutting out from his back pocket.

Parking himself on his bunk, he recalled fond memories of his mates and that rusty bike. He also remembered how much he had loved the woman who took the photo. But since being incarcerated he had never replied to any of her letters. These recollections had come to him every day since his imprisonment eight years ago when he was just sixteen. In the dead of the night, he could hear his friends' voices, backdropped by the gentle rustling of leaves in a calm wind. It was a soothing memory, a quiet natural moment far away from everything else that filled his past.

A tapping at the cell door jolted Carlton awake. Standing at the door was Smokey Davis.

'Ain't ya gonna play any table tennis? Games time over soon.'

'Nah, don't feel like it. I'm bored with it.'

'How about a game of poker or something?'

'Nah, fuck that as well. Been playing table tennis and blackjack every day for years. I wanna try something different. They should bring in a pool table or something.'

'So what're you gonna do? We've only got twenty minutes left.'

Carlton shrugged. 'Read a book or something. And stop Gravesey from kicking the shit out of Wallace.'

'Wallace is a bacco robber.'

'Yeah, he is. It's kinda surprising cos he's new. New people don't get so brave early on. Especially if they can't fight. But Gravesey isn't exactly the archangel Gabriel. He's always beating up the new ones. I wouldn't give a shit but the screws kinda expect me to keep order in this wing. I don't want anything to fuck up my leaving date.'

'Wallace should fight his own wars,' said Smokey. 'What's he gonna do when you're out of here in a few weeks?'

Carlton shrugged again. 'If he carries on robbing he's gonna have to learn to fight.'

Smokey rolled a bacco joint. 'So what're you gonna do when you get out? Have you thought about it?'

Carlton looked at the photo of his friends just above his pillow. 'I dunno, maybe do some joinery that I learnt. I'll be staying with an old friend when I get out. Then I'll try and find a gaff, I s'pose. After that I might look for a whore to grind, if I've got enough money. Who knows, some liberal wanker might wanna give me a job.'

Smokey tossed the roll-up to Carlton and began to roll his own. 'I've always wanted to ask – who are the other guys in the photo?'

'None of your business, that's who they are.'

'Sure you don't wanna play any table tennis?'

'You want me to print a statement?'

'Yeah, alright. I get your drift.'

Smokey left. As he made his way downstairs, he wondered why he could never work Carlton out. Carlton had saved his arse twice, literally, and rescued his hide once. In the time he had known him, he found it impossible to sway Carlton to talk about his past – any attempts always resulted in Carlton becoming aggressive.

Remaining in his cell, Carlton stared at the photo of his friends. He placed his roll-up underneath his pillow, saving it for the night. 'Glenroy, *where* are you?' he whispered. He spat out the remains of the matchstick and found a fresh one on his bunk. He inserted it into his mouth and gnawed violently. The small muscles around his jawbone bulged as the tissues within his eighteen-and-a-half-inch neck danced to the rhythm of chewing. His head sat on a body of perfect strength; within the prison he had plenty of admirers, though none of them were forthcoming with their praise.

The only thing that scared him was the prospect of being free of the prison walls. Being locked up, he didn't have to worry about paying rent or when his next meal would arrive. In prison, he was king, the fittest of the fittest; even the screws respected him and invited him to 'deal' with the convicted perverts, with just one rule: *don't* mark the face. But in the outside world, he would be a nobody, a back-marker in the rat race that he would have to join to survive.

Maybe he could brutalise a shirt-lifter to extend his sentence, Carlton suddenly thought. Fuck up his face. Or pick a fight with one of the screws, fist one of them for no reason. That's bound to cause an extension to his sentence. Nah, fuck that, he reasoned. Don't wanna do that isolation shit. Had enough of that already. He looked at the images of trees surrounding his bunk. He still couldn't understand why they held such a fascination for him. He could never express it in words, but he felt that trees were more alive than people realised. They could manipulate you, instruct you to do things. Like kill people.

Bullet felt his guts sink and remain on the ground floor as the lift raced to the viewing platform of the CN Tower. A Korean tourist fretted in her own language, while an American kid, dressed in a Michael Jackson T-shirt, sang 'Thriller'.

Monty, Bullet's one-and-a-half-year-old son, blinked wildly as the lift door opened and natural light flooded his eyes. His wife, Linda, touched Monty on the cheek before smiling at her husband.

Bullet's brown hair was cropped short, as if he still wanted his army life to be acknowledged. Brown freckles dotted his face, almost entirely covering his dented nose. Thin lips and a hard chin hinted at his determination.

Bullet led his family to the large, angled windows that presented a view of the Toronto skyline and Lake Ontario. The buildings below looked like stepping stones for giants and the blue brilliance of the lake forced Bullet to squint. The sails on the yachts far below pricked the calm waters like white bayonets.

Linda took out her camera and started taking snaps of her family. 'Smile then,' she said. 'At least pretend you're enjoying yourself.'

Bullet forced a half grin. Monty had no time for the camera. 'Let's get away from it all, you said,' Linda snapped. 'You're about as miserable as when we were back home. What's the matter?'

'Nothing.'

Bullet passed Monty to his wife and looked out onto the lake. Suddenly, he saw himself peering out from the highest point of the Pinewood Hills. The first time Curvis had shown him the view of this particular slice of Surrey countryside, Bullet was ten years old. From that day onwards, he always wondered what went on in the outside world. A world away from Pinewood Oaks Children's Home.

Well travelled with the army, Bullet had now seen many countries and many peoples. He felt that the evils he had thought confined to Pinewood Oaks were everywhere – in Northern Ireland, the Middle East, Hong Kong. Children are always the big losers, he concluded. They're the ones who suffer from war, poverty, hunger and the rest of it.

Turning around, he gazed lovingly at Monty. He then thought of Glenroy, Carlton and Curvis, the only real friends he had. His wife, tired of waiting for him to react to her warm smiles while serving from the mess canteen, had made the first move. In the army you're forced to get on with everybody. He knew he had swapped one institution for another. Now he had to face the outside world. At least he had the memories of the Pinewood Hills. No pointless war, hunger or poverty could take that away. One moment of freedom in his life that nobody but his friends could understand.

'Did I tell you Carlton's coming out in a few weeks' time?' said Bullet.

Linda's smile died. 'How could I forget? It's all you talked about on the plane over here.'

'It's gonna be great,' said Bullet. 'We're gonna be together again. As soon as he gets out we should take him for a meal.'

'When's the last time you took *me* for a meal?' Linda glared.

'I took you on this holiday, didn't I?'

'Remember what I said last night. Me and Monty are *the* priority in your life now.'

Bullet didn't reply. He stared out to the horizon and saw a light aircraft gliding high over the lake. 'It's a shame Glenroy won't be there when Carlton gets out.'

Linda rolled her eyes. 'So you keep on saying.' She took Monty a few yards away to look in a different direction.

Lost in the past, Bullet didn't notice his wife walking away. He closed his eyes. 'Glenroy, where are you?' he whispered.

Carshalton, Surrey, May 1985

Glenroy felt a massive sense of achievement as he successfully made himself a cup of tea. It had been two weeks since he was discharged from the mental hospital, and only now was he beginning to think he might cope. But only if he could remember to take his medication. He needed to find out where his nearest chemist was, for when his pills ran out.

A community nurse was supposed to call on him the day before to check if he was okay, but they never arrived. Even though he was in the outside world, he felt like a young skylark that had just watched his parents fly away. Two days ago his sworn enemy, Panic, had found a secret entrance to his brain, causing him to smash his head on the cold water tap in the bathroom. He cut his scalp and ended up putting his head in a bath full of cold water, holding his breath for as long as he could before dunking again.

When Panic finally departed, he ate a dinner of cold sardines and boiled lemonade and retired to his bed, fully clothed, adopting the foetal position. He preferred to keep his bedroom window wide open because the sounds of the birds at dawn soothed him. Only now, two days later, had he emerged from his sleeping place.

He was frightened of this outside world. The shopping trip to the supermarket unsettled him. So many people, all in a crazy hurry, it seemed to him. They all knew where they were going. When he finally reached the cashier, he thought Panic might run amok inside his head again. 'Eight pound fifty, please,' the cashier asked politely, recoiling at his eighteen-stone frame and his wild hair. Glenroy felt the sweat sogging his eyebrows and watering his untamed beard. Should he give her the blue note or the brown one? It took an eternity to decide. 'I haven't got all day, you know,' the cashier snapped. Panic, Glenroy's eternal shadow, was very near.

He gave her the brown note. Glenroy expected a fierce rebuke. The cashier opened the till, giving him change of one pound fifty and a receipt. He stood for a long second, smiling widely. Panic had to retreat. Mission accomplished! *Yes!* He congratulated himself.

Hours later, he sat down in his kitchen, downing his over-milky tea and eating a Mars bar from the collection of sweets he kept in a fruit bowl. He recalled the day he left the hospital. His eyes hurt from tears at leaving his friends behind. Everyone said he'd be alright and that he was better, that he would be okay to go home now. But the hospital was his home, and there he knew what he had to do every day. Make your bed in the morning, breakfast followed by chores. Eleven was games time; Glenroy always hogged the table tennis table. Lunch at twelve thirty. Training in the afternoon, where he learned to cook, count money, read essential shopping lists and fill in various forms.

Dinner was at five thirty followed by another games session. At nine, he would politely ask for his supper of a chocolate roll or fairy cakes, then he would watch a bit of telly; his favourite programme was the *Young Ones*. Ten p.m. was lights out.

In those quiet hours of darkness, he wondered about his life before coming to the hospital. He was told he had spent his childhood in an orphanage. But that's all he knew. His pre-teenage memories were lost in a fog of tablets, injections, beatings and straitjackets.

Almost every night he dreamt about an enchanted forest, where the terrain was hilly, the trees were incredibly tall and the sun baked the grass brown. Now and again, a little girl would appear in these dreams. She looked very poorly but she had an abundance of energy as she danced in the woods, inviting Glenroy to play tag. She only ever spoke two words. Pinewood Hills. Glenroy guessed it was her name. But he knew he could only play with her when it was light, for when darkness came, she turned evil. From blonde, her hair would change to dazzling white and her eyes to a glowing green. She roamed the forest at night, blackbirds swirling around her head, looking for someone to kill. Tightly gripped in her right hand was a doll's head and protruding from it a three-inch nail.

PART 1
PINEWOOD OAKS

Pinewood Oaks, April 1970

A nervous chimpanzee was performing a card trick for seven cynical gorillas when the nine-year-old Glenroy Richards opened his eyes and cleared his head of his daydream. He focused and sneered at the maths equation taunting him from the blackboard and considered using the chalk to sketch a monkey's face on it. Glenroy smiled. He looked down at the wonky wooden desk above his knees and studied the black biro sketches of a matchstick mother holding the hand of a matchstick child.

On a table at the back of the classroom, textbooks formed a pillar; with one push they would tumble, but he would leave that for another day. Drawings of families at the beach were Sellotaped on the cream-painted, brick walls. The ceiling of the classroom was high enough for three teachers to stand on each other's shoulders, and the large windows always teased Glenroy as an escape route.

He stared at the wooden floor beneath him and wondered if he would ever visit the seaside with his own mother. But, he thought, maybe the horrible people in that place where his mum was living wouldn't let her go. He wondered if she ever had the same thought. Maybe if he asked Father Patrick, perhaps he could do something.

He looked up at the stubborn classroom clock, willing the time to spring forward.

The rest of the class had been dismissed half an hour ago, leaving Glenroy to contemplate his misconduct. He didn't think he should be the only one in detention; there were others who deserved the same punishment, especially Tommy Whittle, who had pulled a chair away from the soon-to-be-seated Claire Woodhouse. And then there was Billy Crawford, who had made funny faces behind the teacher's back.

Miffed, Glenroy stooped to pick up a pencil from the floor and noticed the chewed marks at one end of it. As he tapped the pencil on the desk and rocked in his chair the classroom door opened. 'Stop rocking on the chair and will you please stop making that irritating noise with your pencil,' rebuked Mr Goodbury.

Mr Goodbury was stocky in appearance, formally dressed in a navy blazer, black trousers and a ridiculous black-and-yellow polka-dot bow tie. His eyebrows seemed to be as thick as the working end of a broom, angled towards the middle of his face where they almost shook hands. There were small red veins criss-crossing his face, as if someone had gone berserk with a thin, red biro. His only hair, apart from the sproutings in his ears and nostrils, was at each side of his round head. Glenroy thought he looked like an aged goblin.

'Right, Glenroy,' he addressed, wagging his right index finger. 'I have phoned your housefather and I'm sure that he'll see that you are further punished for your behaviour in class this afternoon.' Glenroy flinched. 'You are free to go.'

Glenroy's chair screeched as he shot up out of it. As he approached the door, Mr Goodbury warned: 'Let this be a lesson to you that if you continue to disrupt my class with your teasing and name-calling of other children, then you'll continue to have my company after school has finished. Do you understand me?'

'Yes, Mr Goodbury.' I hope Father Patrick doesn't hear about this, he thought.

Normally he had to walk in file but now he sprinted along the empty corridor, his footsteps resounding on the wooden floor. As he turned a corner to leave by the main school exit, he ran into Miss Worthington, his music teacher. 'How many times have I told you *not* to run in the corridors? *Walk.*'

'Sorry, Miss. I wanna catch up to my friends.'

Miss Worthington inspected Glenroy's clothes. His grey shirt was escaping his grey shorts. His black shoes were scuffed and his grey socks were nearer his ankles than his knees. She noted a mischievous but sad look in his eyes. She felt a little sympathy for him. She had learned that Glenroy's mother was certified insane, but hadn't known the full story, just the cold fact that Glenroy owned a mad mother.

'You'd better do something with your hair before you get home. Your housemother won't appreciate *that* appearance. Try and borrow a comb from Carlton Henry if you catch up with him.'

'Yes, Miss.'

Glenroy trotted out of the main exit and into the children's playground, slowing down as he turned corners. He skipped around to see if any of his school friends were waiting for him like they had promised. The playground was empty. At least Carlton, his best mate, could have waited.

The school was a Victorian building with brownish-red brickwork and white-painted window frames. Its gabled roofs and pointed arches gave it a gothic feel, especially at night. Children, up to the age of eleven, who lived in the Pinewood Oaks children's home complex, were educated here. From eleven plus, the children would attend 'outside' comprehensives in nearby villages, to allow the orphans to integrate into the local community. An unspoken rule was that no single secondary school would absorb all the children who had just left Pinewood Oaks junior school. Consequently, the headmasters of the local comprehensives had a nodding agreement that they would share equally the intake from Pinewood Oaks – it made it easier to deflect complaints and arguments from village parents who didn't want their privileged children to interact with '*those savages from the home*'.

A rickety, brown wooden fence, about a metre and a half high, enclosed the playground area. It was the northern boundary marker for the children's home. For seventy years or more, pupils leaped up to grab a glimpse of the outside world. Glenroy approached this fence and jumped up, reaching out with his hands to grip the top of the barrier. He managed to get his head above the fence and searched the neighbouring recreation field. He saw a group of boys playing football, using their pullovers, satchels and bags for goalposts. Dogs were running freely, teenagers smoked cigarettes under an oak tree and a couple were necking on the grass. In the distance, at the far end of the park, he could just make out the buildings of Ashburden comprehensive school. Beyond this was the village of Ashburden itself, full of avenues, semi-detached houses, back garden ponds with watchful gnomes and middle-aged women walking small dogs.

Glenroy looked towards the horizon and there, pricking the skyline, beyond the hills, he believed stood the Eiffel Tower. He had seen it in a book once and he had promised himself to hitchhike to France one day. He climbed down from the fence and ran out of the playground into a tree-lined road, at the bottom of which was a seven-foot-high wooden gate that was locked by a padlock big enough to secure a castle. Boys who were in their last year of education at Pinewood primary and didn't care about the threat of a caning, dared each other to climb the gate and land on the winding gravel track that led to Ashburden. Opposite the school was the playing field where pupils practised gymnastics. The boys were dressed in white vests and black shorts, and the girls in white flannel T-shirts and short, black pleated skirts.

The sound of a confused amateur band coming from a building at the far end of the playing field hitched a lift on a freshening breeze. All that practice and they still sound like a dying dalek, Glenroy concluded.

He scampered up an incline and when he crested the hill, he stopped and looked around. The road headed due south, where Glenroy could see the first of the Georgian cottages which each housed up to fourteen kids. The houses had three-pointed gabled roofs sitting on a rectangle of brick twelve metres high. Large bay windows caught the sun and there wasn't a front door without a porch over it.

To Glenroy's right there was a strip of grass, ten metres wide and about a kilometre long, fringed by nettles, thorn bushes and hard-to-get-to berries. This acted as a border for the western side of the children's home. Beyond this were the lush and well-kept back gardens of Pinewood village. No roads were curved or arched here. They were as straight as the Pall Mall and covered in the same reddish-brown tarmac. This was the prized route for paperboys who worked from Fred Dawes newsagent's on the High Street. A seventy-pound-haul 'Christmas box' wasn't unheard of when the lucky lad cycled around Pinewood village to collect his bonus. No boy from Pinewood Oaks had ever been given the honour. Refuse collectors, who took extreme care not to leave any stray rubbish in their wake, were even more fortunate on their Christmas round.

On hot days, the kids of the orphanage would eavesdrop and peep in at garden parties where French cheese, salmon and watercress sandwiches and champagne was served to women in wide hats and Laura Ashley dresses and men in Bermuda shorts and Fred Perry T-shirts. The orphans enjoyed mocking the job-a-day cubs, who in the summer holidays were spotted pulling weeds, cleaning ponds, painting garden huts and saluting every adult who came into their sight.

Glenroy sensed a commotion coming from the expanse of grass to his left. He strained his eyes and made out a rabble of boys in the hazy sunlight. Not wanting to miss out, he darted across the field, passing one of the imposing Georgian houses, before bolting through a deep dale. He could see the Pinewood Oaks water tower rising over the trees towards the east.

The grass was recently cut, making him sneeze as he neared the pack of yelping boys. The juniors had formed a ring around a strapping, mixed-race boy. A smaller lad was being pushed into the ring, blubbering at the thought of what was to come.

'Get in the ring, Bullet!' cried out a voice. 'You said that Osgood was a sprout head.'

A score of kids started to yell. 'In the ring! In the ring! In the ring!'

Osgood yanked Bullet's arm and lugged him into the centre of the circle. Osgood, who appeared older than his eleven years, was one of the few boys in long trousers. He smirked as he caught Bullet in a vice around the throat and began to check the power of his well-practised right hook. Bullet looked like a defenceless nail faced with an eager hammer. The mob changed its chant. 'Kill him! Kill him! Kill him!'

Glenroy reached the melee and spotted Carlton. He barged his way to Carlton's side and watched Bullet being hammered into the grass.

'What's he done?' asked Glenroy.

'He called Osgood names after Osgood tripped him up in school,' Carlton replied.

Meanwhile, Bullet tried to fight back but it was pointless. His spirited display only infuriated Osgood, who began kicking his victim. When Osgood was satisfied he had inflicted enough damage, he strutted away with his friends and hangers-on, who congratulated him on his latest victory.

Bullet wormed on the ground, silently sobbing, his arms covering his swollen face. Glenroy ambled away. 'Carlton, let's go home.'

Carlton stood still, glancing at the sorry sight of Bullet, who had now sat up, picking off grass and dry mud from his school uniform. Carlton started towards Glenroy but curiosity got the better of him. He turned around and caught sight of Bullet peeping at him from under his arms. 'Let's see how he is.'

'Are you nuts?' said Glenroy. 'Osgood will dent your face if he finds out.'

Carlton strolled over to Bullet, with a reluctant Glenroy following behind. Bullet warily moved his arms away from his face as Carlton studied him. 'Are you mad or something? Why you wanna start calling Osgood names? He's the best fighter in the school. You must be on a death mission or something.'

Bullet's face was bloodied, his brown hair highlighted green.

He wondered why Carlton had stayed behind and hadn't gone

with the others. He hasn't taken any notice of me before, he thought. Nobody has.

'Come on,' urged Carlton. 'Get up.'

Glenroy pulled a face. He marched up to Carlton and pulled him away. He spoke in a hurried whisper. 'We can't walk with him! Everyone hates him! What if Osgood sees us? He's gonna beat the eyebrows off us! Didn't you see what he done to Jerry Collins? He still can't talk and he walks likes he's got a nail in his foot. Elvin told me one of his balls was crushed.'

'Osgood's gone home,' said Carlton.

Glenroy glared at Bullet. The trio trudged on, walking through the rough, knee-high grass that steadily dipped into a valley. They trekked across a sloping football pitch where the wooden goalposts were warped and the crossbars sagged.

Finally, they reached a children's play area. A set of swings and a broken seesaw were being watched over by an arc of huge oak trees. Brave boys would hold contests to see who could climb the highest in the branches, attempting to claim highly prized birds' nests.

The threesome reached a small stone bridge where a stream hastened below. Under the arch was a popular spot for hide-and-seekers. The bold would venture into the tunnel and hide. They crossed the narrow stone walkway. Glenroy caught sight of somebody on the bank of the stream. 'Holy shit bombs! That's Stanton's brother, Curvis. Stanton used to be Osgood's best mate. We're gonna get our heads kicked in! Curvis will tell Stanton we're with Bullet. Did I tell you that Jerry's only got two teeth left?'

Carlton searched the bank of the stream. A figure was sitting in the shadow of bushes, staring into the rushing water. He picked up a pebble and threw it into the stream, trying to imitate a bouncing bomb.

Led by Carlton, the trio approached Curvis. 'What you doing?'

'I dunno,' replied Curvis.

Curvis wore grey shorts. His jutting knees had gathered dried mud. His skinny, aquiline nose suggested that one of his parents was white. His complexion was milky coffee and he boasted a wild Afro.

'Come on, Carlton,' Glenroy insisted. 'What are you talking to him for? I've got to get home. I'm in big enough trouble as it is.'

'Did you see the fight?' Carlton asked Curvis, ignoring Glenroy. 'Osgood beat up Bullet cos Bullet called him names.'

'Don't like fights.' Curvis stared into the water as if something dramatic was about to happen. He then turned around to study the battered face of Bullet. 'Osgood doesn't like anyone calling him names. He's like my brother. They were best mates.' He returned his gaze to the water. 'I'd keep out of Osgood's way if I was you.'

'I tried to keep out of his way,' said Bullet. 'I ran out of school. Osgood's gang ran after me and caught me on the field.'

'He's given you a good slogging,' said Curvis, still studying Bullet's bruises. 'But on the plus side, Osgood doesn't usually beat up kids twice – only if they say something again.'

'Carlton!' Glenroy interrupted.

Glenroy had to wait five minutes before Carlton and Bullet rejoined him. The boys strolled on lazily out of the field under the warm sun until they reached the orbital road that ringed Pinewood Oaks.

A few cars were parked outside the Georgian houses. Children played outdoors, enjoying the spring sunshine. Boys hurtled by on heavy, squeaky bikes. The more adventurous invited injury by piloting wobbly, home-made trolleys. On the grass, teenagers were getting bruised and bashed by a game of British Bulldog. Black-and-white plastic footballs were kicked against outhouse walls where the goals were chalked in white. Girls were juggling greying tennis balls on red walls; others sang pop songs while skipping ropes and playing hopscotch.

On one old, rusty-looking bike, a small boy of about seven was learning how to ride. He was helped by an older girl who was frantically pushing the saddle. 'Brenton! Pedal, you idiot, pedal!'

Glenroy observed the scene and boasted: 'I learned to ride a bike when I was five. He's useless. Look at him. I didn't need any help when I was that small.'

'When did you come up with that fairy story,' laughed Carlton. 'If I remember, you only learned to ride a bike yesterday! And while you were at it, you fell off so many times the nurses at sick bay got tired of you.'

Glenroy and Carlton proceeded to have a mock fight in the road while Bullet meandered a few yards behind his new friends.

After another fifty metres, they neared Bullet's house, Maple. As he viced Glenroy's neck in an arm-lock, Carlton said to Bullet, 'Maple House. Mark Fearon lives in your house, innit. He's the best footballer in Pinewood Oaks. I saw him up the top field the other day and he scored a Bobby Charlton goal. Whassisname, Lloyd Grant was the goalie. Before he moved a stud the ball was in the back of the net. The cameras shoulda been there to show it on *The Big Match*.'

Glenroy tried to squirm his neck free. 'Mark Fearon's not as good as Kevin Annon.'

'Kevin Annon's not fit to screw on his own studs!' countered Carlton.

'And the only dribbling Mark Fearon can do is when he's eating soggy Weetabix!'

As Glenroy and Carlton disputed the serious matter of the best footballer in Pinewood Oaks, Bullet ambled away to the back of his house. Before he opened the back door, he glanced behind at the quarrelling boys on the road.

Realising that teatime was pushing on, Glenroy and Carlton jogged the rest of the way home. They passed the blue-painted nursery building, topped off by a flat roof. On many a summer's night, boys would climb on top of the nursery and peer through the bedroom windows of the houses nearby. This custom continued until a housefather spotted them and hailed them down, threatening untold varieties of physical punishments.

Screwed into the brickwork of one house, was a green-painted placard, white letters spelling the word Holly. Carlton ran to the front door of this house and shouted to Glenroy, 'See you later. And Mark Fearon's *definitely* the best player in Pinewood Oaks.'

'No he ain't!'

Remembering his trouble at school, Glenroy slowed down to a walk and eased open the front door of the house next to Carlton's. It was named Heather.

Once inside, Glenroy wiped his feet on the large, bristled mat. Then he stepped up the three red-carpeted stairs before him. He entered the hallway. He always hated the painting of a crying child that hung on a wall to the left of the entrance. The wallpaper wasn't much better – a flower-patterned, light-grey reaching right up to a high ceiling. To his immediate right was a mahogany staircase, complete with polished banisters.

A four-year-old boy tottered in front of Glenroy in excited pursuit of a toy car. The child looked at Glenroy and smiled. 'Everybody, Glenroy's home!' Glenroy brushed passed the child, turning right along the hallway. 'Get out of my way,' he said. 'You always get in the way with your stupid cars.'

The child picked up his car and stared at Glenroy in silence as he stepped softly along the passage.

Passing the kitchen on his left, the housemother, who possessed arms big enough to stir a barrel of porridge, caught sight of Glenroy. 'And what time do you call this? Just look at your hair. Have you been fighting again?'

'No, Auntie Mary.'

The first rule a child learned on entering any of the cottages in Pinewood Oaks was to address the staff as 'Auntie' or 'Uncle'. Washing hands before any meal was compulsory and talking after bedtime invited a hard slap or three. For those who dared to wander out of dorms at night, a much more severe fate awaited them. Any photographs, certificates and other documents the orphan might have in their possession were taken away and filed. They were shown their place at the dinner table and cautioned about the wastage of food. Lastly, they would be told in the strictest terms *not* to infringe on the properties of Pinewood village or other out-of-bound areas. Following an anxious night's sleep the new child was measured for clothes, checked for lice, had fingernails clipped, teeth and gums inspected and was told of the weekly chore rota. The next afternoon the child found himself or herself naked in the sick bay, the resident doctor running a check from toe to scalp, asking the child's social worker about any rashes or symptoms that might be contagious.

Taking off her oven gloves, Auntie Mary inspected Glenroy from head to foot. Then she suddenly smacked his face, causing Glenroy's head to jolt ninety degrees. '*Don't* lie to me!' Glenroy squinted at the moment of impact. He raised his arms automatically, backing away. The housemother raised an open right hand again, deciding whether one smack was sufficient. 'Uncle Thomas said he wanted to see you as soon as you get in from school. So you'd better wash your hands and look tidy – then go to the study.'

Soothing his face with his right palm, Glenroy thought his housemother was the young devil's babysitter. He wished the bogeyman would capture her and dunk her fat head in the rushing water under the bridge, and then she might melt away, like the green witch in *The Wizard of Oz*.

He turned around and walked back along the hallway. He headed for the washroom, opposite the entrance of the house. The walls were painted beige and the door frames and skirting had recently been glossed a brilliant white. The marble-like lino floor was bare. The room contained two sinks, two toilet cubicles and a cupboard where the cleaning ladies stored their items. The smell of disinfectant invaded Glenroy's nostrils. He gripped the hot water tap and imagined it was Auntie Mary's neck. He clenched his teeth. 'I *hate* her,' he whispered. 'And *him*.'

He washed his hands while gazing into the mirror above the sink. He wondered what punishment he'd receive. He swabbed away the hatred in his eyes. 'Don't wanna let *her* know she can hurt me.' After drying his hands, he took a plastic comb from a wall cabinet and proceeded to tear into his tight Afro curls.

Five minutes later he trudged into the hallway, expecting the familiar beating. He almost stumbled on his way to the study door, his entire body trembling like a chocolate trifle. At the end of the hallway, he bumped into seven-year-old Lisa. She was gripping the string hair of a tatty doll. 'You're in trouble.'

'Shut up!'

Lisa ran up the stairs giggling as Glenroy sweated on his fate, his heartbeat accelerating. Carlton had told him to bite his finger when he received six wallopings. That way the pain on the backside won't be so bad. Glenroy thought he should try it.

The study was at the end of the hallway, near the staircase. He knocked on the door once, giving it a light tap.

'Come in!' boomed a voice from within.

Glenroy inched his way into the study where he saw his housefather writing on a bureau in the light of a lamp. Aged about forty, he had balding ginger hair. His brown eyes were close together. His skin was pale. He had the build of a hardworking labourer who enjoyed his beer. Glenroy likened him to a ginger-haired troll he had seen in a children's fairy book.

The room was dominated by a mahogany table which had a chessboard upon it with exquisitely carved wooden pieces. All the figures were present in their starting positions, apart from one pawn. A red two-seater sofa was beneath the window. Various pictures and paintings of boys were on the walls and window sills, most of them displaying some sporting pursuit or other. Glenroy always wondered why there weren't any pictures of girls.

The housefather trapped Glenroy with his stern eyes. He fingered his scraggy ginger beard. Glenroy guessed he was deciding on some evil punishment. His thin lips were unforgiving.

'How many times do I have to tell you *not* to misbehave in class?' the housefather ranted. 'I'm sick and tired of Mr Goodbury ringing me up and complaining about your behaviour. The way you're going, you'll end up in Hell. Don't they tell you in church that boys have to behave themselves or otherwise they'll go to Hell? It seems like no punishment is good for you. God! I've tried everything with you. I've a good mind to speak to Father Patrick. Do you want to end up like your mother? Do you want to be crazy? You'll end up like she did, totally useless to society. Well? Do you want to end up like her?'

'No, Uncle Thomas.'

Glenroy couldn't remember what his mother looked like. The only facts he learned about her were from Thomas. He had been told from a very early age that the children's home would keep him safe from his dangerous mother and that he was lucky that the country provided such a compassionate service for children like him.

'Sometimes you haven't got the sense you were born with – just like your bloody mother,' Thomas ranted. 'Look at you! You're fat, black as the coal we use and ugly – spitting image of your good-for-nothing mother. They should ban all mothers from having children if they're going to turn out like you. I've got a good mind to give you the slipper. That's what you deserve. But I'm too busy, too much paperwork to go through. After you have your tea, you'll go straight to bed. If I hear you speak to anybody or make any trouble with the younger children I'll put you in the outhouse until dinner's ready. Maybe that'll work for you. God! I don't know what else I can try.'

Glenroy flinched. He'd rather have the slipper than be sent to the outhouse. There'll be nobody to talk to. Perhaps Uncle Thomas would give him colouring pencils and paper. That's all he had the last time he was confined to his dorm. Glenroy sketched images of what he thought the devil looked like – he prayed for a ginger crayon.

He glanced at the chessboard, wondering how the game was played. He noticed that one pawn was missing from the black set and searched the table to see if he could find it. Thomas interrupted him. 'So get your ugly, black face out of my sight and I don't want to hear your mouth this evening. Is that clear?'

'Yes, Uncle Thomas.'

Glenroy's head dropped. He left the office, carefully closing the door behind him. He walked along the hallway and as he went by the kitchen, he spotted his housemother stirring something in a large, grey pot. She caught sight of him. 'Come here!'

Glenroy slowly shuffled up to her. She grabbed his ear and tweaked it into a fold, pulling Glenroy's head towards her. He grimaced and nearly lost his footing. 'Have you washed your hands? Dinner will be ready in ten minutes. Sit down and behave yourself or I'll give you what for too!'

He lumbered to the end of the hallway and into the dining room. Two large dining tables were on either side, set for the evening meal. A tiled mantelpiece on the far wall had a solitary birthday card upon it, sent to one of the children by a social worker. Below this was an unused coal fireplace. The walls were painted in a dull blue and the large sash windows had no net curtains or drapes to soften the hard edges. To the left of the entrance from the hallway was a hatch in the wall, about the size of a chessboard, through which Glenroy could see his housemother preparing the gravy. In the middle of the room was a bean bag. He walked towards it and fell upon it. Why won't they let me live with my mum, he thought. Perhaps Father Patrick could...

Suddenly, a toy car sped into the room, followed by the frantic patters of an excited boy. Luca. Five years old. Pushing his vehicle around the legs of the dining chairs, Luca looked at Glenroy. 'Look at this!' Luca propelled the three-wheeled car into a wall. Glenroy glared. 'What are you staring at? And stop playing with your stupid cars near the dinner table or I'll tell Auntie Mary.' Picking up his car, Luca crawled out from under the dining table. He swept his long black hair from out of his eyes and stared at Glenroy.

'Go and play in the hallway,' Glenroy ordered, wondering why Luca always looked at him strangely.

Luca just sat down near the table, spinning the wheels of his car, and started crying silently.

'Will you stop that,' Glenroy said. 'Ever since you've come here, all you do is cry. You're getting on everybody's nerves. No one's hit you yet!'

'They ... they took me away,' Luca stuttered.

About to say something, Glenroy paused. He gazed at Luca, wondering if they called his mum mad too. 'That's what they do, Luca. You'd better get used to it. Wash your hands before dinner.'

Ten minutes later, the household settled down for dinner. The smaller children, accompanied by three staff, sat at the table near the hatch, while four teenagers, dressed in various shades of school uniform, dined on the big table beside the window. From an old wireless, perched on a shelf on the end wall, the news of the day voiced out on a low volume.

Placed at the head of the big table, opposite his wife, Uncle Thomas trained his eyes on Glenroy. 'I hope you don't waste that,' he said, as Glenroy fiddled with his food. 'You know I hate waste. You *sit* there until you finish every last morsel. You should be lucky you've got a meal to eat. Your mum always forgot to feed you.'

Glenroy stared into his plate and forced himself to eat.

Sitting beside Glenroy was Lisa. She was unable to kill her smirk. Mary caught sight of Lisa's wide grin and, without warning, stood up and smacked the girl's face, forcing the food in her mouth to dribble over her chin. '*No* laughing at the table or you'll be the next one who goes to bed early.'

Lisa stifled her sobbing. It sounded like hiccups. She resumed eating her sausages and mash. Glenroy was silent beside her, his eyes never moving from his plate. The other children glanced at Lisa, then returned to their meals as if nothing had happened.

Dinner at the children's table went on with only the sound of knives and forks against plates, backdropped by the sports report on the crackling wireless of Chelsea's FA Cup run. The only conversation taking place was at the teenagers' table, where they swapped tales of teachers, canings, football and the latest pop tunes. Glenroy enjoyed his dessert of apple crumble and custard, scooping his plate clean.

After dinner, Glenroy climbed the stairs. He glanced behind at Auntie Mary watching his slow progress. On reaching the top of the stairs, he walked into the boys' dormitory, still lit by the fading, amber sun; the girls' dormitory was at the other end of the hallway. He meandered his way to the bed nearest the door. He found his pyjamas under his pillow and began to undress. Just as he was slipping on his pyjama bottoms, he spotted the fourteen-year-old Ivan Torrance. Long fair hair rested on his shoulders. He wore a cruel grin. His severe acne didn't endear him to the girls in the children's homes complex and nor did his skinny build. He fixed his eyes on Glenroy and started cackling as he watched Glenroy climb into his bed. 'Wog-a-matter? Feeling all browned off? Niggermind, you might feel all white in the morning, when you have your coon flakes.'

Ivan continued laughing and strutted towards Glenroy. He lifted his right foot onto the bed. 'Kiss my foot, Sambo. Go on, *kiss* it. Or you know what'll happen to you on the way to school.'

Shaking, Glenroy gazed at the white football sock. He noticed the dust and tiny carpet strands. He slowly stooped and touched his lips on the sock of his tormentor. Ivan smiled triumphantly. He turned and opened the door. 'Know your place, nigger.'

Pulling the covers over his head, Glenroy pressed his pillow against his stomach. He curled into the foetal position. His body refused to feel tired as bitter resentment surged through him. How can Father Patrick expect me to forgive things like that? he asked himself. When I get older, I'm gonna smash up all the Ivans, Auntie Marys and Mr Thomases in the world and I don't care what Father Patrick might say.

He pressed his palms together and slammed his eyes shut. 'Dear God, sorry for being bad in class today. But I wasn't the only one. I didn't start it. Got a favour to ask. Can you please, please make Mum better so she can take me away and look after me. Amen. Oh, one more small favour. Can you have a word with the devil – I guess he's not your favourite person but you might still talk to him. Anyway, if you can, have a word with him and tell him about Ivan. I don't think he can be saved.'

He pulled off his covers to check if Ivan had left the room. Satisfied, he stood on his bed and looked out of the window towards the orchard, half expecting to hear a demon on his way to feast on Ivan. Two seconds later, he was back under his bed sheets.

He wondered what his mum looked like now and promised himself that when he grew up, wherever she was, he would find her and take her away to live in a big house with seven bedrooms. And, with his mum, he'd definitely behave himself.

Glenroy refused to sleep. He was frightened of his dreams but didn't tell anyone about his nightmares. They'd laugh at him. They'd tell him he was as mad as his mum. He often tried to count a thousand conkers but he never made it to a hundred. Maybe all kids had nightmares, he thought, but they kept it secret. He tried to keep his eyes open but someone seemed to be pulling them closed. He had prayed to God to spare him from this torment but He never seemed to listen. Father Patrick said that God always listened to prayers, even to prayers from kids who live in far-off countries. Maybe He doesn't listen to prayers from kids in a home. Maybe He only listens to kids who hold hands with their nice parents on their way to church.

'Dear God. I can't sleep, so sorry for this second prayer. I know you're probably really busy listening to prayers from kids in starving countries, but this is my last prayer for the night. You have to help me. I live with a witch of an Auntie and an Uncle so wicked he should be one of the adults in the *Oliver* movie. I've asked once already but I'm gonna ask again. You might've been busy when I prayed about this before. So here it goes. Can you make my mum better so she can take me away to live in a big house? If you do this I promise I'll be as good as Ronnie Moran who lives in Acacia House. While we were playing football the other day, Ronnie went out to the bushes and picked some blackberries – his Auntie made a crumble out of it. Anyway, I'll be as good as Ronnie so you can't send me to Hell. Amen.'

Soon he was asleep, but something inside him was alert. He felt himself rising, as if he was a kite on a friendly breeze. He found himself careering on a misty, floaty journey. Images began to appear. A crazed male lion was gnawing one of its own cubs while the cub's mother was lying dead just a few feet away. The left side of her face was missing. Then a wailing, teenage girl, wearing rags and a glittering tiara, laid a newborn baby at the gates of that place where important people argue.

The vision changed to a naked woman behind a counter in a shop, selling her heart to a whip-lashing ugly man who had hooves instead of feet. The vision blurred, then cleared to show a handcuffed headless woman, being escorted to a castle's dungeon by elderly guards with white wigs but no faces.

The journey ended. Glenroy found himself sitting on a cloud. He was mesmerised by the mysterious figure of a man. Eyes lit by a thousand November the fifths stared through him, seemingly examining his thoughts. Locks of hair, like the multi-coloured ropes of a Maypole, danced above his head. In his right hand he held a book, which was ten times thicker than any book he had ever seen. Gripped in his left hand like a great king wielding his sceptre, was what looked like a gigantic tree trunk, twenty times taller than the mightiest oak in Pinewood Oaks.

He sat on a chair that glowed like a peeled tangerine when raised against the sunlight. His chameleon skin changed colour when he moved. When he spoke it was like the sound of a dinosaur stomping below the ground. He opened the book and beckoned Glenroy over. Glenroy's eyes widened as he watched the book reveal a live landscape, a new world. He saw a dazzling green land with zigzagging rivers of milk. Golden sycamore trees were gently blown by the breath of the mysterious man sitting in the gleaming chair. Lions with green-glowing crowns strode proudly.

The lions watched over their cubs and silver-coloured lambs. Happy angels, playing long trumpets, glided through the sky with wings of cotton wool. Birds, with a multitude of eyes on their wings, like tiny flying daleks, sang songs of praise to the man sitting on the shiny big chair. Red-coloured bushes, shaped like hearts, bore green and golden berries. Rich green fields, stretching for a mile, were dotted with conker trees.

Trombones blared out as if trying to speak. Another page was turned. Glenroy found himself nearing a pit surrounded by sharpened, rocky teeth. He shook with fear and he couldn't blink. Trembling, he looked down into the never-ending abyss. Petrified, desperate men tried to avoid falling by holding on to the jagged teeth protruding from the walls of the pit. But they had no hands or feet. They were being pursued by horn-headed, five-legged dogs with long forked tongues.

Birds, boils and burns on their faces, flapped in the chasm, finding it impossible to fly upwards. Smoke, worse than in any war film, rose up out of the void, making the birds cough. From the mouth of the pit, a monster with ten dragon heads clambered out. From seven of these heads, seven tongues snaked out like the whips of old Alabama slavemasters. Its body was that of a man and its legs that of a horse. Glenroy shuddered in terror.

Between its legs was a two-headed, flame-coloured snake and impaled on its spiked body were screaming children. Horrified, Glenroy backed away. Not even Tarzan, Superman or Doctor Who could fight this monster.

A mighty roar from the beast, like the death scream of a million Red Indians, rattled the conkers of the trees and caused the red bushes to uproot themselves. The milky rivers turned a red-brown. The lambs and cubs struggled to maintain their footing. Towards the east the sun seemed to drop out of the sky and in the west a violent storm gathered, shadowing the entire land. The air became very hot despite the raging wind. Glenroy thought he would surely die.

A battle raged between the lions and the monster. Glenroy saw that no animal was a match for this appalling brute. Fifty lions met their death within the first minute of the clash. The beast, crawling on all fours, moved towards the cubs and lambs.

It was at this moment that the man sitting on the throne struck his stick at the edge of the pit with earth-shattering force. Far-off mountains crumbled and the entire land began to crack. Long-haired angels carried tornado winds towards the monster, forcing it back to the mouth of the hole. It stumbled while cursing the man sitting on the throne. It fell back into the smoking gulf. While falling, it caught itself on the jagged teeth, tearing its body apart. A volcanic death cry shook the ground. The yelping and screaming faded as the beast fell into the core of the world.

The man, who was now standing, hurled an enormous black metal lid, which landed perfectly over the top of the pit. The angels sealed it with liquid. A sweet-smelling smoke filled the air. Raindrops that tasted of honey healed the ground. Before Glenroy's eyes, the trees grew branches to a full length. He heard soothing music that instructed him to walk towards the mouth of the pit. He recognised a wailing, deep within the ground. But it was impossible to reach its source. He stood still and wept.

Diving into Trouble

Glenroy parted the royal-blue curtains to reveal a golden dawn. The orchard was still, yet to be aroused for the day ahead. He heard the rhythmic pecking of a raven that had taken a peculiar liking to the bruised door of the outhouse beneath the dormitory window.

As his eyes adjusted to the morning sunlight, the images from his terrible dream came back to him. He shuddered as a chill caressed his spine, causing him to blink rapidly and shake his head. Maybe that horrible place in his nightmare was the Hell that Uncle Thomas was always talking about. He thought about asking Father Patrick if the monster he had seen in his nightmare was the devil – but thought better of it. He willed himself to think of chocolate cakes.

Looking out the window, the grass fields beckoned him out to play. He spotted squirrels hurrying along the branches of oak trees. Skylarks swooped down to the ground, capturing worms between their beaks.

Closing the curtains, he looked around the dormitory and saw that the others were all asleep. The room, apart from three double wardrobes and three chests of drawers, was bare. The tiled floor was uncovered, save for the small mats beside every child's bed. Games and toys were stacked precariously on top of the wardrobes. Pictures of football teams were Sellotaped to the cream-painted walls. Comics, including the *Beano*, *Whizzer* and *Chips*, *Tarzan* and *Spider Man* were kept in a cabinet beside the end wall. School books, pencil cases, notepads and erasers lay on bedside tables. In Glenroy's bedside locker was a pad of paper, pencils, an armless Action Man, three marbles and two greying tennis balls.

Next to Glenroy slept the eleven-year-old Ian Banks, and at the bottom of his bed rested a book about the adventures of Robin Hood. Glenroy recalled that on Ian's last birthday he had asked Auntie Mary if he could have the novel *Oliver Twist*. It was denied him.

Listening to the hum of various breathing patterns, Glenroy decided against telling Ivan that he snored loudly. Collecting his torn, itchy dressing gown, he went downstairs as quietly as his tread would allow him. He heard Auntie Mary whistling to herself in the kitchen.

The housemother had made two mugs of tea and Glenroy caught her picking the sleep from her eyes. She glared at Glenroy then glanced at the kitchen clock above the cooker. Seven fifteen. 'What are you doing up so early?' she scolded. 'Can't you have a lie-in like the rest of the kids? What's a matter with you? Eh? Can't I get any bloody peace in the mornings?'

'I … I woke up early, Auntie. I went to bed early yesterday.'

'And the same thing will happen again if I hear a squeal from you today!'

Mary stared blankly at the mugs of tea; one was for her husband. She considered her day ahead, thinking of the endless shrieks, moans and misbehaving that the day would surely bring. She comforted herself that at least it was Saturday and if the weather was generous, she could tell the younger kids to play outside and out of her way. For a short moment, she reflected on her naïve young days, when she was filled with such great purpose and desire to help unfortunate children. Now, she just looked forward to the end of the week, to the end of the month, a day nearer to retirement.

'Can … can I have my breakfast, please?' Glenroy asked, hoping he would not be sent back to bed.

'Yes, alright then. As long as you're quiet. But if you start running around and waking up the other kids, I'll give you what for! Go on with you! Wait inside the dining room and I'll bring you some toast.'

'Thank you very much, Auntie.'

Glenroy walked into the dining room and sat down at the far end of the junior table. He looked at the chair where Uncle Thomas always sat, and he started seeing images from his nightmare. The big throne where the giant watched over his kingdom, Glenroy thought. He shook his head, blinking furiously as Mary entered carrying a plate of toast. 'What's a matter with you? Eh? You got ants in your pants? *Sit* at the table properly and take your elbows off. Where's your manners?'

'Sorry, Auntie Mary.'

As Mary laid the plate in front of him, he noticed the toast was burned at the corners. 'Thank you, Auntie Mary.'

Glenroy reached for the jam jar and a knife. He covered his toast as if he was plastering a wall. Auntie Mary tutted. 'I hope you've learned your lesson.'

'Yes, Auntie Mary.' *Bleeding* wicked witch from the east and west! Glenroy thought. One day I'll walk to France and go to a home there. And I'll stay up as long as I want!

Squirts of jam stuck on the corners of Glenroy's mouth as he sank his toast. As he wiped his mouth clean with a napkin, he stiffened when he saw Thomas approaching from the hallway. 'I've just booked the swimming pool for ten o clock,' he announced cheerfully. 'So make sure you do your morning chores. You're allowed to invite one of your friends along, perhaps Carlton from next door? He's always well behaved, a good lad. Make sure you get permission from his housemother though. I wish you could be more like him. Maybe if you played football with him more often instead of sitting down drawing things all the time you'd lose some of that flab.'

'Yes, Uncle Thomas.'

An hour later, Glenroy walked out the back door and trotted down the steps. He skipped along the pathway to next door's back entrance and knocked loudly. He waited patiently for an answer as he tried to straighten his hand-me-down football shorts.

He saw a shadow coming towards the door and heard a friendly voice. 'Is that you, Glenroy?'

'Yeah.'

The door swung open to reveal a smiling woman. Glenroy returned her good humour. She had dimples in her cheeks. Red, curly hair topped off her petite frame and her forty-one years were not betrayed by her unlined face. Glenroy always wanted to ask her if she had ever heard Uncle Thomas serving out scoldings and spankings in his study from the other side of the wall where she worked.

She ushered Glenroy inside. 'Carlton's just having his wash. I'll tell him you're here – wait a moment.'

She smiled at Glenroy before leaving the cloakroom. Glenroy was left to study the children's footwear in the wooden stack of lockers. Each cabinet had a name tag on it, unlike the wire mesh rack in which he placed his footwear at home. He noted that one kid was lucky enough to own a pair of Gola trainers. Maybe his family bought them, he thought. He heard someone splashing about in the washroom.

Moments later, Carlton appeared. 'Wotcha, Glenroy. You're a bit early.'

'You wanna come swimming?' Glenroy asked excitedly. 'We're going at ten o'clock. Uncle Thomas asked for you to come.'

'Nah. I'm going around the dump to see if I can get a wheel for my trolley this morning,' Carlton replied. 'And anyway, the stuff they put in the water to make it clean itches my skin. It makes it go all grey.'

'You *never* come swimming with me,' Glenroy complained. 'But when you ask I always go with you.'

'You always ask when I'm doing something,' Carlton replied. 'You know how long it took me to find a decent seat for my trolley! I wanna get to the dump early so I can get some good wheels. And I did go swimming with you two weeks ago – that time your Auntie Mary took us when Uncle Thomas had flu.'

'Yeah, but that was the first time in a long time,' Glenroy recalled. 'I thought you were my friend.'

'I am your friend but I have to get to the dump. I was gonna ask you to come with me.'

'Why can't you go to the dump in the afternoon? I'll go with you then.'

'Cos I'm going shopping with Auntie Josephine – she's buying us some clothes.'

'You don't have to go. I don't have to go when Auntie Mary buys my clothes. You just don't wanna go swimming cos you don't wanna do stuff with me any more! I bet you'd go with Bullet if he asked.'

'Stop your moaning! Everyone's right at school when they say you're too sulky. You're like a girl! And anyway, none of your clothes fit you cos you're never there when Auntie Mary buys 'em.'

'I'm not sulking! And who wants to spend a Saturday afternoon going shopping? What's wrong with ya? Wanna hold Auntie Josephine's hand to the bus stop?'

'Keep saying that and you'll be eating my fist. At least Auntie Josephine buys me clothes that fit me.'

'Auntie Mary bought me a new pair of plimsolls the other day. They fit me.'

Carlton grinned. 'You're only allowed to wear 'em at school.'

'At least they'll last!'

'Auntie Josephine's buying me Golas. That'll make ya sulk.'

Glenroy opened the back door and stormed out of the house. 'You're the one who's a sulker!'

Dejected, Glenroy trudged along the road. Passing the nursery, he watched the milk float wheezing up the hill on its round, the bottles tinkling and the orange crates shifting from left to right. It formed a backdrop for the larks in the oak trees. Gentle breezes caressed the leaves and cooled Glenroy's temper.

He looked to his left and searched the field. He noticed it was polka-dotted with sprouting buttercups. Spring had arrived. The early morning mist that had veiled the bushes in the valley of the buttercup field was now thinning, and a rich, green tapestry of tree-tops filled the horizon, underneath a clear blue sky.

He watched a fox chase after a flock of birds. He made a mental note to venture down the valley later to try and locate the fox's den. He ran down the road for another fifty yards until he came to a pair of cottages on his right-hand side, identical to his and Carlton's homes. He trotted up to the back door of the house nearest the road and knocked loudly. The heavy door creaked open to reveal a black teenager of about fourteen years old. Dressed in football kit and a tracksuit top, he looked down at Glenroy as if he was an underling. 'I s'pose you want Elvin?'

'Yeah. Please,' Glenroy replied, remembering his manners to an older boy – those who didn't were regularly thrown into the stream on the way to school.

'Elvin! Glenroy's at the back door.'

The youth departed, not giving Glenroy a second glance. The slim figure of Elvin appeared. He had an acorn-shaped head with sad, dark eyes. His short, tufty hair was crying out for hair oil and his knees looked like sandpapered doorknobs.

'You wanna come swimming?' Glenroy asked.

Elvin's eyes came alive. 'Yeah! If I'm allowed.'

'My uncle Thomas booked it for ten o'clock, so make sure you get permission. Then call for me at quarter to ten.'

'Are you allowed two mates?' asked Elvin. 'Did you ask Carlton an' all?'

'Yeah, but he's doing something.'

'Did you see the fight yesterday? Osgood beat up that new boy.'

Glenroy wiped his nose. 'I was there. Didn't you see me? That new boy, Bullet, he's a bit of a div. Everyone knows to stay miles clear of Osgood. We tried to tell him that on the way home.'

'You walked home with Bullet?' asked Elvin. 'You'd better mind Osgood doesn't beat you up an' all.'

'He won't.'

'He will!' Elvin raised his voice. 'Osgood's on a mission to beat up everyone in our class. You'd better learn to fight.'

'I can fight!' Glenroy countered. 'It's just that you lot haven't seen me in action lately.'

Glenroy launched himself into shadow boxing, throwing a right and a left uppercut, weaving and dancing around. '*Punch like a rhino, uppercut like a giraffe, by round four you'll be taking an early bath!*'

Elvin collapsed into giggles. When he recovered, he looked above

Glenroy's head, hearing the sound of the milk float. 'That Bullet's weird. When the teacher's not looking he takes out his toy soldiers from a jamboree bag.'

Glenroy laughed. 'Serves him right he got beat up if he plays with little boys' toys.'

'Elvin!' An adult voice boomed from the kitchen. 'Your breakfast is ready.'

Elvin bade farewell and closed the door.

At 9.55 a.m. Glenroy and Elvin, towel and swimming trunks under their arms, hared towards the swimming pool, taking a short cut through the orchard along a narrow, twisted, dried-mud path. The orchard, fronted by unclipped hedges, grew thicker the further they ran, where the trees quit and dense blackberry bushes grew wildly, along with head-high stinging nettles. No daring teenager made a secret camp here.

As Glenroy and Elvin left the fruit trees behind, they entered a field of long, pale grass that climbed to their waists. Grasshoppers debated loudly, hornets buzzed, dragonflies fizzed and daddy long legs crawled.

'Africa country' stretched out for over half a mile, until it met the orbital road where an enterprising housefather had set up allotments to grow potatoes, tomatoes and cabbages. Fifty yards beyond the allotments, bisecting an untamed field, a chicken-wire fence marked the eastern border of the children's homes complex. Beyond that, rising up into the distance and sweeping through the Kent border, were farmlands.

Elvin and Glenroy left the field through a gap in the hedge on its south side. Their footsteps sounded heavier as they skipped along the tarmac approaching the swimming pool building. Standing guard in the background was a blue- and red-bricked water tower. The two boys often wondered how old the swimming pool building was – with its red-slated, angled roofs, concrete walkways and a network of black pipes that were almost big enough for a football to be kicked through.

They could both smell the hot steam that came from the laundry and they heard the irritating din of work tools echoing from the engineers' depot. Council workmen loathed working in this location because of the walking distances; it was two and a half miles to the nearest bus stop. Carlton had got on friendly terms with a painter who worked at the depot and on many occasions Carlton was dispatched to the shops to buy a drink for the decorator, and rewarded with ten pence for his five-mile round trip. In the summer months he spent his earnings on strawberry-iced jubblys and teased Glenroy with them.

Pinewood Oaks had its own team of carpenters, plumbers, engineers, glaziers, gardeners and many other workmen, mainly performing repair and maintenance tasks. In the factory beside the water tower, part-time female staff darned socks, repaired clothes, laundered bed sheets and sewed council name tags on garments for the new arrivals. The workforce were discouraged from building any sort of relationship with the children and it was strictly forbidden for any workers to take a child outside the grounds of the complex, even on a trip to the shops.

Elvin and Glenroy sprinted the rest of the way to the swimming pool. Uncle Thomas's mud-splattered jeep was parked outside the blue doors. The boys entered and were met by a riot of squawks, ricocheting around the pool's red-painted walls.

'Uncle Thomas never gives me a lift to the swimming pool,' Glenroy moaned, walking towards the cubicles that were situated on the right-hand side of the pool.

Entering the booth next to Glenroy, Elvin replied. 'That's probably because you're one of the oldest now. The little ones will get knackered walking all this way.'

'What about Colin? He's ten and he got a lift! Little pissing conker head!'

Elvin closed the door of his chamber and secured the small lock. 'That's because he's not in your house, you divo! I heard that Uncle Thomas promised Colin's housemother he's gonna teach him how to swim.'

'Oh yeah,' said Glenroy. 'I forgot about that. But last time I came with Carlton he gave us a lift.'

Minutes later, the two boys joined the fray in the pool. The able swimmers dive-bombed and jumped into the deep end while the not-so-floatable were schooled by Uncle Thomas. Polystyrene white floats drifted like miniature icebergs on the pool's surface.

The older children fought for the use of a single pair of goggles. Glenroy and Elvin played tag in and out of the water.

'How many times do I have to tell you?' barked Uncle Thomas. '*Don't* run. *Walk!* Someone might get hurt.'

Before the children knew it, the time had crept up close to eleven o'clock. Thomas beckoned everybody out of the water. The house-father dried himself while walking up and down the length of the pool, making sure everybody had returned to their cubicles. He grabbed another towel from a chair and paced quickly towards the cubicles where Elvin and Glenroy were changing. He came to a halt and banged on Elvin's door.

'Elvin! I have your towel,' Thomas said in a kindly manner. 'You must've left it on a chair.'

Elvin held his cubicle door ajar. Following a quick glance over his shoulder, Thomas stepped inside. Elvin was naked, dripping with water. Confused, he looked at the towel. He placed his hands under his jaws. The scent of chlorine lingered on his body. Thomas smiled. He stroked Elvin's wet hair. Elvin flinched and grabbed the towel. Not letting go of the towel, Thomas proceeded to dry Elvin's back. His other hand stroked Elvin's genitals. He grinned again. 'Did you enjoy that?'

Unable to move, Elvin stood frozen. Petrified. Every nerve repulsed the presence of the older man. He so wanted to wrench the towel off Thomas and cover himself. But he couldn't. He gazed at the wet floor and pushed his elbows into his belly. Thomas finally relaxed his grip on the towel. Elvin grabbed it immediately and wrapped it around his waist. He recoiled again as he spotted Thomas's penis bulging inside his trunks. Elvin turned around, facing the wall. He made a fist and gripped onto his towel. He became conscious of the sound of his own breathing. He closed his eyes. He felt a rough hand stroke his hair then caress his shoulders. His neck and back muscles locked tight. His throat became dry. He felt Thomas's hand slide over his backside before leaving his body. For a few seconds he couldn't exhale. He then heard the door click and close again. It was a long minute until he turned around to confirm that Thomas had indeed departed. He sat down with his back pressed against the wall and pushed the towel into his face.

On the way home through the orchard, Glenroy asked Elvin: 'Did Uncle Thomas tell you off for messing about with your towel near the water?'

Elvin walked with his eyes trained to the ground. 'Yeah ... he did,' he stuttered. 'But ... before I jumped in the pool I put it back in my cubicle. Someone ... someone must've taken it out again.'

They walked on in silence. Normally, they would play a game of tag on the way home or hide behind bushes and shrubbery making jungle sounds as they watched others go by. 'Did he hit you?' Glenroy wanted to know.

'No. He ... he sort of ... told me off about the towel,' replied Elvin. 'And, he, er ... yeah, he said that I should come to swimming classes. Cos, er ... yeah. He said there's something wrong with my front stroke. But ... I don't wanna go.'

Glenroy kicked a twig. 'Why not? You said he didn't hit you? You're the lucky one! If that was me he would've sent me home and given me a beating later when he got back.'

'I *don't* like him,' Elvin insisted. He quickened his pace. It turned into a sprint. 'I'm not coming swimming with you again! No way!'

'What's-a-matter with you! He didn't beat ya. Flipping daisies! He only told you off about the towel!'

Elvin kept on running.

Glenroy chased his pal and leaped on his back. 'Gotcha, acorn head!' he cried as they fell forward. The front of Elvin's T-shirt turned an instant light-brown as it kissed the dried mud. Elvin twisted and squirmed free. 'GET LOST! LEAVE ME ALONE!'

Glenroy attempted a grip he had seen on Saturday afternoon wrestling. 'Say you submit, acorn head! Say you submit!'

'GET OFF! GET YOUR FAT HANDS OFF ME!'

Elvin shoved Glenroy away. Tears fell down his cheeks. He scampered off as quickly as his legs would allow him. Giving up on the chase and realising it wasn't a game any more, Glenroy stood still and watched. Maybe I called him acorn head too much, he thought. But he shouldn't moan. He calls me fat all the time! He turned around, stared at the trees for a while and jogged the rest of the way home.

PART 2
TIGHT CIRCUIT

2 June 1976

Curvis worked the rusty spanner around the nut of the front wheel of a bike, securing it to its axle. He hoisted the front forks and spun the metal hoop, searching for any signs of a kink. Smiling, he was satisfied with his work. 'That's a lot better, innit,' he said proudly. 'It's got a little buckle on it but you can hardly see it.'

Inspecting the spinning disc like a jeweller, Carlton agreed. 'Yeah. It's going around straight. I'll give you that. But if I fall off the thing, I'm still gonna blame you though.'

'Blame me! If it weren't for me you wouldn't have a bike,' said Curvis, wielding his spanner in mock anger. He spotted a speck of oil on the bike frame and wiped it off with a cloth.

'What d'you mean?' argued Carlton. 'It was me who found the frame at the dump. And I was the one who painted it. And I got the brakes.'

'Got the brakes?' Curvis laughed. 'Is that what you call it? You took apart that bike that was outside the chippy last month. D'you think we don't know that? You're crookier than a burglar's back! How would you feel if you came out of a shop and saw that some thief had taken your brakes?'

Carlton smirked. 'I'm sure whoever it belonged to, their parents can probably buy a substitute; especially those posh people who live behind the chippy.'

The two friends were inside the outhouse behind Carlton's cottage, surrounded by bits of wood, bike frames, nuts, bolts, washers, worn spanners, chipped screwdrivers and small, empty oil cans. Curvis had grown to almost six foot and there wasn't an ounce of fat on his taut body. His misshapen Afro was left to its own devices and his slender fingers had grown unusually long. Not as tall, Carlton had fully developed shoulders and owned a chest that promised perfect power. His limbs had thickened considerably and his jaws had squared into a face of determination. Crippled bike frames, punctured tyres, mangled spokes and broken trolley wheels were piled in an undignified heap in a corner of the dusty room. A snow sledge, with a frayed rope attached to it, waited for the winter months in another corner. Forgotten, headless Action Men and one-eyed dolls were kept in a cardboard box with other broken toys beneath the window frame.

Carlton peered through a cracked, blackened window. 'Hey! Bullet, Glenroy! Get your arses inside.'

Bullet and Glenroy were trying to head-lock each other in a grappling contest. Just over five foot tall, Bullet had grown his hair long. He owned a pair of powerful, squat legs that offered him the speed to compete for the local schools sprint championships. He had big hands with fleshy fingers that enabled him to negotiate the most challenging trees. The cheek in his eyes attracted teenage girls in Pinewood Oaks, although he was unaware of it. Glenroy now weighed over fourteen stone. His round, cherubic features had developed faint laughter lines. His double chin was nearing completion. They untangled themselves and looked towards the window. Carlton beckoned to them. Two spanner turns later they entered the damp of the outhouse and watched Carlton sitting imperiously on his bike as Curvis picked up his tools from the floor.

'Can't you two keep your hands off each other even for a second?' mocked Carlton. 'You're like two poofs!'

'Takes one to know one!' returned Glenroy.

'Least I don't play kiss chase with boys,' Carlton sniped.

'You're just saying that cos you haven't got the bollocks to take us on in a wrestling match,' countered Bullet. He right-hooked the air in front of him.

'Take you two losers on?' Carlton laughed. 'I could beat the two of you even if I was in a straitjacket.'

Without warning, Glenroy sprung upon Carlton, strangling him, while Bullet grabbed Carlton's left arm and twisted it behind his back. The bike fell to the floor. 'Mind the bike!' Curvis yelled.

He was ignored.

'Say you submit,' Bullet urged.

'Aaaarrggg! Get off, you wankers!'

Bullet tightened his hold. 'Say you submit!'

'Uuhhhggghh, aaarrrgghhh. Alright! Alright! I submit.'

Bullet grinned triumphantly. He loosened his hold. 'Easy … What was that bollocks you were saying before?'

'Hummpphh. I didn't hear any starting bell,' complained Carlton. 'You just caught me by surprise. That's the only way you'll beat me. You're still amateurs.'

Everyone laughed save Curvis who shook his head, staring aghast at the damaged paintwork on the bike.

'So you're going in the race with that?' Glenroy pointed at the bike with contempt. 'You've got about as much chance of flying in a space rocket.'

'At least I can fit in a space rocket,' retaliated Carlton.

'Ain't no way you're gonna beat me.'

'All because you bullied Elvin into lending you his bike for the race,' said Carlton. 'By the way, how did Elvin get the money for his new bike?'

'Uncle Thomas gave him most of it,' replied Glenroy. 'Elvin helped him teach swimming to the under-elevens last week. They had a long natter in his study. I tried to listen but Auntie Mary told me to scarper. Elvin came out with thirty pound or something. He didn't look too happy about it. *Thirty* fucking pound! If that was me I'd be doing handsprings.'

'Thirty pound!' Bullet repeated. 'With that I could buy the new Adidas Beckenbauer boots, a pair of Adidas Bamba trainers and still have enough money to go to the pictures and buy my comics.'

'Comics!' Glenroy said with contempt. 'You'd waste a lot of that money on comics!'

'What's wrong with buying com—'

'Alright, you two!' Curvis intervened. 'Let's see how this bike rolls.'

Carlton carefully wheeled his bike out of the outhouse and onto a path. The children from his household, playing a game of rounders in the field behind the outhouse, cheered their hero as he mounted the bicycle. 'You're looking at the winner!' he shouted to them, pumping his fist into the air.

Ten minutes later, Carlton and his friends arrived at the rendez-vous point for the start of the annual Pinewood Oaks cycle race. The pedal-off was outside Violet House, whose sports-loving housefather, Mr Brewmington, had organised the event. Some competitors were cruising around on their bikes. Others were completing last-minute checks on brakes, forks, gears and water bottles. Most were dressed in football shorts and white vests. Carlton was wearing cut-down jeans and a yellow T-shirt. Mr Brewmington, a portly figure, who some whispered should do more riding bikes than refereeing races, had his long hair tied in a ponytail. His beard rivalled a black-haired Santa Claus and his sideburns could have carpeted a small bungalow. He strutted his stage, fiddling with his whistle in his England football team tracksuit.

Wearing a grey, nondescript tracksuit, Glenroy searched for Elvin. He looked for him for another five minutes until Elvin emerged from around a corner on his gleaming new bicycle. 'Hey, Elvin,' Glenroy called. 'Have you done the brakes? Have you oiled the cogs and chain? You're s'posed to do those things cos you're my bike engi-neer – Carlton's got Bullet.'

'What for?' replied Elvin. 'The bike's brand new, innit. And cos it's new, don't pull the brakes too hard, otherwise you will go head over tit and knee over bollocks.'

'Me, fall off?' laughed Glenroy. 'You're talking like a tosspot. Have I ever fallen off?'

'YES!' chorused five voices.

Meanwhile, Curvis climbed a tree and perched himself on a branch overlooking the starting line. Hands behind his head, he watched the proceedings beneath him. He spotted Bullet, championing Carlton's case to anybody who would listen.

Twenty-two cyclists assembled together along the starting point. Mr Brewmington formed the racers into a straight line with a level of fuss that suggested he was firing the gun for an Olympic 100-metre final. Glenroy muscled his way into the middle of the line-up, stealing a few inches. He was soon put in place by the eagle-eyed Mr Brewmington, who took the opportunity to test his whistle. Spectators covered their ears.

Carlton's face was rigid with concentration. Mellor, slightly older than Carlton and wearing a Chelsea football club woolly hat, glanced across the line with nervous apprehension. Others had eyes only for the road ahead. It was a flat start. They would race three hundred yards or so before a sharp left in front of the community centre.

Mr Brewmington dramatically marched ten yards beyond the start, whistle primed in his mouth. Then he blew with enough gusto to play the *Star Wars* fanfare. The faces of the competitors strained. Their calf muscles tightened as they pedalled furiously to gain an advantage.

Spectators yelled out their support from under the shade of trees. Elvin joined Curvis in the tree. They both watched the racers disappear into the sun-hazed distance. Curvis looked down at Bullet. 'Save your shouting till he comes round the last bend.'

'On that bike Carlton needs all the shouting he can get,' replied Bullet. 'He said he'll buy us jubblys if he wins.'

'If I was you I'd save my pennies for an ice pole,' someone laughed.

'And if I was you I'd shut my mouth,' Bullet challenged.

'I've seen an elephant with a lighter frame than Carlton's bike.'

'And I've seen a sock puppet with more teeth than you might have if you don't shut your cake hole!'

'Lightwood's gonna win it,' predicted Curvis.

'What makes you say that?' asked Elvin. 'My money's on Mellor.'

'Lightwood's good at cross-country so that means he's got loads of stamina,' reasoned Curvis. 'The others will all rush off and knacker themselves out. Around Pinewood Oaks is about three and a half miles, and the way most of them set off, they're not gonna last.'

'Where do you reckon Glenroy and Carlton will finish?' Elvin wanted to know.

'Carlton will never give up. He hates to lose anything. Glenroy…'

Curvis tailed off but Elvin guessed Curvis had little confidence in Glenroy. 'Will be last?' Elvin completed the sentence. 'I hope he's not too fat for my new bike. He might squash my thin tyres – they use them kind of tyres in the Tour of France.'

Meanwhile, at the front of the race, Glenroy had stolen a lead of three bike lengths. The riders behind him were tightly packed. Beads of sweat marked every brow. They were reaching speeds of thirty miles an hour as they raced downhill. Kids stationed in the 'piggery' were cheering and shouting. Others lined the pavement, willing on their favourites. They saw one racer hit a kerb, fall and slide on his back across the unforgiving asphalt.

The bikers rode through the valley. Their expressions creased as they climbed the hill that would take them by the nursery building. Skateboarders frantically rolled off the road. They made hurried landings on the grass as the bikers pedalled towards them. The sharp rise had exhausted Glenroy. His thighs seemed to be carrying lead weights. His calves had stiffened like setting glue. Mellor had caught up with him on the left-handed bend at the top end of the orchard. Carlton and Lightwood positioned themselves in the middle of the pack, waiting to pounce for the final push in the home straight. They raced under the shade of a sycamore tree; Carlton knew this was the halfway mark.

Mellor glanced at Glenroy. He gained inspiration from his obvious fatigue. He surged ahead to take the outright lead. Widening gaps began to appear between the racers. They flashed past the swimming pool – sun rays ricocheted off its glass, wire-meshed roof. Carlton made his calculated move. He neared the leaders. Lightwood stalked him, taking huge gulps of air and trying to control his breathing.

The peloton swooped downhill. Past the blue-bricked water tower that shadowed them for three seconds. The race began in earnest with everyone realising that to fall behind now would mean certain defeat. No slowing down to ride over the ramps. The children playing in the vale near the stream had spotted them, and moved accordingly. They raced over the bridge all in their top gears. They braced themselves again for the ascent that would take them past another children's play area. Glenroy's legs simply couldn't respond to his will. He rocked from side to side, gnashed his teeth. All reserves of energy abandoned him. He was eventually passed by the peloton. He dropped substantially behind the leaders, slowed and gave up the race. 'Aaaarrrgggh! My leg!' he feigned injury.

Up front, Mellor had a two-bike length lead but was being chased by Carlton. Gradually and surely, Carlton reached Mellor's back wheel. The leader glanced back in alarm while frantically shifting his gears. They crested the brow of the hill and turned left into the finishing straight. Carlton was just half a bike length down.

The spectators, two hundred yards away at the finishing road ramp, spotted the leaders. Carlton summoned every muscle in his body as he forced himself past Mellor. Curvis and Elvin jumped down from the tree, shouting encouragement. Other supporters, including Bullet, did likewise. 'COME ON, CARLTON. PUMP THOSE FUCKING LEGS!'

With a huge effort, Lightwood went by Mellor and was now closing on Carlton. Fifty yards to go. Carlton was one bike length ahead. Twenty-five yards to go. Carlton's face twisted and twirled, his calf muscles glistening in the sun, his arms taut on the handlebars, his fingertips turning red. Head down. In a flash Carlton glanced at Lightwood and saw his doom. The two leaders came dangerously close together. Lightwood emitted a desperate grunt, his backside off the seat. He was inches away from the lead. Carlton had no more to give, his body yielding to exhaustion. Lightwood was ecstatic as he rolled over the ramp centimetres ahead of Carlton. His friends all performed jigs of delight and they ran after him.

Mellor came home in third place, about twenty yards behind the first two. As soon as he dismounted his bike, he collapsed on the grass underneath a tree, panting furiously. A girl went to tend to him with a bottle of water. Carlton lay on his back on the pavement, breathing hard, unable to move his limbs. Curvis and Elvin ambled towards him, proud of their friend's efforts.

'Flying blue tits!' exclaimed Curvis. 'When you came into the straight I thought you was gonna win.'

Carlton's spent face turned into anger. 'So did I!' He abruptly got to his feet and kicked the front wheel of the bike. 'Fucking Lightwood! He only won cos he had a better bike than me. I'm gonna ask him for another race tomorrow … Can't believe I lost.'

'Don't take it out on the bike,' scolded Curvis. 'D'you know how much time I spent on that?'

'But you done better than expected,' said Elvin. 'You pushed Lightwood as close as you could get. Must've been inches.'

'Don't matter how close,' Carlton replied. 'I still lost! Someone get me a fucking drink.'

Elvin ran over to a girl who was carrying a bottle of water. He returned to Carlton and handed it to him. Carlton half-emptied the one-litre bottle in one go. 'Can't believe I lost,' he repeated.

Examining his stopwatch, Mr Brewmington declared, 'Lightwood! That was a Pinewood Oaks record. Well done, son. That was the best finish for years. You'll get your tenner later on.' Mr Brewmington then turned to Carlton. 'Good effort, Carlton, we all thought as you came around the last bend that you had it in the kit bag. Hard lines. Perhaps you need a better bike?'

Carlton's face betrayed his devastation. 'By the way, what happened to Glenroy?' Mr Brewmington enquired.

'What? Hasn't he finished yet?' Carlton replied. He searched the finishers sprawled on the grass and tarmac.

'No sign of him,' said Mr Brewmington. 'He didn't fall, did he?'

'Probably,' one passer-by quipped.

Getting to his feet, Carlton walked as if he had custard in his legs.

'I don't think so,' he said. 'I passed him just by the bridge near the stream.'

'He probably gave up,' said Curvis.

Elvin picked up Carlton's bike. 'I hope he hasn't mashed up my new bike. I'll push him into nettle dike if he has.'

'We'd better go and look for him,' suggested Bullet. 'Knowing Glenroy, he probably crashed into a tree.'

'Poor tree,' said Carlton.

Elvin wasn't amused.

The friends set off across the sloping field. They could see the stream sparkling silver in the distance underneath an amber sun. Young girls played rounders in the twilight. 'Fuck Glenroy, let's watch this,' Elvin laughed.

They ignored Elvin and continued to stroll downhill across the baked grass. The street lights, set about thirty yards apart, came on, illuminating the orbital road.

Elvin mounted Carlton's bike as the others trudged on. Bullet leaped onto the stone wall, the stream five feet below him. Underneath the umbrella of branches and leaves, he spotted Glenroy throwing stones in the water.

'There he is,' pointed Bullet. 'Down there.'

The quartet looked down along the banks of the stream and saw Glenroy with his head bowed. Elvin pedalled towards him, anxiety spreading over his face. 'Where's my bike?'

Turning around, Glenroy watched Elvin approach him with a blank expression. He said nothing. Elvin located his bike lying on the grass near a cluster of bushes. He dismounted and went over to run a check. 'Why are you on a sulkathon?' Curvis chuckled. 'Someone threw a pine tree in your spokes?'

'My foot slipped and I fell on the grass,' Glenroy lied. 'I just missed crashing into the wall. It wasn't worth rejoining the race. But I could've won if it wasn't for that.'

'And then the little piggy shitted on the moon,' laughed Carlton. 'Why are you lying? You were knackered.'

Curvis and Bullet both held back belly laughs.

'No, I wasn't tired!' Glenroy stormed. 'I was saving myself for the finish! Like them professional bikers in the Tour of France.'

The others giggled as Glenroy threw another pebble into the stream. Elvin ambled towards his friends, satisfied that his bike was not damaged. 'Hey, Elvin,' Carlton called. 'Glenroy reckons his foot slipped off the pedal and he nearly crashed into the wall of the bridge.'

Elvin grinned. 'None of us need to watch *Jackanory* tomorrow – we'll just listen to Glenroy. Mellor told me he was burnt out and gave up.'

'Mellor's a liar!' Glenroy raged. 'You always believe anything he says. If it weren't for Elvin's stupid bike I would've won. I was *pretending* to be tired.'

Glenroy's friends laughed again, collapsing to the turf. Abruptly Glenroy stood up. 'I'm going home. I dunno why you lot came to look for me if all you can do is take the piss.'

'Stop sulking!' Carlton rebuked. 'Fuck the daisies! Sometimes it's like we have a seven-year-old with us. Hang up, I'll go with ya. But I don't wanna hear you stropping in my ears all the way home.'

Carlton mounted his bike and quickly caught up with Glenroy. 'What's a matter with you?' he asked. 'Today's gotta be your biggest sulk yet.'

Glenroy didn't reply. He walked on, head down.

'For fuck's sake!' Carlton called after him. 'You're in a moan just because of the bike race?'

'NO!'

'Kendo Nagasaki lost to Mick McManus in the wrestling last Saturday?'

'NO!'

'Then what is it?'

'Why should I tell ya? You just wanna take the piss.'

'Oh, for fuck's sake!'

'It's Uncle Thomas.'

Carlton leaped off his bike and led it by the handlebars. 'What's Uncle Thomas done to you now?'

'He reckons I stole ten pounds,' Glenroy replied. 'And he's gonna speak to my social worker tomorrow. And he told Father Patrick. He wasn't gonna let me out this afternoon. I had to beg. Uncle Thomas says he's had enough of me and threatened to send me to Stanford House.'

'Stanford House!' Carlton repeated. His expression softened. 'Sweet nobblers. You don't wanna go there. That's where they sent Curvis's brother two years ago, and you know what happened to him, right?'

Stanton, Curvis's older brother, had been sent to Stanford House for continuous violent outbursts at his children's home in Kent. It all began four years ago when Stanton was refused permission to visit Curvis. Stanford House was a youth detention centre with a bad reputation. Tales of baton-wielding staff and metal straitjackets drifted to Pinewood Oaks. Some whispered that Stanton had lost his mind.

Glenroy nodded. 'Yeah, I know. But I didn't nick the ten pounds. And you know my social worker is gonna believe him – they always do. Fucking social wankers!'

'Didn't I did tell ya to change that useless cow of a social worker you got?' Carlton said. 'Didn't I tell ya?'

'She did take me to a Wimpy,' Glenroy cited. 'She bought me a Knickerbocker Glory. No one's bought me one before.'

'But she don't do fuck all for you!' Carlton raised his voice. 'Haven't you told her about the way that cunt treats ya?'

Glenroy shook his head.

Carlton closed his eyes and took in a deep breath of frustration. 'She's more interested in what biscuits she's gonna be offered and how much sugar she wants in her tea.'

'I wish I was in your house,' Glenroy lamented.

Carlton nodded.

'I'm not going to Stanford House,' Glenroy promised. 'I'll do anything than go to that shithole. I'll even run away.'

Carlton searched Glenroy's eyes and realised he was very serious, as serious as he had ever seen him. He stopped to pick up a blade of grass and inserted it inside his mouth. He started chewing. 'You run away,' he mocked. '*You*! What do you know about running away? Look at that time years ago when you started walking to France.'

'Back then I didn't know it was over the sea.'

'You turned around at the back gates. You wouldn't survive a day on your own.'

Glenroy smiled knowingly. 'Who says I'm going on my own,' he said.

Carlton struggled to respond. His eyebrows angled. 'Not going on your own?' he stuttered. 'It's Curvis, innit. You're gonna go with Curvis?'

'Yep,' Glenroy replied, his grin reaching his ears. 'We chatted last week about it but he's been on punishment until today, so we haven't had a chance to go over it. He's still mad about his Auntie not letting him see Stanton. He still won't talk to her.'

'I thought cos he was allowed out today, Curvis sorted it all out,' Carlton said. 'He's still not talking to her?'

'Nope. He told me today he'd rather go Stanford House than talk to that pale, witch-queen dragon. Yep, that's what he called her.'

Carlton laughed, nearly dropping his bike. 'A pale, witch-queen dragon,' he repeated.

They approached the orchard. Carlton tried to change Curvis's mind. If Glenroy and Curvis were about to run away, he would be obliged to go with them. Bullet would too. They were his friends and besides, the authorities would put intolerable pressure on him, pressure that Auntie Josephine could not protect him from. What am I gonna do?

Carlton turned to Glenroy again. 'You two are serious about this, innit? You're not fucking about just to wind me up?'

'Nope, we're not fucking about. I'll swear on my next toad in the hole and my next rhubarb crumble. Ain't no way I'm going Stanford House. Fuck that! They beat you up three times a day and put you in straitjackets there. They stop feeding ya and give ya funny pills. No fucking way!'

'Have you told Bullet about this?'

'Nope. I was gonna tell him today, but he was too busy wanting to give me a Johnny Kwango headbutt and a Giant Haystacks bellyslam – we wanted to tell you lot together.'

'We'll have to chat about this – all four of us,' Carlton suggested. 'You must realise that if you and Curvis go on a runner, they'll be asking me and Bullet loads of questions, and they'll be watching us all the time.'

Excitement spread over Glenroy's face. 'When are we gonna chat about it?' he asked. 'Tomorrow after school?'

'Nah. I've got sports for the rest of the week after school. It'll have to be Saturday. When you see Curvis and Bullet tomorrow, tell 'em.'

'So would you come?' Glenroy wanted to know.

Carlton couldn't hide his reluctance. 'I … I dunno. I want to know what Bullet makes of it. I know life for you lot in this place is shit. But Auntie Josephine treats me…' Carlton tailed off and glanced up through the branches. Stars were appearing in the night sky. 'If me and Bullet didn't go it would fuck up things for me and him.'

Glenroy cut his eyes at his friend. Carlton suddenly laughed. 'Imagine it,' he said. 'All four of us on the run. That'll give Uncle Thomas and the rest of 'em something to moan about. And it would wipe the snobby smile off Curvis's bitch of a housemother. Bullet's Uncle Rodney will probably call it desertion, fucking army-loving wanker. If I was Bullet, I'd tell him where to stick his shoe inspections and all that standing-to-attention bollocks. Why doesn't he fuck off outta here and join *Dad's Army* or something.'

'So you coming then?' asked Glenroy once more.

'I dunno. We could all end up in Stanford House. And they'll have one big problem finding a straitjacket to fit you.'

'I'd give you a Giant Haystacks bellyslam but I'll let that one go,' Glenroy said. 'You're still pissed off cos you lost to Lightwood. If you don't leg it with us, we'll go without you and you can stay with your *nice* Auntie Josephine and kiss her arse for all I care.'

'Not my fault I'm lucky and living in her house. She's been good to me. I know you lot have lived through shit. But I haven't got any big reason to do a runner.'

'That's alright for you to say,' Glenroy said. 'What did you say last year? That we're all brothers and we should do everything together. Some brother you are! I bet Bullet comes. He wouldn't care if he had a *nice* Auntie Josephine in his house. He'd come anyway. And that'll leave you on your tod.'

Carlton recalled a summer's day last year. He and his friends had watched a western on a rainy Sunday afternoon. All four had been mesmerised by a scene in which an Indian and a white man had slashed their palms and clasped their hands together in an act of brotherly love. It was Bullet's idea to re-enact the scene in the darkness of the damp orchard, all of them masking their pain with locked lips and taut cheeks. Curvis had stolen a small tube of antiseptic cream to prevent infection. Carlton and Bullet said they didn't need the cream, reasoning that the cowboy and Indian hadn't used it. Glenroy smothered his right palm with the lotion. They vowed to stand together and support each other, no matter what happened. As they went home that night, they sensed a kind of family belonging that had been denied them all their lives. Carlton knew that it was a bond that couldn't be broken. 'If everyone agrees,' he finally said, 'I'll go with you. But it has to be planned *good*. None of this Tommy Cooper make-it-up-on-the-spot crap.'

'Of course it'll be worked out! It'll be a proper mission. You know Curvis. He's probably looking at maps and planning it now.'

Gnats orbited their heads as they strolled home. The first hooting of an owl could be heard from a towering oak tree. 'So we definitely gonna have a meeting on Saturday to talk about all this?' Glenroy wanted confirmation.

'Yeah. I s'pose so. So don't piss off Uncle Thomas and get grounded.'

Before entering his home, Carlton spotted Auntie Josephine through a dining room window. She was preparing a table for breakfast. He felt a surge of guilt.

Democracy

Situated in the centre of the homes complex, sitting beside a children's play area which consisted of swings and seesaws, was a metal climbing frame. It looked like a big metal football with gaping holes in it. Draped on the frame were three male teenagers. A stocky figure perched on the top, balanced perfectly. He had long, brown hair and infant sideburns. Small pimples collected around his nose. His face seemed more red than white. He was wearing a blue sweat-stained vest. Below him, the debate raged.

'I like that, oh yeah, I like that,' disputed Bullet. 'You expect me to convince Carlton that we should leg it! What's next? If you decide to jump naked into the stinging nettles up by Skunkers Dike, would you expect us to do that an' all? You can't expect me and Carlton to come with you just because we're best friends.'

Curvis shook his head. 'You said to me the other week how you were fighting with your Uncle and how he beat you up. What did you say at the time? That if you was offered a bed in a kids' home in Siberia, you'd take it! Did that happen? No, it didn't! Even your social worker didn't believe you. Uncle Rodney's been picking on you for years. You seemed to have forgotten how he caned your arse every other day with that marching stick. Why don't you look at your arse in the mirror? I'm sure it's got a groove in it.'

Bullet wiped his runny nose. Curvis continued, 'If you do a runner, then they'll have to take you serious, innit. They're bound to give you a transfer. Just tell your social worker that you ran away cos Uncle Rodney keeps using you as a punch bag. Look at that time he busted your mouth wide open and he took you to the dentist. He told 'em you fell off a bike. You haven't even got a fucking bike! Whatever marbles Uncle Rodney had in his head have gone a long time ago. He thinks he's still fighting the Germans. The kids in your house might as well be wearing SS uniforms and doing that worm-crunching march.'

'Yeah,' Glenroy laughed. 'If I lived in his house I'd hit him with a coal shovel.'

'I can't remember you ever hitting Uncle Thomas back,' countered Bullet. 'And you didn't exactly kick him in the bollocks when he used to lock you up in the outhouse. You didn't even smash the windows to try and escape. So *don't* come with your Victoria Cross shit about fucking coal shovels.'

Curvis held Bullet's gaze. 'When did Uncle Rodney last hit you?' he asked Bullet.

'In April,' admitted Bullet. 'After me and Elvin nicked tomatoes from Uncle Sam's allotments. He hasn't touched me since.'

'You don't even like tomatoes,' remarked Glenroy.

Bullet shrugged. 'Elvin does.'

'He might not have touched you since the tomato raid,' said Curvis. 'But he still gives you stupid punishments. Look at that time he wouldn't let you stay up and watch the Ali fight? You only forgot to clean your football boots! It's not like he's gonna wear 'em to his army parades.'

'Yeah,' Bullet nodded. 'He was a right cunt for that. Believe me, that night I wanted to do him something in his sleep.'

Curvis half smiled.

'Alright, alright!' Bullet raised his voice. 'Say we all run away. Where are we gonna go? How are we gonna live? Fuck if I'm living on blackberries in the bushes! I bet you haven't thought of that, have you? You haven't planned fuck all! None of us has any rich uncles who live in mansions beside golf courses and who we can stay with.'

'What are you talking about?' said Curvis. 'I dunno what Glenroy has told you but I know where I'm going!'

Bullet turned to Glenroy, eyeing him like a teacher watching an unruly pupil. 'Alright, Glenroy. Where're you gonna go? Our old camp in the orchard? Paris? Hong fucking Kong? Pluto?'

Glenroy picked off the seven petals of a bright, colourful flower he had found while strolling near the allotments. His expression betrayed his confusion. 'Er … with Curvis, innit.'

'See. He don't know where the fuck he's going,' laughed Bullet. 'If you do decide to go on a runner, *don't* give him the compass!'

'I do know where I'm going,' countered Glenroy. 'I'm not gonna tell ya if you're not interested. You'll probably grass on us anyway.'

Bullet's eyebrows angled sharply. 'Fuck you! I ain't no fucking grass! Have I grassed on any of you since I've known ya?'

Bullet searched his friend's eyes and his fierce gaze unnerved Glenroy, causing him to slip and lose his grip on the climbing frame. He stretched out an arm and grabbed onto a bar. The flower he was holding, now only with three petals, danced in the air. Curvis watched it drop softly to the ground as Glenroy composed himself. 'Yes, you have!' Glenroy said. 'What about that time we were nicking wood from the top of Acacia's outhouse the night before bonfire night?'

'That was years ago,' replied Bullet. 'How old were we? About ten or eleven. You can't bring that up.'

'You said you haven't grassed,' sniped Glenroy. 'But you have! You're such a big grass I'm surprised they haven't asked you to roll yourself out so they can play tennis on ya.'

Curvis burst out laughing. He almost lost his grip on the frame.

'If I remember rightly, it was your fault I got caught anyway!' snarled Bullet. 'You were s'posed to be my lookout. Didn't look very good, did ya? I would've done better if I had a blindfolded Stevie Wonder with me with a brown bag on his bonce! I mean, how can you miss somebody with one of those giant battery torches in his hand and his Alsatian running about like it hasn't been fed for a month!'

'I couldn't see properly. It was misty that night.'

'Misty that night! The only mist around was inside your brain!'

'It was a stupid idea anyway,' Glenroy argued.

'Maybe stupid but you're still a *grass*. I'm surprised your Afro hasn't turned green.'

'Carry on and see if your head doesn't say hello to the nearest nettle bush!'

'You can come and try if it doesn't knacker you out too much by throwing a punch,' challenged Bullet.

Curvis watched his two friends, shaking his head. He looked around to see if Carlton was approaching, but couldn't see him. The row raged on.

'Alright, you two,' Curvis finally intervened. 'If this is what it's gonna be like on the run with you two, I might stay here for another year or five.'

There was peace for a few seconds. Gnats hovered above the climbing frame. Something disturbed the shrubbery. Curvis was the first to turn around, but whatever it was had gone. Glenroy changed the subject. 'You hear what happened to Kevin Annon?'

'Nah,' Curvis answered. 'What's he done now?'

'You know he plays for the Crystal Palace youth team,' Glenroy replied. 'Well, he was playing a game for them when a defender called him Oliver Orphan. Kevin went after him, give him a Johnny Kwango special headbutt and then he took off his football boot and gave him a wider smile.'

'All because someone called him Oliver Orphan?' remarked Curvis. 'That's what outside kids call us all the time. Kevin better get used to it if he wants to be a footballer.'

Bullet shook his head. 'Kevin's a nutter. But I might've done the same thing. No outsiders are gonna call *me* Oliver Orphan and get away with it.'

'Kevin's funny,' said Glenroy. 'You can call him virtually anything and get away with it. But if he hears someone call him Oliver Orphan he goes mental. Don't you remember last year when he nicked the carving knife off his Auntie and chased after Lightwood. That all started cos Lightwood called him the Fartful Dodger. Then it got a bit deep when they started having a go at each other's mums.'

'Kevin's roasted with salt on top,' said Bullet. 'A complete nut.

And he's lucky he hasn't gone Stanford House. If it weren't for football he would've gone by now.'

'After last night, Mellor's on punishment,' said Curvis.

'Why? What's he done this time?' asked Glenroy.

'You know Sonia's housemother is giving him grief cos Sonia goes out with him. She banned him from the house. Mellor decided that nothing's gonna stop him. So he climbed up the drainpipe to Sonia's bedroom the other night. Sonia wasn't there, but little Katie Puckrik was. She thought she saw the bogeyman.'

Everybody laughed. The gnats backed away. Curvis continued, 'Last night, Sonia sneaked Mellor into her house. He was hiding in the stairway cupboard with a white bedsheet over him. He waited till about eleven o'clock when Sonia's Auntie Mildred was switching off all the lights in the house. When she came to turn off the stairway light, Mellor came out shouting "Wooo! Wooo! Wooo!" The sheet was over his head. Sonia told me Auntie Mildred screamed as if she was giving birth to a Brontosaurus. Mellor just stood there, trying to say it was just a joke. But he forgot to take the sheet off. Then he did a runner. Auntie Mildred was traumatised. Uncle Maurice had to call out the doctor for the silly cow.'

They laughed, enjoying the break from the serious matter of the day.

'He's a nutjob too,' chuckled Bullet.

'What happened to Mellor?' asked Glenroy.

'He's not allowed within a hundred yards of Sonia's house,' replied Curvis. 'And he's grounded for two weeks.'

Carlton emerged from one of the paths that twisted its way from the bush. Dressed in a red Adidas T-shirt and blue jogging bottoms, he jogged to the climbing frame.

'You're late,' yelled Glenroy.

'Shut up,' spat Carlton, not in the mood to put up with Glenroy today.

A fizzing dragonfly had followed Carlton from the bushes. He had sensed its presence, waiting for the moment to pounce and destroy it. Suddenly, he set off in pursuit of the insect, cursing as he went.

'Leave it alone,' said Curvis. 'What's it done to you?'

'One of them things stung me the other day,' said Carlton, pointing to a blemish on his right forearm. He nevertheless gave up the chase and made his way to the climbing frame. He leant on it, looking at each of his friends in turn. 'So you lot come to any decision or you've been arguing like you usually do?'

'We're serious, you know,' said Glenroy. 'We're not messing about. Me and Curvis are definitely doing a runner.'

Carlton turned to Bullet. 'What do you reckon?'

Bullet thought about it. 'To be honest,' he finally answered, 'Uncle Rodney doesn't beat me up so much now but I can't take his stupid punishments. A few weeks ago he had me polishing all his boots and then he scuffed them up on the grass and asked me to polish 'em again! I'd rather take the beatings – at least it's over and done with.'

'He thinks you're a POW,' Curvis said. 'They should put him in an old war plane and push him out over El Alamein, Iwo Jima or Dunkirk.'

'I haven't got too long to go here but I wanna move out of Uncle Rodney's house,' continued Bullet. 'We've always said that we'll do everything together.'

Bullet gazed at the scar on his right palm. 'So, er, I'm up for it. I'm gonna go.'

Glenroy grinned. Curvis nodded. Bullet searched the eyes of his friends. Carlton's expression was hard to read. He half shrugged then fiercely side-eyed Glenroy. 'What have you been telling him?'

'What?' Glenroy replied. 'To Bullet? Nothing! He made up his own mind, innit.'

'You lot have put me in an impossible position. It's not my fault I live in Auntie Josephine's house and she treats me alright. It's not my fault you live in houses where you get shitloads of grief. But if I go with you lot, it'll be like kicking Auntie Josephine in the guts. And the chiefs will think she treated me bad.'

'I *want* them to know they treat us bad,' cut in Glenroy.

'That's the first sensible thing you've said all day,' said Curvis.

'Kids are treated like shit here,' admitted Carlton. 'Uncle Thomas is an evil cunt who should be shot in the bollocks. But I'm just not sure about running away.'

Curvis stared at Carlton. He leaped down from the frame and picked up a small twig. He pointed it at Carlton and it had the desired effect of claiming everyone's attention. Carlton looked bemused as he gazed at the twig. Curvis finally broke the silence. 'All these years I've known you,' he said to Carlton in a slow, gentle voice, 'you've had it easy. Nothing ever bad has happened to you that I know of. We don't even know why you're in this damn place. You've never told us.'

Carlton's lips moved, as if primed for retaliation. He swallowed saliva and stood still, only offering Curvis a blank stare. Curvis resumed: 'We all know each other's stories, apart from yours. Glenroy's mum is in some mental place. Bullet was left on the doorstep of some social services office, and my old man thought the reason people had kids was to beat them up as soon as they could walk. But you, I don't know. I don't really want to know. I s'pose you'll tell us when you're ready. But I know this. For what? Six years? We've done everything together, helped each other build our own bikes and trolleys, got in trouble, lied for each other, played knock-down ginger, ran about playing British Bulldog and tim-tam-tommy, and been in punch-ups.'

Feeling more uncomfortable with Curvis's harsh gaze than his words, Carlton spotted another dragonfly winging its way towards the climbing frame. Curvis continued, 'I don't think you get it what us three go through. Auntie Josephine spoils you. When was the last time you weren't allowed out?'

Glenroy and Bullet wondered if Carlton was about to reply with a right hook. Instead, Carlton shrugged, dropped his head and ambled to a logged enclosure that fighting kids had used as a boxing ring. He climbed onto the top rung, pondering what to do. He stooped down and plucked a long blade of grass. He inserted it into his mouth. Through the trees, he could make out the road that led to his home.

He thought of Auntie Josephine sitting up late at night to stitch his football shorts. He remembered her pride as he was named man of the match for the regional school cricket final. He stole a quick glance at his friends. It would be intolerable if he was left on his own. Deep inside, he knew that every waking moment his mind would dwell on them. He spied another look at them.

'Hey, Curvis,' Glenroy whispered. 'That was a bit strong, wasn't it?'

'Yeah, but sometimes he lives in his own spoilt world,' Curvis replied. 'For us everything is not cups of teas, chocolate fingers and jam scones with Saint Josephine.'

'I'm gonna see how he is,' said Bullet, leaping off the frame.

'*No!* Leave him be,' insisted Curvis. 'Let him think.'

Five minutes later, Carlton slowly loped back to his mates. He wore a defeated expression. He eyed Curvis. 'Yeah, I'll go,' he said quietly. 'I mean, someone has to look after Glenroy if you do a runner, innit.'

'I don't need anybody to look after me,' retorted Glenroy.

'Oh yes, you do,' laughed Bullet.

Glenroy stole behind Bullet's back. He licked the palm of his right hand then smacked him on the back of his neck. Bullet spun around, only to see Glenroy scampering towards the bushes. Bullet was quick to take up the chase. 'Come here, you nutter!'

Carlton and Curvis watched them, chuckling. 'Them two will be chasing each other when they're old men,' said Curvis.

Carlton picked up a fresh blade of grass and placed it in the corner of his mouth. Curvis wondered if Carlton had been a cow in a previous life. In between chews, Carlton asked, 'So when and where do we go? Or haven't you yet thought about that small detail?'

'I've been thinking about it for the past few weeks. It's kept me awake at night.'

'So what have you come up with?' Carlton wanted to know.

'I don't think it's a good idea to hide in the grounds of Pinewood Oaks,' said Curvis. 'We should go to the Pinewood Hills. I know the area by the soles of my feet and the backs of my hands.'

Carlton inspected the grass he was gnawing then put it back in his mouth. 'Speak for yourself. At night I still get lost in the orchard.'

'While you guys are playing football or something, I go up there to check it out,' Curvis revealed.

Carlton nodded. 'We know. Don't take this the wrong way but everyone apart from us lot thinks you're weird. They don't say it in front of me and Bullet. Can't you at least play in goal now and again? Just to shut 'em up.'

Curvis shook his head. 'No! Why do something I don't like? Don't give a fuck what anyone else thinks.'

'Alright!' Carlton raised his palms. 'Only asked.'

Curvis lowered his tone to a whisper. 'There's a place up there that the scout's use when they go camping. Hopefully, when we go up there, there won't be any of 'em around.'

'And what if there is?'

'Then we'll just hide out in the woods,' Curvis replied. 'Nobody will find us. I know the place too good.'

'I've been there once when me and Bullet went up to the golf course. We nicked the balls from the greens and then watched from our hiding places. It was a right laugh – something to do on a boring Sunday afternoon.'

Curvis scratched his long nose. 'Can you think of anywhere better than the hills?'

'Er … no. You're right. We can't hide in Pinewood Oaks. They'll probably get the locals to search for us in the piggery with pitch forks and clubs.'

'And torches of fire,' Curvis giggled. '*Find those boys dead or alive!*'

'Yeah, Pinewood Hills will make it hard for 'em,' Carlton agreed. '*They* won't be expecting that. I don't know about Glenroy though. He gets lost in his outhouse.'

'He'll be with us, innit,' Curvis assured. 'He'll be alright, as long as we keep a leash on him.'

'You can lead him,' said Carlton.

Curvis nodded. 'We'll take turns.'

'Hold on a sec,' said Carlton. 'What happens if you die or something? The rest of us will be fucked.'

'Carlton, I'm not gonna fucking die on you. Promise.'

'You'd better not.'

'Don't worry! I'm not about to climb the tallest tree in the hills and jump off.'

Carlton kicked a clump of grass. 'So … *when*?'

'Next week. We're gonna have to nick some money, blankets, food, you know, things to help us.'

'What's this Glenroy's been telling me about your brother?' asked Carlton.

'Stanton was moved from his detention centre in Ashford,' replied Curvis. He looked down at the ground. 'He'd only spent a few months there after he was at Stanford House. And my Auntie won't tell me where they moved him. I think he beat up some screws in Ashford cos they moved him to a lower cell on ground level – he couldn't see the fields from his new cell and he freaked out. Went mad. He got put in isolation. Anyway, I wrote a message to my Auntie telling her I'm not speaking to her until she tells me where he is. *Fuck* her.'

Carlton climbed the grey frame and found a metal bar to rest on. 'Stanton can look after himself,' he said.

'Not if he doesn't see me,' returned Curvis. 'When I saw him last month, he looked like he was about to crack up. He was saying how he wanted to kill all the screws and police. My Auntie says he's a bad influence on me. I don't know why she says it cos I don't get into serious trouble. Never have.'

'That's gonna change,' said Carlton. 'When this is all done and dusted you really think they're just gonna ground you and send you to bed without your apple crumble?'

Curvis thought about it. 'No,' he said finally. 'But I don't give a fuck any more. My life can't be worse than it is now.'

Carlton searched the bushes looking for Bullet and Glenroy. His gaze finally returned to Curvis. His attention was then drawn to the field sloping upwards from the play area to where it met Lime House at the crest of the hill; Sonia and two of her younger sisters lived here with seven other children. Bare-trunked housefathers had set up a variety of outdoor activities including rounders and tip-and-run cricket. Meanwhile, an endless procession of piloted trolleys and customised bikes raced downhill, doing their best to evade footballs, tennis balls, kites, Frisbees and small children.

'From where we are it looks like the best place in the world,' Carlton said.

Curvis nodded. 'It's the luck of the draw,' he said. 'There's what? About two or three houseparents that really care in this place. The rest of 'em don't give a shit. They're just here for their pay packet.'

'Your housemother is a witch and a half,' said Carlton. 'I couldn't put up with a quarter of the shit you lot put up with. It'd do my head in.'

'I have to admit it,' said Curvis, 'we're all a little jealous of you having Auntie Josephine as a housemother. Especially Glenroy. It's hard for him cos he knows you live alright and you're just separated by one wall. One *fucking* wall is the difference to being loved and being abu— hated.'

Carlton wondered if Curvis knew his secret. He avoided Curvis's gaze. 'That's one thing me and Auntie Josephine still argue about,' said Carlton. 'Growing up we heard all the screams and banging, *him* hitting the kids. And Auntie Josephine hasn't done fuck all about it. Even now I tell her to report that ginger-haired cunt. But she never has. Sometimes I've seen her cry about it at night. She's probably thinking of the little kids in Glenroy's house. He's just a bully. Sometimes I feel like killing him myself.'

'Who's she gonna report him to? Eh?' asked Curvis. 'They're all the same.'

Away Day

While the other children were sleeping in, Glenroy, who had risen with the sound of a raven pecking the outhouse door, took the opportunity to finish his weekend homework. Uncle Thomas had praised his efforts the previous day for his essay for the religious education class. His piece of writing had told the biblical story, in his own words, of how Joshua broke down the walls of Jericho. 'Well done,' Thomas commended. 'You're obviously not as stupid as you act.'

Following the final full stop to his essay about the Industrial Revolution, he made his way out the back door and hared through the orchard, beyond the long pale grass, to Curvis's cottage. Glenroy squinted as he adjusted to the already bright sun. He heard crickets squawking as he ran through 'Africa country'. He wanted to see Curvis before he left Pinewood Oaks for the day to visit his blood uncle in South London.

As he approached the cottage, he spotted a housefather tending to his allotment. Some of the older kids in his charge had to work on his patch of land as part of their chores. 'Go around!' the man warned Glenroy. 'Don't you dare walk across *my* land.'

As Glenroy considered a reply, he spotted Curvis emerging from his front door. He wore a T-shirt, knee-length cut-off jeans and carried a plastic bag. 'Curvis! Curvis!'

Curvis looked up and noticed his friend jumping up and down and waving his arms. Curvis started slowly towards him, mindful of the housefather's eyes upon him. 'Didn't I tell you last night that I was going away for the day?' Curvis said.

'Yeah,' Glenroy replied. He palmed the sweat off his forehead. 'I thought I'd walk up the road with ya.'

'Haven't you got anything better to do?'

'No,' Glenroy quickly replied.

On their way they watched the paper boy struggling with his burden of Sunday papers on an old, heavy bike that squeaked annoyingly. Visibly straining, the paper boy cycled by Glenroy and Curvis, nearly toppling over as he rode over a road ramp.

'Hey, Brenton,' laughed Glenroy. 'You've got a puncture!'

Barely in his teens and dressed in hand-me-down shorts and a yellow tracksuit top, Brenton turned around in alarm to check his back wheel. He was relieved to find it still in shape. Glenroy let out a manic giggle.

'What's a matter with you?' Curvis glared at Glenroy as Brenton zig-zagged down the road. '*Don't* bully the young *uns*.'

'Wasn't bullying – just having a laugh.'

The road steadily rose towards the Lodge. The fields to the left sloped down to a valley of thorns, berries and bushes. A mild breeze disturbed the buttercups and daisies. The boys often wondered what life was like for the kids playing in expansive back gardens beyond the narrow strip of grass that was fenced off to their right.

'What happened about the ten pound Uncle Thomas reckoned you nicked?' asked Curvis.

'He phoned up my social worker about it and he's coming down for a case meeting in two weeks. Uncle Thomas wants to send me away. He reckons I've been nicking all the time.'

'He's probably thieving the money himself,' replied Curvis. 'He looks worse than a thief. I wouldn't trust him to look after a sixpence. After running away, you might get a chance in a different house. That'll be a good result.'

'There's lot of young kids who are scared of him,' Glenroy said. 'Elvin used to hate him too. Now he's started to help him give swimming lessons! Can't blame him – he got a bike out of it. How many kids round here get a brand new bike? You can count 'em on the paw of a cat.'

Curvis wanted to change the subject. 'When you and Bullet decided to play tag for the rest of yesterday afternoon, me and

Carlton thought the best place for us to go is the Pinewood Hills. We can make camp there. We might go next week – if we can get all our supplies.'

'Pinewood Hills! That's a march and a half. What supplies?'

'What do you mean what supplies?' scolded Curvis. 'Do you think we're gonna do a runner and take nothing with us? I dunno about you but while we're on the run I'm not gonna live on dock leaves and berries! We've got to make sure we've got money, blankets, extra clothes and food – if we can get it.'

Five minutes later, Curvis and Glenroy reached the southern exit to Pinewood Oaks. The red-brick perimeter wall had a gap big enough for one car to enter or depart. Pinewood High Street ran parallel to the wall. It had a grocer shop, baker's, florist's, newsagent's, confectionist's, antique dealer's, an estate agent's, post office and the Pinewood Inn; a sign outside the pub informed drinkers about the wonders of its beer garden. Tree-lined avenues led off the High Street where semi-detached houses with smart porches and brightly coloured patios boasted the latest brand cars in their drives.

They spotted a green bus climbing up the main road, heading east. Black exhaust fumes trailed behind it. The boys turned left and headed for the newsagent's. Curvis bought a Curly Wurly chocolate bar while Glenroy stood outside, remembering that only one Pinewood Oaks' kid was allowed inside the shop at any time. They crossed the road and walked past the Pinewood Inn to the bus stop. A fat, middle-aged woman wearing a flower-patterned dress and carrying a brown sausage dog was already waiting. She looked at the two boys with such contempt that Curvis thought that kids from the Home might as well have their own bus stop.

'So, what time will you be back?' whispered Glenroy.

'About six, earlier if possible. I don't like going to my uncle's. It's boring. All he does is drink beer and watch cricket on a Sunday.'

'At least you're getting out for the day. I gotta go back.'

'Not for long you don't, Glenroy. Can you imagine the look on old ginger chops when he realises you're missing.'

Glenroy grinned.

A green double-decker bus arrived twenty minutes later. Curvis boarded it and bade a fond farewell. The bus picked up a fair speed heading west, leaving the village of Pinewood and passing through narrow roads with large houses fronted by well-kept gardens and neat hedges. Sitting in the upper deck, Curvis admired the landscape of the Surrey North Downs. To his left, partly hidden by hills, was the hamlet of Spurleigh Town. To his right, expanses of green were polka-dotted with sheep and cows. The fields were criss-crossed by a network of hedges and rust-coloured paths that failed to keep to a straight line.

Curvis thought about his father. Maybe if he had had two shillings to rub together, he might not have taken out his frustrations on his family. His uncle had told him how his father had always struggled to hold down a job. Curvis remembered how he cowered in the corner of his small bedroom, gripping Stanton around the neck. He could still hear the terrified screams of his gravely wounded mother. She could do nothing to help. Her nose was broken and her left eye had swollen. Blood was seeping from the back of her head. All there was to protect him was Stanton. And it was he who took most of the blows that were intended for Curvis, his father already satisfied with the damage inflicted on his mother. Even now Curvis could smell the stench of beer from his father's breath, and the image of his mother's face had never left him; the slowly closing eye when death finally claimed her. From then on *that* memory was implanted inside his brain, like a one-page photo album.

Curvis could not remember much about his mother, although if he wanted to he could sketch a true portrait, capturing her very essence. But the words she said, the motherly things she offered him were distant to him. It was a cruel fate, he thought. All that was left to him was *that* image.

Fifteen minutes later, he reached the village of Claremont, a little bigger than Pinewood. The bus stopped outside its two-track train station. He caught a train to East Croydon, the journey lasting sixteen minutes. Jumping off the train, he boarded a bus for Stockwell, South London. He wished he had bought a comic to eat up the time.

Arriving in the city, Curvis noticed how everyone walked much quicker there. He wondered how the residents in the council blocks could tolerate living stacked on top of each other. He cautiously looked around, fearful of the teenagers idling in the forecourt. They all seemed to be observing his every move.

Broken masonry lay near a large, metal bin. A skinny dog inspected a rotten apple. A communal door leading to a tower block had a busted lock and twisted handle. Next to this was a splintered window frame surrounded by shards of glass. Children ran along the balconies yelping and shrieking. The possibility of living with his uncle in this place was not one Curvis would ever entertain.

He trotted up the litter-laden steps of the block, trying to ignore the stench of waste and rotting food from the dustbins. Reaching the fourth floor he walked along the balcony, taking in the view of central Stockwell. He felt claustrophobic as he scanned the concrete jungle all round him. Looking north in the distance he could see the chimneys of Battersea Power Station and beyond that he spotted the Post Office tower. He tapped the letter box of the third door along the balcony.

'Ah who dat?' boomed out a suspicious voice.

'It's me,' Curvis replied. 'Curvis.'

The door opened. Curvis was greeted by a middle-aged West Indian man with a three-cans-of-beer-a-day stomach. His receding hair was greying and his expression bore the look of constant annoyance.

Curvis followed him past a cramped kitchen that had empty, takeaway chicken boxes on the floor. He spotted his uncle's British Rail jacket hooked on a peg in the undecorated hallway. Reaching the lounge, where the main feature was a framed portrait of Muhammad Ali looking proud in a black jacket and bow tie, Curvis was ushered to sit down in a tatty armchair.

'So you t'ink 'bout wha' I was talking 'bout last time when you was 'ere?' Cecil asked Curvis. 'I did talk to your social worker and him say it would be a good idea.'

Curvis didn't want to show he was ungrateful for the offer. 'I dunno,' he shrugged. 'It would mean having to change schools and everything. And I don't really like it around here. I wouldn't fit in. I'd miss my friends.'

'Listen me good, bwai,' Cecil raised his voice. 'Me nuh understand you. You always complain 'bout de way dem people treat you inna de home. Me nuh have to invite you to stay. I'm doing dis of my own free will. But you treat me offer like it no big t'ing!'

Curvis glared at Cecil, wondering why he was so keen now to give him a home but not so charitable in the past. His uncle had puffy cheeks below a pair of dark, severe eyes. He guessed he hadn't shaved for a few days; salt and pepper stubble appeared very dry on his square chin. He probably drinks just like my old man, Curvis thought.

'Why now?' asked Curvis. 'It would've been alright if you wanted me to stay when I was a kid. But now? It will take time for me to get used to—'

'Listen, bwai. Me's de only family you 'ave. Be t'ankful for dat.'

Curvis bit his top lip and stared at the floor. His mind yelled. *Stanton was the only family he had!*

Cecil continued. 'Alright, me place is small-like and me live inna council block. But it's 'ome and it could be your 'ome too. De way you describe dat place where you is, dat can never be called a 'ome for children. It's not my fault my brudder killed your mudder. Lord bless her and may she rest in peace. Me jus' want to do my part.'

'It's too late,' Curvis said almost in a whisper.

'Wha' you say?'

Just then, a white woman entered the room. She was wearing a dressing gown, her long auburn hair masking half her face. Curvis guessed she was about thirty. Cecil smiled at her, thinking of a recent, pleasant memory. He hauled himself upright. 'Curvis, dis is Maureen, my woman.'

Curvis didn't look at her for more than a second. 'Morning, Maureen,' he greeted politely.

'So you're the one Cecil has been talking about,' Maureen said. 'He tells me that you're gonna live with us soon. That's brilliant news, isn't it? We'll be one happy family.'

Curvis side-eyed his uncle. Maureen continued, 'He's very concerned about you, especially after what happened to your brother.'

Cecil winced as Maureen mentioned his other nephew. Curvis fixed his eyes on his uncle, refusing to blink. In a slow, hushed voice, he asked him: 'Did my social worker tell you where they moved Stanton?'

Unnerved by his nephew's gaze, Cecil hesitated. 'Er … yeah. But everybody decided dat there is no point in you knowing where him der. He's a bad influence on you. Dat's de trut' of de matter.'

Curvis said nothing. Instead, he intensified his glare. Cecil tried to smile away the obvious tension as Maureen looked at them both.

Finally, Curvis released his gaze. He spoke in that deliberate way of his, every syllable clear and precise. 'You know, that's what they all tell me in the home. I didn't expect to hear it from your mouth. Maybe those meetings you had with my social worker and the others, where they give you nice little biscuits and coffees in nice little mugs, have brainwashed you. Maybe you believed in their nice aren't-we-good-people smiles.'

Cecil made a fist and covered it with his other hand.

'Stanton *is* my brother,' Curvis resumed. 'It seems that no one understands that, including you. He has looked after me better than anybody else can or might do. Now it's up to me to look out for him. I know he needs me.'

Cecil glanced at Maureen, searching for a reassuring look. Then he looked at his nephew, recognising that his slow vocal delivery was just like his father's. It chilled his bones.

'Look after you?' Cecil finally countered. 'So beating everybody who has so much as looked 'pon you is minding you? Stanton love to fight too much. Did dem tell you wha' he done to de man inna detention centre?'

'No. I was told he just beat him up,' Curvis casually replied. 'The man must have done something to him for Stanton to do him.'

Cecil reclined into his chair. 'The whole t'ing kick off jus' because de man call him somet'ing like mixed-up skunk. Stanton beat up de man so badly him still mash up inna hospital. Stanton too violent, man! He mus' ah get it from his fader.'

'After the life he had, it's a little wonder why Stanton grew up so violent,' Curvis spat back. 'I can remember when he used to stand up to my old man, trying to defend me and Mum.'

Cecil's head dropped. Maureen gently shook her head. Cecil stood up as Maureen went to the kitchen. He walked lazily to the window where the paint was cracked and peeling on the frame. He took in a long breath. He decided to change the tone. 'So you want put flowers 'pon your mudder's grave come dis July?'

'Yeah … it will be nine years,' Curvis replied in a near whisper. *That* image returned to his inner vision.

'I know t'ings 'ave been rough wid you, but we nuh want you following Stanton,' advised Cecil. 'De people inna de 'ome don't want dat. There is some 'ope for you.'

'And none for him?' Curvis shot back. He scowled and spoke quicker. 'So everyone has given up on him? I will *never* do that. *Never.*'

'Wha' do you want me to do?' asked Cecil, raising his hands. 'Me cyan't help him now, can I? Me never tell him to t'ump down de warden. Me never place him inna jailhouse.'

Curvis's eyes betrayed his fury, but his voice remained calm and controlled. 'I'm gonna try and help him. I'll find out where he is without your or anyone else's help. I'm not gonna leave him where he is. To rot. Like *you're* doing.'

Cecil could not hold back his frustration any longer. 'You nah go near him! Y'hear me, bwai. Dat kinda foolishness will nuh do anyone any raas good! Keep away from him!'

'And what you gonna do if I see him? Beat me up.'

The tension eased when Maureen re-appeared carrying a tray of drinks. Cecil snatched his milk and rum and disappeared into the bedroom, leaving Maureen and Curvis sitting opposite each other. Curvis ignored his glass of orange squash. Maureen tried a reassuring smile. 'He's only trying to do the best for you,' she said.

'Is he?'

Curvis spent most of the afternoon on the balcony, sniffing the smell of roasting chicken and boiling vegetables. He sipped cold drinks and watched young kids playing tip-and-run cricket in the forecourt of the block. Concaved dustbins were wickets and a tennis racquet was employed as a bat. Other teens idled around in groups, bantering and laughing. Their slang words were foreign to him. Mid-afternoon Cecil tried to persuade him to go downstairs and try to make friends. Curvis declined. Maureen busied herself in the kitchen, while Cecil lay horizontal in the lounge watching cricket. 'Shot him, boss!' he would exclaim as the West Indian batsman, Viv Richards, stroked the ball for yet another boundary.

Curvis wondered what Stanton did on Sundays. He looked up to the sky and thought it was cruel to keep prisoners inside their cells in this relentless heatwave. No looking up at trees, no birdsong, no scent of morning dew. Then his thoughts turned to running away from home. It'll be a plus if the sun keeps shining every day, he thought. It'd be a bonus if the superintendent of the home and the police knocked on Cecil's door asking about my whereabouts. He'd hate that.

He had his own name for the Pinewood Hills – Mum's Garden. Every week he would trek up there, locating the same isolated spot. Reaching his destination, he would sit down and talk to his mother, telling her all the things that had happened to him during the past seven days, and informing her about Stanton.

He would listen attentively to the stirring leaves, the shrill language of the larks and the pockets of breezes that curled around the pines, sure in his mind that in the mist of all this natural sound, the gentle voice of his mother was beckoning him.

Curvis had no doubt that once he and his friends reached the haven of the Pinewood Hills, his mother would watch over him, guiding him at night and looking out for them during the day.

The clamour from the dining room as the children prepared themselves for dinner was unrelenting. The younger children wanted to sit in different places, resulting in a tug of war with two chairs and colourful name-calling.

Forgetting what he had been like as a child, Bullet shook his head in exasperation at the commotion. Feeling a sense of responsibility as the eldest in the household, he tried to establish order. 'Donna! Sit in your usual seat!'

'But I don't wanna sit next to Lester!' Donna shrilled, her seven-year-old hands wrenching a chair off another child.

'Sit there or I'll tan your backside,' warned Mrs Hordbuckle, the housemother. She had just entered the dining room wearing an apron. Oven gloves draped over her right shoulder. She was a slight woman, nearing her fifties, but her voice carried the weight of someone a few stones heavier.

Sulking, Donna released her hold on the chair and plonked herself down at the table next to her housemother's place; kids in the household called this the slap chair. Donna and Lester swapped threatening glares.

Bullet was last to be seated at the far end of the table. He silently seethed at Uncle Rodney's refusal to allow him to eat his dinner on a tray in the front room watching television. Behind him stood a radiogram, which was big enough for two small children to hide in. For as long as Bullet could remember, Uncle Rodney would switch the wireless on at five to six in the morning, sip his black coffee, nibble a single finger of shortbread and listen to the six o'clock news.

The privilege of sitting at the foot of the table was offered to Bullet by his housefather last year when the eldest boy, Vincent Chapman, left home to start life in the army. The last Bullet had heard, Vincent had left the army and was seeking help for alcoholism.

Mrs Hordbuckle patiently served the roast beef, boiled potatoes, cabbage, greens and carrots to the hungry horde, making sure all the younger children had the same portions. The din of children's voices and Mrs Hordbuckle's rebukes cancelled out the clattering of knives and forks against plates.

The sound of the front door opening and closing had a bewitching effect on the children. A man sporting a white shirt, blue tie and navy-coloured blazer marched along the hallway and into the dining room. The children fell silent. 'Aren't you forgetting something, children?' Mrs Hordbuckle prompted, dropping her tone to a near whisper.

In perfect unison, the children greeted the man. 'Evening, Uncle Rodney.'

Loosening his tie, Rodney stood still, inspecting his charges, his proud countenance learned from many years in the armed forces. His tall, lean frame was sculpted by the exercise regime he had performed faithfully every morning for as long as Bullet had been in the home 'Have you been behaving yourselves, children?'

As one, the youngsters answered. 'Yes, Uncle Rodney.'

Rodney smiled and sat down at the head of the table, acknowledging his wife with a nod. They had been married for years, but the only time Bullet ever saw any affection between them was when Rodney offered his arm to his wife on their annual pilgrimage to Whitehall for Remembrance Sunday.

Dinner was consumed quietly, the children displayed impeccable manners. Bullet was the first one to finish his meal. Following his request to be excused from the dinner table, he ambled along the hallway, passing the kitchen on his right and the lounge on his left. At the end of the passage, facing Uncle Rodney's study, he turned right into the room where all the shoes were kept in a wire-meshed rack. An airing cupboard was opposite, its hot vents escaping through a gap beneath the door. Next to this, and below a sash window, were two deep sinks, large enough to bathe two-year-old baby twins. At the far end of the room, just beyond the downstairs toilets, sunlight stole through the wire-meshed window of the back door, creating a visible beam.

Bullet found the shoe polish and brushes in a bottom compartment of the rack and began buffing, knowing that Rodney would inspect his work upon completion. Twenty minutes later, Rodney strode into the room with his hands held behind his back. He regarded Bullet for a long second. 'Brian, when you finish your duties, I want to see you in my study.'

'What about?' replied Bullet.

'You'll find out,' Rodney replied.

Two pairs of polished shoes later, Bullet entered Rodney's study. A large, framed portrait of the Queen boasting all her regal robes watched over the room from the end wall. On the mantelpiece were framed black-and-white photographs of RAF personnel, grinning in uniforms with the backdrop of Spitfire fighter planes; Rodney's Christmas gifts to Bullet when he was seven, eight and nine years old had been Airfix model planes.

Rodney was standing beside his desk at the other side of the room. He poured himself a shot of whisky and invited Bullet to sit in an armchair in the corner of the room. Rodney, straight-backed, strode over to the large sash windows with a view of the orbital road of Pinewood Oaks. He tutted as he noticed boys and girls riding their skateboards over the road ramps. 'Have you thought about what you're going to do when you leave school?' Rodney asked, still looking through the window.

'Er … kind of,' Bullet replied. 'I'd like to be a footballer. I reckon I can make it.'

'Everyone your age wants to be a footballer, but only one in ten thousand can make it into another Bobby Charlton.'

'I can,' said Bullet.

Rodney turned around to face Bullet. 'Hmm. I've been reading your school reports. They're not brilliant, are they?'

Bullet rested his chin on his right fist. Rodney gently shook his glass and downed the contents. He winced as the whisky hit his throat. 'A young man like you needs discipline!' he said. 'So you can learn right from wrong and be a decent citizen. A few years in the army never done anyone any harm. Look at me! Born into a poor family in Huddersfield. Apart from the pits I had nothing going for me. But with the army I fought for King and country and travelled the world.'

'I can do that playing football,' cut in Bullet. 'Bobby Charlton played in Mexico and that country next to Spain. What's it called? Begins with P.'

Rodney cut Bullet a fierce glare. 'Old people are being mugged in the streets. Louts are fighting each other at the football. I used to go to the Arsenal when I was a boy. Watched the best players of the time like Alex James, Charlie Drake, Tommy Lawton and Dixie Dean with sixty or seventy thousand others. There was *never* any trouble. If you were too small to see they would hand you down over a thousand heads to the front. But now? Now, kids have *no* respect for their elders and none for the police. They should've never scrapped National Service.'

Bullet made himself comfortable in the armchair, preparing himself for an Uncle Rodney long speech; he hoped he wouldn't venture into the often-told details of the Battle of Britain or any Churchill speeches. Rodney resumed: 'Brian, I think you should enlist in the army. They will teach you a trade and give you all the discipline you need. You're interested in cars, aren't you? The army can teach you everything about them. After you have completed four years' service or so, you will come out equipped to be a respectable young man.'

Bullet stared at the carpet. 'But my PE teacher reckons that I should be good enough to go off for trials. All my friends say I'm good enough as well. They reckon I should go for it. I … I want to go for it.'

Rodney raised his voice. 'This is not about what your friends think. They don't live your life and you can't make a decision just because they think they're right. It was your friends who told you to go and make trouble on that National Front march at the end of April. I mean, you're not Jewish or coloured. These National Front people are not against you. It's got nothing to do with you.'

Bullet lifted his head. He took in a deep breath. 'Most ... most of my friends are coloured. Most of the kids *here* are coloured ... or half-coloured. That's who my—'

'I don't like the influence they have on you,' Rodney interrupted. 'I mean, I'm not a racist. But it's a fact that coloured people can't be as well disciplined as the rest of us. It's not their fault. They've only been here for twenty years or so and they haven't caught up in education and other things. Some of them do try hard.'

Bullet dropped his head again and closed his eyes.

Rodney continued: 'Coloured kids are more likely to get into trouble than you. That's a fact. They find learning difficult and you can't blame them for that. The best hope for your coloured friends is to take up athletics or boxing. It helps to give them discipline.'

Bullet tried to find a counter. 'Carlton's brainy.'

'Yes,' Rodney nodded. 'Maybe he is. But he's the exception to the rule. Besides, he has serious problems with his discipline. And he's got a chip on his shoulder. So many of them have. Isn't he always getting in fights? He should consider joining the army too.'

Bullet fidgeted in his armchair. He wanted to shout at his housefather, but years of conditioning stopped him. He wished he had Curvis's ability to find the right words.

Bullet stood up. 'Is that all, Uncle Rodney?' he asked politely.

'Yes. Go on with you.'

Half an hour later, Bullet heard a knock on the back door just as he was slipping on his trainers. He was still thinking about his meeting with Uncle Rodney. He talks to me like I'm a little kid. *Go on with you!* I shoulda told him to stick his army boots where the breezes can't blow. He opened the door to a grinning Elvin. 'You coming out, Bullet?'

'Yeah, just getting ready.'

The two friends jogged out of the back door beneath a setting sun and headed to a field where a game of cricket was in full slog. The players had an audience of four teenage girls, someone in a tree overlooking the square-leg boundary and Mellor.

Bullet and Elvin jogged up to Mellor. 'Where's Carlton, Glenroy and Curvis?' Bullet wanted to know.

'Glenroy's at swimming,' replied Mellor. 'His Uncle's teaching the posh kids from outside this evening. And Carlton and Curvis went off somewhere – don't know where.'

'What way did they go?'

'Didn't see,' Mellor said. 'Funny that Carlton missed out on a game of cricket – he's the second best player in Pinewood Oaks, behind me, of course.'

'He's the *best!*' protested Elvin.

'Another non-believer,' chuckled Mellor. 'One day you'll discover the madness of your ways. As I said, he's gone off with Curvis. Maybe them two are bum chums.'

'Takes a bum chum to know one,' snapped Bullet.

'Alright, alright. Keep your jockstrap on. Just joking.'

'Hi, Bullet!' one of the girls who was watching the cricket hailed, waving her right hand. 'Come over 'ere.'

Bullet pretended he didn't hear. Instead of responding, he watched the bowler begin his run-up. The batsman found the boundary again, hooking the ball expertly to the road, the fielders not even moving.

Accusation

The school sports hall echoed to the sound of teenage male voices as a competitive game of basketball was underway. Ten pairs of thundering soles shook the wooden floor. Two PE teachers, both dressed in T-shirts and loose tracksuit bottoms, ran up and down the sidelines of the court, shouting out instructions to their respective teams, pointing and gesturing as if their lives depended on the result.

On the court, a black, stocky teenager had skilfully stolen the ball from the opposing team. He bounded his way to the unguarded basket, attempting to lay up to score. A defender pushed the attacker forcefully in the back, propelling the youth to an unfriendly greeting with the wall. A whistle was blown. Frustrated shouts came from the team that was about to secure victory. The dazed teenager groggily got up to his feet. Any sense of sportsmanship evaporated. He rushed towards his grinning fouler. 'Who're you pushing?'

Without warning, the teenager swung his right fist and connected with the left jaw of his fouler, sending him to the floor. A brawl broke out. The two teams swapped kicks, punches and obscenities. The teachers rushed onto the court to try to stop the fracas. 'Carlton! Get to the changing rooms right now!' Carlton's PE tutor, Mr Banks, pointed a rigid finger.

'But he's been pushing me all through the game! He deserves a kicking.'

'*Move* or you'll be looking at a suspension,' Mr Banks warned.

'Didn't you see the push,' yelled Carlton. 'I smashed into the fucking wall!'

The players in both teams stopped the pushing and jostling. Carlton reluctantly made his way to the changing rooms. Once inside, he threw himself on the wooden bench and reached for a towel from inside his sports bag. He buried his face in the towel before wiping the sweat off his face. He felt that once more, Mr Banks had made an example of him.

Two heated arguments later, Carlton could hear the game restart and the shouts that accompanied it. He ambled over to one of the sinks by the showers and ran the cold tap, splashing his face to cool not just his head but his temper. He sat back down again, beside the peg that held his school uniform. He dressed slowly and whispered to himself, 'I'll have him outside school. Banks only picks on me cos I live in a fucking home.'

Carlton had achieved considerable respect for sport at his school. He was the first-choice centre forward in the football team – they had just won the Surrey schools cup. He was a fearsome opening bowler for the cricket team, modelling his extra long run-up on the West Indian bowler, Michael Holding, and he could sprint a hundred metres in eleven seconds dead. He impressed at field events too, especially the long jump.

At home he had all his certificates framed, hung above his bed in his dormitory. His medals were displayed in Auntie Josephine's study. But Carlton felt there was no pleasing Mr Banks.

By the time he laced up his shoes, the game had finished. His teammates trudged into the changing room. Their heads were down. 'Did we lose?' Carlton asked.

'No. We won 55–48,' replied Valentine. 'That tosser who pushed you into the wall was sent off after he barged Hillsey. If he didn't go there would've been another roll.'

'I might get the wanker when we're going home,' spat Carlton. 'See if I don't!'

'No, you won't!' roared Mr Banks who had entered the changing room. 'How many times have I told you not to retaliate when you're provoked? *How many times!*'

Mr Banks locked Carlton in a stare, hands on hips and a whistle dangling around his neck. Sweat mingled with his greasy slick-backed hairstyle. 'They can't beat us so they try and get you wound up. And they *did*. Didn't they? For Christsakes! They didn't have to try that hard!'

Carlton searched his teammates' eyes, trying to buy their sympathy. Some of them looked away.

'If their teacher reports that you punched one of their players, starting this free-for-all, then the whole team might get banned. And I'm not going to risk that happening again.'

'So it's alright if some wanker slams me into the wall and I have to get up and shake his hand?'

'I'm *not* going to have you risking the team's chances of winning this league all because you can't help losing your temper,' Mr Banks raised his voice. 'So you won't be playing again. I've had enough.'

Carlton's teammates drew in a synchronised breath. It took Carlton half a minute to find his tongue. 'What do you mean I won't be playing again? That wanker started it! Why can't you see that? D'you want a slow-motion replay?'

'But you shouldn't have retaliated,' Mr Banks snapped.

'Aren't you listening to me or don't you care?' Carlton argued. 'Yeah, go on! Blame me for starting everything! You always do.'

'*He* would've got disciplined if you gave me the chance! *You* have blown your top once too often.'

'Maybe if you were on *my* side I wouldn't need to blow my top.'

'*I'm* the referee! Get that into your thick head! I'm sick and tired of it! You go against everything I tell you.'

'Maybe if you talked any sense I wouldn't have to.'

'I'm *not* taking talk like that. I've stood up for you in the past, and without sport you are nothing … *Nothing!*'

Carlton folded his arms. 'So some of the other teachers always tell me.'

Mr Banks gauged the reaction of Carlton's teammates before fixing his stare on Carlton again. 'This'll be your last game.'

Carlton lifted his head. He glared at Mr Banks for a long second. 'Nothing.' His voice was calm. 'So you think that as well. *Nothing*. Fuck you!'

There was a silent stand-off.

'Carlton's our best player,' blurted one of Carlton's teammates. His support wasn't seconded.

Carlton's hard gaze didn't leave Mr Banks. He looked like a relic from the rock and roll era, he thought. Those ridiculous black sideburns don't look cool at all. Not at his age. I wonder if he can fight? Probably got a solid punch but I'd be too quick for him. I would fuck him up if we ever come to blows. No way could he handle me. I'll let you off this time, you greasy-haired knob. But next time I'll have ya. Call me nothing again and see what happens. I'll slam you into the fucking wall.

Carlton finally looked away.

Satisfied he had established some kind of authority, Mr Banks said, 'Hurry up and get dressed, I want to lock up.' He then left, leaving Carlton staring at his fists.

Half an hour later, Carlton walked home with Hillsey. They reached Pinewood High Street and ambled into a shop. They were watched closely.

'Hey, Hillsey, got two pence?'

'Yeah, hold up.'

They bought themselves a bar of chocolate each.

Hillsey waited until they were out of the shop to ask his question. 'So you gonna watch from now on then?'

'Nah. There's only two games left before we break up anyway. Banks knew that wanker was causing trouble from the start, but he didn't do anything about it. And if Banks bans me from playing basketball, then I'm not running in the athletic finals either. Banks can go and have an accident with a javelin or something.'

'What about cricket?'

Carlton quickened his stride. 'Fuck that as well. The whole school can go and fuck themselves. I'm not playing any more sports for the school. You heard him. *Nothing* he called me.'

Hillsey didn't try to persuade his friend to change his mind. He decided to change the subject. 'What do you think Miss Osbourne's gonna do about the detention you never went to?'

'Miss Osbourne can't take a joke,' Carlton chuckled. 'When I asked if she bought her dresses from Oxfam, I was only fucking about. Jeez! It's not like I called her the worst bitch to have walked these lands since Cruella Deville bought a dog leash.'

Hillsey laughed hard. When he composed himself, he said, 'We don't think you're nothing, not by a long way. I don't think none of us had the balls to say that in front of Banks though.'

Carlton nodded. 'Thanks, Hillsey. You're alright. So are most of the team. We're gonna have to work on Boxall though. If Banks asked him to scrub out all the jockstraps with his own toothbrush he'd do it.'

After bidding goodbye to Hillsey, Carlton entered the grounds of Pinewood Oaks. He spotted the old man sitting behind the counter in the Lodge, talking on the phone. Behind him was a selection of keys hanging from nails on a wooden board.

The grass on either side of the road, tormented by the harsh sun for many days, was more yellow than green. The large trees, mostly oaks and chestnuts, began to boast their seed. The drive sloped gently downhill. A hundred and fifty yards inside the complex, Pinewood Oaks unfurled into a beautiful rural open estate, as leafy and mani-cured as anything the aristocracy could offer.

Feeling pangs of hunger, Carlton marched on quickly – he still had a good mile to walk. The first of the cottages, Almond House, stood to his left. Lining his right were trees that gave way to thick bushes and clusters of ferns and nettles. He heard a muffled voice. 'Carlton, why you so late?'

A coloured head protruded out from the shrubbery. Carlton rec-ognised the face. 'Elvin, what the daisy bottoms you doing there? You've got a green Afro!'

'Last night we were playing run-outs and I lost ten pence.' Elvin began to shake and swipe his hair. A shower of grass formed a halo around his head.

'You're trying to find ten pence!' Carlton laughed. 'You'll be looking for it till you've got a grey Afro.'

'I know I lost it here so I might as well look for it,' Elvin said. 'Don't want no other tosser to find it and run off to the shop and buy some gobstoppers or a jamboree bag.'

Carlton doubled up in hysterics. 'If you find it, you can look for all the money I've lost in the fields and bushes around here. I'll give you half of what you find.'

Elvin hacked away at the shrubbery with his feet. 'Do you think I'm stupid or what? Look for your own money!'

Shaking his head, Carlton started for home once more. 'I might see you later. If you find that ten pence you can buy me a packet of crisps. But don't look too hard, will ya.'

'Alright then. Bullet was around here somewhere. He knocked for you about half an hour ago.'

'What does he want?' Carlton asked.

'Something secret. He wouldn't tell me. He reckons I've got a big mouth.'

'You have, Elvin. They don't call you the Dartford Tunnel for nothing. If you see Bullet, tell him I'll see him later.'

'Yeah, alright.'

Carlton jogged on, veering off the pavement to his right, crossing a baked field that sloped down to a valley of thorns and nettles. He ran along a dried-mud path that bisected the undergrowth. Dust accumulated on his shoes and the hems of his trousers. He could hear younger children playing in the distance. 'Tim-tam-tommy, tim-tam-tommy, coming ready or not!' a young voice cried out. Carlton smiled, a memory hitting a sweet spot.

He emerged from the scrub into yet another dry field. He saw the flat rooftop of the nursery on the horizon, shimmering in the evening June sun. He sprinted up the hill, deviating to his left where he joined the orbital road. Children were riding down the incline on two- and three-wheeled bikes. Others rolled down on second-hand roller skates, trying to pick up speed as they went over the newly laid road ramps.

'Carlton, look at me! I can ride a bike now!' said a kid on a bike.

'About time and all. Thought you'd never get it. Who's on duty tonight?'

'Auntie Josephine.'

Carlton smiled. He didn't stop running until he reached his front door. He leaped up the three steps and only slowed when he set foot in the hallway, mindful of the rule against running in the house. The passage was decorated in silver-coloured wallpaper with white flecks. Two waist-high green plants stood at either end, resting on a tough-wearing, brown carpet. Carlton made his way to the kitchen where he spotted Auntie Josephine wiping a table.

'Good evening, Carlton,' Josephine greeted him with a warm smile. 'Did you win?'

'Er, yeah, we won.'

'Great stuff! How many? What do they call it? Baskets?'

'Yeah, that's right.'

'How many baskets did you score?'

Carlton couldn't remember. He guessed. 'About twelve, maybe fourteen.'

'Great stuff,' Josephine repeated. 'You're turning out to be the all-round sportsman, aren't you?'

Carlton blushed. He didn't want to spoil Josephine's cheerfulness by admitting he had been sent off the court. He looked fondly at her. 'Say I don't make it in sports, Auntie, do you think I could get a decent job?'

'Of course! You're very bright. What brought this up?'

'Er, nothing. I was just thinking in case I got a bad injury. It does happen.'

'What did I say to you about thinking negative?' Josephine stressed. 'Think *positive* ...' She regarded him kindly and stroked his hair. 'Why don't you change out of your school uniform. I'll heat up your dinner.'

'Thanks, Auntie.'

'I wish the council would thank me better,' Josephine said with a sigh. 'Working in the kitchen in this weather is bloody murder! It must be over ninety today.'

A change into a pair of jeans and a Crystal Palace football shirt later, Carlton was seated downstairs enjoying his dinner of lamb chops, roast potatoes, cabbage and carrots. Opposite him sat Josephine smoking a cigarette, making sure she blew her smoke away from him.

'When are you gonna be late again?' asked Josephine. 'I'm off tomorrow, so I'll have to tell Auntie Margaret and Auntie Sophie whether to save your dinner or not.'

'No. I'll be coming home normal time tomorrow.'

'I suppose you'll need your rest. You've been doing sports all this week, haven't you? Maybe tomorrow you can catch up on your homework?'

Before Carlton could think of an excuse, Petrula came running into the dining room. She was six years old. Tears were smudged down her cheeks. 'Auntie! Auntie! Phillip pushed me over on purpose.'

'Where's Phillip!' asked Josephine. 'Can't you kids play quietly around the back? Tell Phillip I want to see him. It's nearly half past seven and it's time to come in and have your hot cocoa. Then bed!'

Petrula wiped her cheeks, couldn't restrain a grin and ran into the hallway yelling. 'Phillip! Phillip! Auntie wants you *now!*'

Josephine sucked hard on her cigarette. 'No rest for the good, is there?' She managed a smile.

A minute later, seven-year-old Phillip walked slowly into the dining room. His head was bowed. He tried to defend himself. 'She started it, you always blame me.'

'She's a year younger than you,' said Josephine. 'How many times have I told you? Play away from her.'

'She follows me around!' argued Phillip.

'What did I say would happen if you laid a finger on Petrula again?'

Phillip thought about it. 'Bed,' he said finally.

'Go on with ya,' ordered Josephine. 'And brush your teeth!'

Phillip tramped out of the dining room. The floor resonated under Carlton's feet. Josephine stubbed out her cigarette and watched

Carlton finishing off his last potato. 'So, you haven't told me how you did in that geography test today?'

'I think I done alright. I got a bit stuck about those olden days crop rotation and all that stuff. But apart from that, I reckon I done alright.'

'Didn't I tell you to brush up on what you learned to get a top mark?' said Josephine. 'But *you* wanted to play football with Brian and your other friends! You can't play football every night. You have to find *some* time for homework.'

Carlton nodded. 'Yeah, you're right. But it's hard staying in doing homework when everybody else is out, especially in this weather.'

'I know that,' replied Josephine. 'But you have to think about your future.'

Mr Banks gatecrashed Carlton's mind. *You're nothing!* He resumed eating his dinner while Josephine lit up another cigarette.

An hour later, the younger children were in bed, but not until there had been more pushing, pinching and yelping. As Carlton watched *Love Thy Neighbour* on TV, he heard a loud knock on the back door. Josephine shouted, 'I bet that's Glenroy making that din. How many times have I told him not to bang on that back door when the kids are in bed! For the life of me! If he does it again I'll give him what for! Isn't this his church youth club night?'

Carlton rose from his armchair. 'Yeah, it is his church club night. I hope he hasn't skived off. You know what Uncle Thomas's like.'

Josephine didn't reply.

Carlton wearily ambled along the hallway and turned right, entering the laundry room. Through the frosted wire-glassed back door, he made out the lean frame of Curvis.

Carlton opened the door. 'Are you coming out?' Curvis asked. 'You're not too tired, are ya?'

'Yeah, I'm knackered. I also had a ruck.'

'With who?'

'Some wanker who pushed me into the wall during basketball.'

'You didn't *do* him, did ya?'

'Didn't get a chance to,' replied Carlton. 'As usual, I got the blame. Got banned.'

'Sorry to hear. Teachers always blame home kids.'

'Yep. Ain't that the fucking truth. Give me a sec. Let me put something on my feet.'

Two minutes later, they were sitting down in a deserted field. Curvis wrapped a buttercup around his index finger while Carlton gnawed a blade of grass.

'So on Saturday,' Carlton began, 'we're still gonna meet up the top field by the sycamore tree?'

'Yeah, it's the best place,' Curvis nodded. 'No one's gonna be there in the middle of the night. We can go through the bushes and climb over the fence, which goes to an alleyway. It leads to a road outside.'

'Did you chat with Glenroy and Bullet today?'

'Yeah, everyone knows what to do.'

'Why can't we just walk out the front gate?' Carlton wanted to know. 'No one's about that time of night.'

'Yeah, but you never know,' Curvis replied. 'It's too risky – someone might be up at the Lodge. And Mr Williams sometimes drives up and down in his car on patrol. If we go the top field way then no one will see us.'

Mr Williams was the Pinewood Oaks' troubleshooter; every incident was reported to him, and he was the link between the council and the staff who ran the cottages. Every Monday morning he would drive up to London to report to his seniors on matters arising within Pinewood Oaks. He lived in a rent-free cottage within the grounds with his own family.

'Mr Corporal Williams!' Carlton mocked. 'The lazy wanker should try and do some work in the daytime so he doesn't have to prowl about at night. Doesn't he ever sleep?'

'Yeah, he does actually,' Curvis chuckled. 'His kids are not allowed to disturb him from one in the afternoon till six in the evening. If they make any noise they get grounded.'

'Fuck the buttercups! Even for kids who live with their parents here it's like Colditz.'

'Maybe, but at least we don't have to tunnel out,' Curvis laughed.

'We still have to cross the main road,' said Carlton. 'You know what the residents around here are like – they see a black face they'll be on the phone quicker than a fly on warm dog shit.'

'I know, I know,' replied Curvis. 'But it's better we come out of a side road than coming out of the entrance of Pinewood Oaks … We might be stopped by that vampire Williams before we even get out of the grounds. Some great escape that'll be. We'll all be sitting in tiny stone cells bouncing tennis balls like Steve McQueen.'

'Two in the morning we meet by the sycamore tree?' Carlton wanted confirmation.

'Yeah. Any earlier someone might be up and about. The house-father in Laburnum is always up late on a Saturday night. He's a weird freak. Mr Brooke Martin. He plays solitaire in his study for hours when everybody is asleep. You and Glenroy have to pass Laburnum on the way to the top field. Keep close to the bushes and *don't* shine your torches! Oh, and don't wear bright clothes. Tell Glenroy his yellow cords are a no-no.'

'I'll tell him. But you know we're in the middle of summer, Curvis. You know it gets light about half four in the morning?'

'Yeah, but by then we should be safe in the hills. I reckon it'll take us one and a half hours. Hour and a quarter if it weren't for Glenroy.'

'You sure you know where you're going in the dark?' Carlton asked. 'You can easily get lost up there. Some of those scouts get lost in the daytime.'

'I'm gonna nick my housemother's big torch,' said Curvis. 'She keeps it under the stairs. And Bullet is gonna nick Uncle Rodney's. I just hope the batteries last – they're expensive.'

'I still don't feel easy about nicking the petty cash box from under Auntie Josephine's bed. It's like betrayal. Can't see why one of you lot can't nick a petty cash box.'

'We don't know where the fuck they hide it!' reasoned Curvis.

'*You* know where Auntie Josephine keeps hers. And it won't be like you're nicking from her. It's council money and they'll replace it. Don't worry about it. Can't last with our own money.'

'Fuck knows what I'll do if she wakes up.'

'You'll be alright. Just pretend you're wriggling through the grass and scaring girls like we used to do in Africa country.'

'Alright for you to say.'

'Don't forget to nick all the grub you can,' reminded Curvis. 'I told Glenroy not to bother cos he's too clumsy – you know what he's like. He'll probably bring down a shelf or two. Besides, I think they lock the larder in his house.'

'They do,' confirmed Carlton. 'I wouldn't be surprised if Uncle Thomas had one of them castle padlocks on it. When Glenroy's housemother bakes cakes, she gives most of 'em to the staff to take home. The kids only get treats when the Marks and Spencer van comes with their out-of-date grub.'

Carlton yawned and Curvis took this as a cue for taking his leave. He stood up and glanced skywards. The heavens had darkened. 'Carlton, you realise you can't take your bike.'

'I thought about that,' Carlton said. 'Who knows if I'll see it again? I can carry it on my shoulder.'

Curvis shook his head. 'We're going to the hills. Not even you can ride it up there. Your arse will be rolling down a slope.'

'Not planning plan to ride it. I can hide it somewhere.'

'Carlton!'

'Alright! Keep your Afro on. I won't take it. Thought you'd want me to keep it considering all the work you done on it.'

'We've gotta let things go,' said Curvis.

Carlton thought of Josephine. He wiped an imaginary tear. 'I s'pose so.'

Two hours later, Curvis sat up in bed. He spot-lit the dormitory with his small torch and found all his roommates fast asleep. Someone had forgotten to pack away a snakes and ladders board that was left on the blue-carpeted floor. Overlooking a child's bed, a poster of the Liverpool football team had Kevin Keegan's head missing. Another boy's best clothes were laid out neatly next to his bed, draped on a chair. Stan's social worker must be coming tomorrow, Curvis guessed.

Having trouble getting to sleep, Curvis lifted the covers off his chest. Then he stood up and pushed up the sash window to its limit. The night breeze cooled his skin. He looked up; the half-crescent moon shone brilliantly. Staring at the stars, he offered a whisper. 'We're gonna be on our way soon, Mum. I feel scared thinking about it. Maybe Carlton should be the leader. Don't wanna lead all my best mates into trouble. Don't want 'em to end up on punishment. God knows what that cunt Thomas will do to Glenroy. Maybe I should go on my own?'

Ten thirty. The warm night air was heavy. A lone lamp-post, its dim, yellow light flickering, stood like a sentinel outside a dull beige-bricked building; it could not challenge the half moon's brightness. Halfway up a hill, a hundred yards south of Pinewood Oaks primary school, the flat-topped youth club was sheltered by oak leaves. The trees had no breeze to make them murmur.

The bruised, graffiti-daubed blue door of the building opened. From the exit, noisy teenagers filled the road. They were shouting, joking and cursing just like teenagers do. The din filtered through to the surrounding fields.

Three adults stepped out of the youth club with one of them locking the door behind him. He glared at his rowdy charges. 'Will you *please* go home quietly! Come on now. You've all had a good evening. *Don't* spoil it.' The man sighed, expecting more complaints from the staff of Yew cottage, fifty yards further up the road.

Darting around, pestering two girls, Glenroy ignored the youth worker's pleas. 'Glenroy!' one of the adults barked. 'Leave Sandra and Brenda alone! You've been annoying them all evening.'

Glenroy made a face before running to catch up with his friends.

Curvis, Carlton and Bullet made slow progress across the field, the crescent moon their guiding light through the dark grass. The lamp-posts, spread fifty yards apart, pin-pricked the trees and bushes. They formed long, ghost-like shadows. Realisation dawned on them that this might be the last time they trekked home from the Blue Peter club together.

'Tomorrow is it,' announced Bullet, hands in pockets. 'I can't believe it! The day came so quick.'

'Don't forget the blankets, will ya,' added Carlton. 'And whatever you do, don't forget to wake up. I know you love your sleep. Just remember, *be* at the sycamore tree up by the top field by three o'clock.'

'Three o'clock?' queried Bullet. 'I thought it was two o'clock?'

'I changed it,' said Curvis. 'Don't you listen to anything I tell you? That mad housefather in Laburnum house might be up at two.'

'Don't worry about me,' reassured Bullet. 'I'm not gonna fall asleep. I'm staying awake.'

'Which one's the sycamore tree?' asked Glenroy.

'How many times do I have to tell you?' Curvis raised his voice. 'It's the tree that's got those things that fall off – they look like tiny boomerangs.'

'Oh yeah. Of course.'

'All of you should get as many blankets as you can,' stressed Curvis. 'We're gonna need them to sleep on. And Carlton, you sure you know where Auntie Josephine keeps the petty cash?'

'How many times have you asked me that this evening? For the millionth time, underneath her bed. She's kept it under there for years now.'

'Your Auntie still bakes cakes on a Saturday afternoon?' Curvis asked Bullet.

'Three o'clock on the dot,' replied Bullet. 'Every Saturday without fail. You could set your watch to it. She keeps 'em in a biscuit tin in the larder.'

'Does your Auntie lock the larder door at night?'

'Nah,' Bullet chuckled. 'Are you having a laugh? In our house everyone's too shit scared to do a larder raid. If Uncle Rodney caught ya he'd probably ask the Germans to reopen Colditz and send you there for sixty years.'

'And don't forget your sports bag,' added Curvis.

'I can get some biscuits,' said Glenroy. 'We've got some ginger snaps in our larder.'

'Get them if you can,' said Carlton. 'The biscuits would be cool but they're not *that* important. You don't wanna get caught in your kitchen when we're about to leg it. Just make sure you get all the clothes you can carry and put them in a bag.'

'I won't get caught,' replied Glenroy. 'Our larder is always locked but there's a window at the back. I think I can get through. I'll be like a cat burglar.'

'More like a hippo on a greasy tin roof,' Carlton joked. 'Forget it! I've seen the window at the back of your larder and even a very flat gingerbread man would get stuck.'

The quartet had reached the northern fringes of the allotment area that was protected with flimsy fencing. It was fronted by tall, fir-like trees that looked out of place in a landscape dominated by oaks and chestnuts. Curvis peered into the blackness. 'What's that?' he called out. 'Did you see that? Someone's in the allotments.'

Silently, the friends climbed the fence and took cover underneath a tree. Thirty yards away, four silhouetted figures lifted netting and plucked something from the ground. Eager to get a better view, Glenroy wriggled closer. 'It's Johnson and his mates,' he whispered. 'Them guys who live in Ashburden.'

Curvis beckoned Glenroy with his right hand. 'Let's go home,' he said. 'If they wanna nick tomatoes and stuff, then let 'em. Why should we give a fuck?'

Carlton inched towards Glenroy. 'Nah. We shouldn't let guys from outside Pinewood Oaks come here and nick from the allotments.'

'Why should we care?' repeated Curvis. 'It's not like they're growing it for us.'

'We should care cos we'll probably get the blame for this,' reasoned Carlton. 'We don't want Williams coming round to our houses in the morning with his *Columbo* face on.'

Bullet nodded. He followed Carlton on all fours. 'Let's give 'em a kicking!'

Glenroy inadvertently sneezed. One of the night raiders turned around and spotted Glenroy crawling on the grass. 'Hey, Johnson,' the thief called. 'It's that dunce in your class. Glenroy.'

'Why are you spying on us?' Johnson demanded, emerging out of the darkness. He carried a sports bag full of ill-gotten veg. 'It's not your allotment.'

'It might not be mine but it's on *our* grounds,' Glenroy challenged. 'I live round here so why don't you fuck off back to your area.'

Backed up by his accomplices, Johnson ran towards Glenroy with serious intent. Simultaneously Carlton and Bullet sprang to their feet. Curvis remained by the tree, shaking his head. Seeing Carlton, Johnson stopped short of Glenroy and glared at him in a promise of revenge for another day. 'Who are you telling to fuck off, you fat piece of shit,' Johnson cursed.

'He's telling you to fuck off,' Bullet sniped. 'What's a matter? Are your ears full of shit?'

Johnson quickly ran his eyes over Carlton's physique. He backed away a step. Carlton walked slowly towards Johnson. Bullet prowled behind him, his fists clenched in anticipation. 'If you wanna take your goods home, you're gonna have to fight for them,' warned Carlton. 'We don't like wankers coming in here and nicking from our grounds.'

Johnson thought about it. Ten seconds later he raised his right arm and beckoned his mates to follow him. He emptied his bag. Tomatoes, potatoes and other vegetables dropped to the ground. 'Come on,' he ordered. 'If they're gonna squeal about it, let's go somewhere else.'

Giving Carlton a wide berth, Johnson's crew made for the fence. They scaled the barrier and scampered into the nearest field, disappearing into the dark. Forgetting that he might have to confront Johnson again at school, Glenroy held up his left hand in an uncomplimentary gesture. 'Tossers!'

Bullet grinned. 'They bottled it.'

Carlton looked around to find Curvis – he was still sitting down underneath a tree. 'What's a matter with you?' Carlton asked.

'Nothing,' Curvis replied. 'Just watched a lot of bollocks that wasn't called for. Why didn't you leave 'em to it?'

'Cos this is our patch,' answered Bullet. 'If we let knob-heads like

Johnson come in here and push their weight around, then more will come and take the piss.'

'Our patch?' Curvis argued. 'Have you forgotten that we're leaving this shit of a patch?'

'You're right,' Carlton agreed. 'But if we don't come back, other kids have gotta live here somehow. It's bad enough without the likes of Johnson.'

Glenroy went over to where Johnson had spilled the vegetables. He picked up a tomato and examined it. 'These tomatoes aren't even ripe,' he remarked. 'We should've let Johnson take 'em. By morning they would've had shit running down their legs.'

Carlton and Bullet laughed. Curvis jogged towards the fence, climbed it with ridiculous ease and walked off. He didn't look behind him. Carlton set off after him. 'What's a matter now?' he called.

Curvis waited until Carlton caught up with him. 'I had a really bad feeling last night,' Curvis admitted. 'Felt it in my gut.'

'Felt what in your gut,' Carlton asked. 'It might've been your Auntie's shepherd's pie.'

Curvis wasn't amused. 'Couldn't sleep,' he said. 'I dunno if we're doing the right thing.'

'It's a bit late to get all jumpy about it,' Carlton snapped. 'I wasn't sure about it but now the time has come, I'm really looking forward to it.'

'Maybe I should go on my own,' Curvis proposed. 'I'm the one who wants to make a point to them cunts.'

'What do you mean?' Carlton pulled Curvis by the arm and trapped him with a fierce glare. 'We all have our reasons. We're all up for it.'

Curvis was distracted by Bullet and Glenroy. He waited until they caught up before speaking again. 'I don't wanna be the leader,' he announced. 'Look at what just happened! I'm about as much help in a fight as a cotton wool jockstrap. I don't wanna be the weak link.'

Carlton placed his arm around Curvis's shoulders. 'We're doing the right thing. Think about all the shit that goes on here. No matter what happens, whoever's in charge of this place is gonna be asked questions if we do a runner. Can you imagine Williams going up to London trying to explain that we've done a runner? It'll wipe the snidey grin off his face.'

'Yeah,' Bullet nodded. 'Williams drives up and down the place and expects us to salute him or something. *Fix your tie, young man. Button up your shirt. Have you combed your hair today?* Fuck that!'

'I still don't think running away will solve all our problems,' replied Curvis. He stared at the ground. 'And I can't even fight for myself. I get the shits every time you lot are involved with something. And tonight? I kept telling myself to help. But I couldn't.'

'You didn't have to help,' said Carlton. 'So stop getting your brain in a twist about it. We'll look after you. Your problem was that when Stanton was here, he slugged anybody who so much as flicked you. By the sounds of it, he's not coming back. Get used to it! Me, Bullet and Glenroy had to fight for ourselves.'

Curvis recalled an incident from the past. He had been beaten up by two school bullies. The pain of the beating had faded but the image of his father that gatecrashed his mind at the time was an experience he'd never forget. Two days after the assault, Carlton, Bullet and Glenroy arrived at Curvis's school seeking vengeance; Stanton would have been the first one to show up, but he wasn't there any more. Curvis remembered the cuts and bruises his friends suffered on his behalf while he hid behind a school dustbin. He often wondered why they wanted him as a friend.

In silence, the friends made their way across the field towards the banks of the stream that sparkled under the moonlight. An unseen owl disturbed the peace. Glenroy found a burrow and searched for a fox. Before he could get down on his knees to get a better look, Bullet jumped on his back and they started round 678 of their eternal wrestling match. Carlton and Curvis laughed. Glenroy won this particular bout by body-slamming Bullet into the turf and sitting on his shoulders.

They jogged towards the stream, moving silhouettes against a murky backdrop. They could now hear the rush of water, hurrying its way under the stone bridge. Curvis peered through the trees that fronted his cottage. He could see his dining-room window lit by a naked lightbulb from one hundred yards away.

Carlton plucked a blade of grass and wrapped it around his right index finger. He studied it as if it held the secrets of the world. 'I think we're all getting nervous,' he said. 'I can't believe we're gonna do this ... but we are.'

Curvis nodded.

'Auntie Josephine's gonna hate me for this,' Carlton continued. 'She's been good to me. Not gonna lie about that. She's probably the only decent member of staff in this place. I was thinking of writing her a note, telling her I didn't run away cos of her.'

Lying belly-down on the grass, Curvis watched the flow of the water. 'Yeah, you should,' he said. 'She's alright. The only house-mother in this place who treats her kids like she's their mum. *Don't* tell her where we're going though.'

'I won't,' assured Carlton.

'I *know* you won't.'

They paused for a minute as Bullet and Glenroy yelped, growled and groaned.

'If we asked Elvin, he would've come with us,' said Carlton. 'Why didn't you want me to ask him?'

Curvis considered his reply. 'Two reasons.'

'What's that?' Carlton wanted to know.

'You know that in the past two months his older sister has been visiting him on Sundays. Elvin tells me that if things work out, he might go and live with her.'

'Doesn't she live in a two-bedroom flat? Where's Elvin gonna sleep?'

'On the sofa,' replied Curvis. 'You know what they're like about that sort of thing. If they had their way, no one would ever leave this place till they're smoking pipes. If Elvin legs it away with us, it might fuck up what small chance he's got of getting out of here. Us? We haven't got fuck all to lose.'

'Speak for yourself!' returned Carlton.

Curvis nodded. 'Yeah. Auntie Josephine. I s'pose you got more to lose than the rest of us.'

'You said two reasons,' said Carlton. 'What's the other?'

Curvis took his time in answering. 'Have you heard the rumours about Uncle Thomas?'

Carlton hesitated. 'Yeah … one or two kids talk about it.'

'So you know then?' pressed Curvis.

'That he touched up Elvin years ago?' Carlton stuttered. 'Yeah … I know about that.'

Curvis didn't know what to add.

'When he told me I didn't know what to say,' said Carlton. 'I knew he wasn't lying. Why would someone lie about that? What did you say?'

'Nothing,' replied Curvis. His eyes returned to the wrestling match. 'I just hope that he hasn't done it to Glenroy.'

'Nah. He definitely would've told us.'

'Would he?' questioned Curvis. 'Elvin only told me last spring. It happened when he was *seven*. It's sick.'

'I'm telling ya,' Carlton insisted. 'Glenroy would've definitely told me. He tells me everything that goes on in his house.'

'You're right,' agreed Curvis. 'But I just can't help wondering.'

'Can you imagine living in his house with that shit going on?' said Carlton. 'I would sleep with a cricket bat in my bed.'

'Keep your voice down,' advised Curvis. 'Elvin made me promise that I'd never tell Glenroy.'

'Elvin made me promise too,' said Carlton. 'He's probably safe now cos I reckon that fucker's only interested in young boys. It's probably why Uncle Thomas wants to get rid of him. He wants to get in fresh meat.'

'*Sick!*' Curvis raised his voice.

'Tell me about it,' nodded Carlton.

'I'm not sure that he gives a shit what age the boys are,' said Curvis. 'But something boggles my head.'

'What's that?'

'I just can't see how Elvin can work at the swimming pool with that cunt.'

'If it was me,' said Carlton, 'I swear, if he tried it on me I'd have to *do* him. I wouldn't stop. Fucking nonce. Maybe he doesn't try it on teenagers cos they would fight back.'

Curvis noted a primal rage in Carlton's gaze. He didn't say anything, deciding to wait until the anger faded.

Carlton changed the subject. 'It's well humid tonight, innit.'

'That suits us,' said Curvis. 'At least we don't have to bring our anoraks.'

Carlton watched Bullet and Glenroy still grappling each other. 'Can you imagine them two wrestling in the Pinewood Hills? Will we get any sleep?'

'Probably not,' chuckled Curvis, rising to his feet. He expected a familiar rebuke from his housemother about his lateness, but he didn't care. He hadn't spoken a single word to her beyond 'thank you' and 'yes, Auntie' for almost three weeks now. He waved his friends farewell as if he wouldn't see them for months.

Bullet was next to start for home but not before slapping Glenroy on the forehead. Carlton and Glenroy jogged through Africa country and through the silent orchard. Carlton couldn't help but wonder if Glenroy had been 'touched' by Uncle Thomas. He recalled his own words. *Uncle Thomas probably wouldn't try it on teenagers cos they could fight back.* Carlton knew Glenroy couldn't fight back.

Emerging from the orchard, they both heard Uncle Thomas's stern voice cutting through the night. 'Didn't I tell you to come straight home from the club! It's nearly midnight!'

Carlton stood still as he watched his friend run the rest of the way home. Uncle Thomas held the back door open for Glenroy. Carlton stiffened as the housefather watched him. He didn't move until the back door was closed.

Carlton enjoyed the quiet and stillness as he entered his own home. Framed photographs of children and certificates of sporting excellence, mainly belonging to Carlton, hung from the walls. Children's drawings and sketches were pinned onto a notice board that was displayed near the front door.

Hearing his housemother working in her study, Carlton made his way there. He poked his head around the office door, and sure enough, Josephine, wearing a pink dressing gown with pen in hand, was surrounded by papers demanding her attention. A portable black-and-white television in the corner of the room silently broadcast a Dracula film. Josephine peered over her reading glasses. 'Oh, hello, Carlton,' she greeted warmly. She checked her watch. 'God Almighty! Hark at the time! Where've you been?'

'Out with my mates.'

'But club finished ages ago. You'll get me in trouble, you will!'

Carlton smiled. 'You wanna cup of tea, Auntie? I'm gonna make myself a snack before I hit the pillow.'

'You're a sweet, Carlton – I'll have mine black … Oh, I have changed everybody's sheets – none of the kids were comfortable sleeping in this heat – poor Suzy was drenched in sweat last night.'

'Thanks, Auntie.'

Carlton disappeared into the hallway. Before he reached the kitchen, he heard his housemother's voice again. 'Don't go straight to bed when you've eaten, I want a word with you.'

Seven minutes later, Carlton reappeared, balancing two cups of tea and a plate of chocolate digestives. Josephine wearily got to her feet and took her tea, offering a smile as thanks. She sat back down and watched Carlton affectionately; she would not admit it to anybody but Carlton had always been her favourite.

Carlton sat down in a red armchair.

'I had a phone call from your mother today,' Josephine said formally. 'She wants to visit you. I didn't really know what to say. So in the end, I told her that I had to speak to you first.'

Carlton stared at the carpet. He was about to say something but he checked himself.

Josephine bit her top lip before resuming. 'For what's it worth,

I think you should give her a chance. She sounds desperate. She's promised she's changed her ways. She blames me that you haven't spoken to her for seven years.'

'Seven years?' Carlton repeated.

Josephine nodded. She sipped her tea. 'Yeah, I didn't realise it was that long either.'

Carlton picked up his tea. 'I don't want her down here. *No way!*'

'But just try and get to know her again,' said Josephine. 'Let bygones be bygones. You can't go through your life hating your mum. It's killing her that you won't see her.'

'NO! I try to forget her. How many times do I have to tell ya?'

'You shouldn't feel shame,' said Josephine. 'No one knows what she's done in the past. It's all confidential. It's not gonna come out on my account. Not even my staff know.'

Carlton dunked a chocolate digestive into his tea and bit half of it. He looked up. '*I* know.'

'You've got to put that behind you. She might've changed into a better person.'

'Put it behind me? How can I put it behind me when she hasn't got a clue who my dad is? When I go out into the world I'll be thinking any black man that I pass in the street could be my dad.'

Josephine dropped her head.

'And how can I put it behind me that she used to leave me on my own at night when I was a baby?' Carlton went on. '*That's* the only thing I can remember about living with her. Being left on my own, screaming the house down. Doesn't it say that in my file? Doesn't it? Isn't that how you lot found me?'

Josephine nodded.

'So I can't put that behind me.'

Josephine sipped her tea again. 'You know, there are some kids in this place who don't know any family. Look at your friend Bullet and the paper boy, little Brenton Brown. They're all alone in this world.'

'Maybe, but I'll bet their mums haven't gone as low as the bitch who shitted me out.'

Silence. Josephine closed her eyes for a long second, absorbing Carlton's bitter words. 'People can change,' she said.

'Why do you want me to see her?' Carlton suddenly raised his voice. 'Whose side are you on? I don't wanna see her again. I don't want a*nything* to do with her.'

'She's your mother. Try and think about how she feels.'

'I wouldn't call her that,' Carlton replied. 'I've got another name for her.'

Finding it difficult to gaze at Carlton, Josephine stared at the papers on her desk. She closed her eyes again as she heard Carlton leaving the room, slamming the door. He hadn't finished his tea or his biscuits.

With a tear in her eye, Josephine went back to her work. '*Damn* her,' she whispered to herself. '*Damn* her!'

PART 3
EXODUS

Half asleep, Bullet dreamed of the future. It was a distant place. He imagined a placard fixed to the wall beside the entrance of Pinewood Oaks. The sign said, '*These are the names of the heroes, sons of Pinewood Oaks, who ran away from evil to freedom – Bullet, Glenroy, Carlton and Curvis.*'

Shaking his head to rid his body of sleep, Bullet willed the time to leap forward. He hadn't thought of it before but he had slept in his bed every night for the past seven years. He wondered what it would be like falling asleep under the stars with tree trunks replacing the walls and leaves forming a ceiling. I hope it doesn't rain, he chuckled to himself. Running away to the Pinewood Hills might get us all in the papers. Who knows? My mum might read about me and ask to take me home.

He tried to visualise what his mother looked like. Maybe she resembled the nice-looking lady in the washing-up liquid advert? Perhaps my dad was a mercenary and got killed in some faraway war. He could've fought in Vietnam, helping out the GIs. He could've been a footballer in the 1950s, playing alongside those famous players that Uncle Rodney keeps going on about. He could've tackled Stanley Matthews! Or jumped for a header with Duncan Edwards! Yeah, he was a hero. Maybe he didn't know he had a son. Who knows? Mum might be dead as well. Yeah, she could've died from a bomb attack while nursing the soldiers in Vietnam. That's how they met. She's a hero as well. Yeah, my parents are heroes.

His mind spinning with what-ifs and maybes, Bullet recalled the day when he, Curvis, Carlton and Glenroy made their first camp in the orchard. Old blankets made a carpet and a tatty car seat that Carlton had dragged from the dump was their throne. Bullet laughed as he remembered they had to take turns sitting on it. He could never forget their oath on that day, taken from a cowboys and Indians film they had all seen, as they bonded with their bloodied hands.

No less than four, mighty are we
Three'll be like cutting off our knees
Two'll be like the sinking of a crew
And one'll be like killing us with a gun.

It was the four friends' secret world, their hideaway where they dreamed of becoming famous footballers, world-class bowlers and war heroes. They hid sweets under tufts of grass and concealed their 'war' weapons beneath ferns in case of attack from another gang. Bullet shaped a sword out of a stray piece of fencing and immediately challenged Glenroy. Bullet named himself D'Artagnan, and Glenroy called himself Robin Hood. Shouts of *touché!* and *olé!* filtered through the hazel and holly bushes. Carlton and Curvis sat on a fallen bough in the glade, fiercely contesting a game of conkers.

Now, years later, Bullet and his friends were about to set up another camp in the Pinewood Hills. But this time for real. Bullet could feel the same adrenaline and excitement he felt then. Everyone would be talking about him back at the home – that would be cool too. Uncle Rodney's gonna get one big shock when he wakes up in the morning!

He slipped out of his bed as quietly as he could. He pulled on his jeans and white T-shirt that were folded neatly on a chair next to his bed. Once dressed, he groped for the large sports bag under his bed. On the dressing table that he shared with a younger boy were his few toiletries. He placed his comb and brush into the bag. He felt his heart thump against his chest. Sweat drenched his eyebrows. The silence was loud. The stillness of the dormitory unnerved him.

He opened his drawer and hurled vests, T-shirts, Y-fronts and socks into his holdall. In the corner of the drawer was his globe money box. Meticulously, he put his savings into his carrier. He pulled open another drawer and found his two sweaters. Might need 'em if we're still in the Pinewood Hills in the winter, he thought. If we make it to then, that'll be one long mission.

He rolled across to the other side of his bed to open his locker. He picked out his torch and penknife. He decided to pack his frayed playing cards. Glenroy might finally learn how to play blackjack, he chuckled. After closing the locker door, he sat on his bed. He looked around at the still shadows created by the moonlight that stole through the curtains. He wondered if he would see his bedroom again, or indeed, his roommates. He offered a silent goodbye to all of them as his heartbeat chugged into a higher gear.

He zipped his bag slowly, stood up and started to creep towards the door. On reaching it, he looked out into the hallway. He scanned the corridor. I'd better take my chance now, he thought. No turning back. Don't wanna let down my mates.

The staircase at the end of the passage seemed further away than normal. He closed the dormitory door behind him and began to cross the corridor, thankful for the carpet that cushioned the squeak of his well-worn trainers. Sweat gummed his hair against his temples and forehead as he passed Uncle Rodney's bedroom. Someone's gonna hear me, he convinced himself. He inched by the staff bedroom. His heartbeat accelerated. Something cracked beneath his right foot. It was a clear sound, like a slap across the face. I'm done for, he fretted. Uncle Rodney might be awake reading one of his war books, or doing one of his stupid exercises. He slinked on, his strides shrinking into chicken steps. Only when the staircase was a few inches away did he relax. Just the girls dorm to pass, he told himself.

He tiptoed down the stairs, concentrating on the patches in the old wooden frame, which after years of experience informed him where the steps creaked. Once downstairs, he felt his way to the washroom where he found his towel and flannel hanging on a peg. Walking on the balls of his feet, he made it to the airing cupboard, making sure he closed the door before switching on the light. He grabbed three blankets. 'So far so good,' he whispered to himself as he headed towards the back door.

He took one last glance behind him and then unfastened the latch. He opened the door and closed it behind him as if he was performing keyhole surgery. He breathed out a long sigh and wiped the sweat from his forehead. He navigated the back door steps as if any undue pressure would crack the concrete. He allowed himself to glance up. *'Done it!'*

Finally, he was in the clear. Freedom. He closed his eyes, breathed deeply in and out again. He then darted into the murk of the field that lead directly from the back of the house towards the piggery. As he ran, the surrounding trees seemed to mutter to each other. He could sense anonymous eyes on him. He looked for signs of life, sure he could detect indistinct sounds coming from the bushes around the field. 'No,' he said. 'My mind's playing tricks on me.'

He stepped on a twig and to him it sounded like a rifle shot. He stopped and peered into the undergrowth once more. He heard something else. He ran, ran as hard as he could.

2.15 a.m.

Desperately trying to control his breathing, Carlton crawled along the carpet of Auntie Josephine's bedroom. He could smell the perfume from Josephine's dressing table. A window was open but no breeze entered. His palms were moist even before he entered the room, his face streaked in perspiration. He could hear his housemother gently exhaling through her nose. Every small fidget from her sounded as if King Kong was trying to find a comfortable sleeping position.

He tried to think of excuses in case she awoke – but he couldn't.

He made out the shape of Josephine's dressing gown, draped over a chair. He stretched out his right arm under the bed and groped with his hand, brushing the bottom of the mattress. All he felt was the texture of the carpet. His hand ran along the rug, searching with his fingers for the hard metal of the petty cash box. *Don't wake up,* he willed. *Don't wake up.*

With his thumb and index finger, he touched the square of the cash box. It felt cold. He nudged it towards him, flipping the sharp corner with his fingers. His lungs filled with pure panic. He couldn't breathe out.

It seemed to take an eternity to prod the cash box out. But finally, he could see it. Metallic black. He slid backwards, towards the door, moving the box along the carpet. Josephine sneezed. He slammed his eyes shut, frightened into stillness. He pressed his face into the carpet, wishing it would wrap over him like an envelope. He heard the rustling of sheets and chanced a look above the mattress.

Josephine returned to sleep, exhaling and inhaling softly. He regained his composure. He swabbed the sweat from his temples. He slithered further backwards. Once past the door frame, he turned his body around and crawled out into the hallway. He stood up, ears and eyes alert. Walking on tiptoes he crept back into his bedroom. I'm now a thief, he cursed himself.

He had already packed his bag with clothes and other necessities. It felt light, but guilt weighed heavy in his mind. He picked up his holdall from just inside his room and placed the cash box carefully inside. Breathing easier, he made his way to the staircase, stepping down sideways.

On reaching the ground floor he stole along the hallway and into the kitchen; the smell of baked chocolate fairy cakes still lingered in the room. He wiped his face once more, unhooked a plastic bag from the kitchen door handle and proceeded to take the fairy cakes from a tin in the larder. He ate one in two bites.

He knew where Josephine had put up her chores rota – pinned against a board above the double sinks. He unpinned the paper listing the jobs for the children to carry out during the week. He found a biro in a drawer beside the sinks and started to write a short note on the back of the paper. His handwriting wasn't his best. His message read: 'I'm not doing this because of the way you treat me.'

He tiptoed out of the kitchen and crept along the passage. He looked up to the staircase and half expected Auntie Josephine to be standing on the landing, staring with accusing eyes. No one was there. Get your feet in gear, he said to himself. No hanging about. It's not like I want to get caught. Is it?

He paced to the back door and pulled on his trainers. Before he departed, he checked behind him one last time. He opened the back door, stepped out into the night and closed the door as gently as he could. Auntie Josephine grew large in his mind. Once down the steps, he offered a glance upwards. 'Sorry,' he whispered.

He then ran into the black gloom of the hushed field with tears stinging the corners of his eyes.

2.45 a.m.

Carlton, Bullet and Glenroy had made it to the rendezvous point. They looked at each other, displaying differing degrees of panic. Curvis hadn't yet arrived. No one wanted to ask where he could be. They waited under the branches of the sycamore tree at the top field, dimly illuminated by the moon and the lamp-post sixty yards away. The hedges were still. The rhythmical hooting of an owl, somewhere in the depths of the orchard, pricked the silence. The sycamore tree itself stood like a muted, dark sentinel. Carlton imagined it was watching him.

As they peered across the field, they all felt a wrenching doubt inside their stomachs. Maybe Curvis got caught? Perhaps he changed his mind. Or, even worse, he might have left for the Pinewood Hills already, deciding to leave on his own.

Glenroy gazed at the heavens; Curvis had once given him a lesson about the stars. He spotted Capella in the south-western sky, shining brightest. He saw shadows in the moon. 'He's bottled it,' he said. 'After all this. He's bottled it! All that planning! *Do* this and *do* that and he doesn't even turn up.'

'He'll be here,' reassured Carlton. 'He better be *here*. Don't wanna sneak the money box back under Auntie Josephine's bed.'

'Maybe that snobby bitch was up and caught him,' Glenroy suggested. 'They might be on the way up here. Curvis might've grassed.'

'Will you take an ice pole and calm down!' Carlton snapped. 'It's not even three yet.'

'But he's always the first to arrive,' Glenroy replied. 'He's never late. He even goes to school early.'

'He's right,' agreed Bullet. He circled on the spot, peering into the dark as best he could. 'Glenroy's right. Curvis's never late. Greenwich Mean Time could set their watches to him.'

The eerie silence unnerved them all. The night air was dense and they could almost feel the moisture creeping out of the earth. Gnats hovered above the hedges. They heard the crickets having a night-time debate in Africa country.

Bullet sat down and picked up a twig. He peeled it with his pen-knife. 'Come on, Curvis,' he willed softly. 'Sneaking back in will be worse than sneaking out.'

'What are we gonna do if he doesn't turn up?' asked Glenroy.

'Will you shut up!' Carlton raised his voice. '*Don't* get all panicky on me. Worst comes to the worst, we can eat all the grub. We'll tell 'em we came here for a night-time picnic.'

'And what are you gonna tell 'em about the money?' Glenroy wanted to know.

Carlton offered Glenroy one of his most brutal glares.

'Curvis's probably here already,' said Bullet. 'Probably laughing cos we're shitting ourselves.'

Everyone looked up into the branches.

'Speak for yourself,' said Glenroy. 'Ain't no one shitting themselves apart from you.'

Bullet heard a rustling from a hedge. Glenroy followed his eyes. Slowly they made out a slim figure emerging from the bushes. Curvis jogged towards them, clutching a holdall in each hand. His friends tasted sweet relief.

'What kept you?' barked Glenroy.

'Nothing,' Curvis replied calmly. 'It just took longer than I thought to pack my bags. It's not quite three yet so why have you got your woodpeckers in your Y-fronts?'

'Glenroy was about to have a fit,' said Carlton. 'He reckoned you bottled it or got caught.'

'He doesn't have to worry,' laughed Curvis. 'I'm here to hold his hand and wipe his nose.'

Bullet honed a sharp point on his twig. 'So this is it then? The start of our special mission. No turning back now, is there?'

'Why d'you say that?' asked Glenroy. 'D'you wanna go back?'

'Why you always starting an argument?' asked Bullet. 'Just keep your mouth shut.'

'You gonna make me?' challenged Glenroy.

Ignoring the start of round 781, Curvis placed his bags on the grass and turned to Carlton. 'How much money did you get?'

Carlton opened the petty cash box. Everybody looked on. There were two notes; one blue and one brown. Carlton counted the coins. 'Nineteen pound sixty.'

'Is that all?' moaned Curvis. 'I've only got three pound.'

Curvis turned to Bullet. 'How much have you got?'

'Four pound and a lot of pennies.'

Bullet headlighted Glenroy. 'And what have you got?'

Glenroy took his time. 'Forty-two pence.'

'Forty-two pence!' Curvis repeated. 'You were s'posed to be saving your money for the last two weeks.'

'I wanted to get that Bruce Lee magazine with the fold-out poster in it,' reasoned Glenroy. 'I'm gonna need something to read while we're on the run.'

'Then you should've broke into the nursery and nicked those Peter and Jane books,' chuckled Bullet.

'I don't believe this guy,' growled Carlton. 'Forty-two pence! That'll buy us about three jamboree bags and a gobstopper!'

'And if we're lucky, we might get a plastic soldier inside,' joked Bullet.

'We've got nearly thirty pound,' said Curvis. 'That's gonna have to do. We can forget about Mars bars and Milky Ways.'

Curvis stooped down to pick up his bags. 'Come on, we'd better get our legs in gear. Can't stand here arguing about forty-two pence until the larks sing in the dawn – and that'll be in another hour and a bit.'

'Oh shit!' Bullet cried. 'With Glenroy going on about his Bruce Lee poster, I've just realised I've left my *Victor* and football comics behind.'

'Aren't you getting a bit old for *Victor* comics?' asked Carlton.

'They're for kids,' Glenroy agreed.

'Grown-ups read 'em an' all,' replied Bullet.

'At least I remembered to bring my pencils and paper,' chuckled Glenroy.

'Well, thank fuck for that!' mocked Carlton. 'The thought of you remembering to bring along your pencils and stuff has kept me awake for nights on end! Can we go now?'

They set off, walking four abreast and heading towards the thick bushes towards a corner of the top field. The terrain sloped gently downwards and they could now see the white football goalposts with their bowed cross bars. The backs of detached houses, fronted by clipped back gardens and spacious greenhouses, came into view on the other side of an eight-foot-high, meshed fence. No lights were on inside. Wild growing nettles created a natural barrier between Pinewood Oaks and normal family life. It would take a brave boy to retrieve the many tennis balls and footballs that were trapped here.

They reached the football pitch. It was too dark to make out any of the white lines marked on the turf. They maintained their march, the sycamore tree now a few hundred yards behind them.

They headed to a corner of the field where the houses quit. Curvis knew that in the winter, the access would be easy, but in the present season, the nettles and thorn bushes had grown substantially to act as a barrier to their intended path. He watched Bullet put his twig inside his bag. Carlton stooped to pick up a blade of grass and placed it in the corner of his mouth. They stopped before the nettles and put down their bags. 'How we gonna get through there?' asked Glenroy.

'By swinging you by the feet and letting your hair clear a path,' joked Curvis.

'Fuck you.'

'Look for a stick,' suggested Curvis. 'Otherwise, we'll have to use our feet.'

Bullet found a snapped branch by the perimeter fencing. He handed it to Carlton who wasted no time in hacking away the scrub, his friends silently marvelling at his strength. They lined up in single file behind him, using their feet to clear a navigable course. They were careful to avoid any flying 'sick bay' leaves. Bullet took out his torch and beamed it forward. 'Doing this makes me feel like we're on a mission,' he remarked.

'It's hardly James Bond,' Carlton laughed. 'That old bloke who gives Bond weapons would have given me something for these bushes.'

They continued into the blackness, which sucked them in like a rabbit hole. Soon the pathway became clear as the vegetation quit. Wild cherry trees, growing no more than twelve feet high, came into view. 'These are the nobbler trees I've always talked about,' said Curvis. 'In autumn, the nobblers are the juiciest in Pinewood Oaks.'

'Thank you, Professor Bellamy,' Carlton laughed. 'I really needed that information.'

'If we're still on the run by autumn we can come back here and pick 'em,' Glenroy suggested.

He received no answer. They threaded through the scrub before coming to a six-foot-high, wooden fence. Glenroy glanced up. 'Tree. I'll be seeing you later.'

'It's a bit creepy in here,' said Bullet. 'It's got a bit of a Dracula feel going on. I won't go on too much cos Glenroy will think the fanged one is following us. I don't wanna scare the bollocks off him.'

'I'd rather Drac than Uncle Thomas,' replied Glenroy.

'What would Dracula be doing in Pinewood?' joked Curvis. 'He's s'posed to live in Transylvania.'

'He might've got a barge and come over,' said Glenroy.

'He's not gonna get a barge,' replied Bullet. 'Barges are for canals! You divo! Besides, Drac's scared of water.'

Curvis was first to climb over the fence. He reached the other side with ease. Carlton passed all the bags over to him. The others quickly followed, Glenroy, being the clumsiest, lost his footing and scraped his left shin.

'Ouch!'

They found themselves in an alleyway strewn with litter, dead leaves and yellowed newspapers. The stench of urine attacked their nostrils. Along one side was the thicket they had just crossed, which stared into the backyards of a dozen semi-detached houses. A cat with luminous green eyes watched them from a back-garden shed. They looked back to where they had come from. Still, not even the slightest of breezes was stirring.

'We're out!' gasped Bullet. 'We're all nutters. We're out!'

'Yeah!' Glenroy exclaimed. He did a disco twirl, spinning around on his feet twice before losing his balance.

'Will you shut your cake holes!' scolded Carlton. 'You wanna wake up the whole of Pinewood?'

'Come on,' whispered Curvis. 'Get your toes in gear. We're not safe yet.'

Curvis took the lead. They followed the alleyway until they came to a side road that led off Pinewood High Street. Distant traffic was now audible from the roundabout where routes led to Ashburden and New Craddington.

'When we get to the main road, watch out for any cars,' Carlton warned. '*Don't* cross the road if a car is coming.'

They started up the cul-de-sac, admiring the expensive cars parked in driveways. They wondered what it would be like to live beyond the trimmed hedges and elaborate porches that fronted the detached houses.

They arrived at the main road, one hundred yards east of the shops on Pinewood High Street. Curvis stopped and listened. To his left the road climbed steeply, snaking a shadowed route deep into the Kent countryside. He spotted a vehicle's headlights in the distance and urged his friends to retreat. The motorist flashed by at a fast speed. Curvis ran a last check. 'Run!' They bolted across the road and hurriedly made their way up another side street, heading south. This was similar to the one before. Semi-detached homes with garages and well-kept front gardens.

'Keep your eyes frogging left and right,' advised Carlton. 'Who knows who might peep out of bedroom windows at this time of night.'

Picking up their pace, they passed a British Red Cross centre before turning left into another leafy avenue. They passed a stone office building filling the space of two houses. The sign outside read Air Corps Training Centre.

'Whassisname, Robson used to go there, innit,' Bullet said. 'He must be some kind of pilot now.'

'Robson?' Carlton laughed. 'Stevie Wonder must be doing the recruiting. If I'd been stranded on a desert island for thirty years and he came to save me in a little plane, he'd have to knock me out before I got in. Did you see the way he drove his trolleys downhill? He broke more wheels than in a Ben Hur chariot race.'

Everyone laughed. 'He only became an air cadet cos he couldn't make anything in the scouts,' Carlton nodded.

'I thought Robson joined the air cadets cos the magistrate in court said he needed to learn discipline,' said Curvis. 'They always want kids from a home to join the army, the navy and the R.G.S.D.F.'

'The what?' Bullet wanted to know.

'The R.G.S.D.F,' Curvis repeated. 'The Royal Get Shot Down Force.'

They laughed again, more relaxed now that they were far enough away from Pinewood Oaks. They marched to the end of the road.

Curvis felt the weight of his two bags. They turned right where the road steadily climbed. The houses increased in splendour, the front gardens more colourful. Ponds and garden gnomes became a feature. They made out a field at the end of the road. Bullet switched on his torch and shone it into Glenroy's face.

'Turn it off!' barked Curvis.

Bullet did as he was told.

They entered Pinewood recreation ground. The field had a football pitch marked in the middle. To their right was a children's play area with swings, a slide and a roundabout. Beyond the children's enclosure was a bowling green, three grass tennis courts and a croquet lawn.

'Anyone brought their racquet?' asked Carlton.

'We can cut off Glenroy's hand and use that,' grinned Bullet. 'It's big enough.'

They started along a dusty footpath that cut across the rec.

'Which way's the Pinewood Hills?' asked Glenroy.

'Straight ahead.' Curvis pointed the way. 'Cross the road, and go left, then right.'

Glenroy peered into the night. He saw the dark grey contours of the hills spanning the horizon. Beyond the road and dwarfing the houses into insignificance were the trees in the forest. The trunks stood imperiously straight and were crowned by moonlit leaves. Glenroy felt something in his stomach, and wasn't sure if it was excitement or fear. Carlton took in a gulp of air and checked if his friends had seen him do so.

They turned right into another cul-de-sac that led to woodland. The houses were spectacular, fronted by tall gates, manicured hedges and arching driveways. Gargoyles, primed to pounce, stared menacingly into the night from atop walls and porches. Glenroy recoiled at the sight of one that lolled out its tongue as if finishing a meal. Curvis put his right forefinger to his lips. 'Sssshhh. Last time I was up here dogs were barking all over the place.'

Carlton thought of wolves. He couldn't rid the sound of howling from his mind. He peered ahead into the forest and took in another deep breath.

They entered the woods. The canopy masked any sight of the moonlit sky. The air tasted different, tangible. It was heavier. They could feel no wind but they heard the treetops rustling, as if they were commenting on their intrusion. Curvis and Bullet switched on their torches. They beamed ahead. Huge hollows and craters scarred the dry ground, as if a titan had stomped lesser beings into the earth.

'How did them holes get there?' asked Carlton.

'Dunno,' replied Bullet. 'Might be bombs in the war or Glenroy's been up here and did a lot of farting.'

'Fuck you!'

In the distance they could see two bright lights – they dipped and rose like a boat tossed in an angry sea.

'Shit!' cursed Curvis. 'The scouts must be camping here. We'll have to go to the other side.'

They turned around and headed back to the cul-de-sac. 'Every summer holiday,' Curvis explained, 'the scouts camp up here – cubs an' all. They've got some huts deeper in the forest but sometimes they pitch up their tents wherever they like. Some of them might have made camps near here. They're always driving around in jeeps and Land Rovers.'

Wary of traffic, Curvis led his company eastwards along the road opposite the recreation ground. They walked swiftly, sensing their vulnerability in a residential area. They could now make out the spire of a church that set a dark gothic challenge to the height of the pines. Glenroy could just make out the gravestones that jutted above the hedges. There was a single light bulb above the arched front door of the church, casting sharp-angled shadows. Glenroy's heartbeat accelerated.

'Are we gonna stop for the night in the graveyard?' Carlton chuckled. 'I bet I'll be the only one who's got the balls to walk through it.'

'You can take my balls with ya,' laughed Glenroy. 'You're on your own on this one.'

'I've heard stories about that place,' said Bullet.

'It's not the one about if you knock seven times on a gravestone and some ghost pops out?' laughed Curvis.

Bullet turned on his torch again and shone it on the spire. 'If you think it's such a joke why don't you go over there and knock seven times.'

Curvis didn't take up the challenge.

Fifty yards on, Curvis found another entrance to the woods. He turned left into a pathway that led south. On his right, beyond a five-foot-high fence, was a secondary school, its playing fields stretching out into the night.

'Curvis,' Carlton called. 'I always thought you wanted to keep as far away as possible from your school.'

'It wouldn't surprise me to see my PE teacher on one of his jogs,' Curvis replied. 'Mr Beecher. He's a running maniac! Even when there's snow on the ground, he makes us go on cross-country runs. All because he loves it.'

'Sounds like a nutter,' Bullet remarked.

'He is,' nodded Curvis. 'His favourite sport is running up mountains. They should send him up in a plane and push him out over the foothills of Mount Everest and tell him to run to the top. As I said, he's a fruit-looping, mountain-hugging, jogging maniac.'

They walked steadily uphill, dwarfed by the pines on their left. Taking up the rear, Glenroy blew hard. He dared himself a glance into the woods and imagined the trees exhaling icy breaths on him. Get lost in there and you'd never find your way out, he thought.

Scouts are braver than I thought. Thank God I never joined, coming to *this* place every school holiday.

Leaving the school grounds behind them, they eventually arrived in a quiet avenue. Bullet switched off his torch. They all heard the whoosh of traffic passing nearby. The New Craddington Road was ahead. Beams from vehicle headlights swished across the trees. Small, thatched cottages with tiny, well-kept front gardens and waist-high wooden gates lined the avenue. The brickwork appeared ancient. Bullet wondered if old people lived in these tiny cottages, preparing to die. At the junction was a small grocery shop where many of Curvis's school friends bought biscuits, crisps and chocolate bars with their dinner money.

The New Craddington Road climbed steeply to their left, its journey ending in another county. To their right it dropped sharply downhill, winding its way to Ashburden. The pines reached their zenith here, almost shielding the moonlight. They grew closer together, daring anyone to enter. The trunks were darker, denied sunlight for seasons untold. There was no horizon. The stench of the pine cones filled their nostrils. Standing perfectly still, Curvis peered into the forest. 'They'll never find us in there.'

Glenroy gulped. 'It looks different at night, innit. More … creepy.'

Bullet switched on his torch again. Carlton zipped open his bag and took out a chocolate fairy cake. 'That's cos it's darker. Ain't nothing different about it. I can't believe you're scared of trees. It's just … wood and leaves.'

'You sure you know the way in there?' asked Bullet. 'You sure it's safe in there?'

'Bullet's asking the right questions for once,' Glenroy agreed. 'I mean … look. Once we get inside we might find all sorts of weirdoes and mad men who escaped from prison or nut houses.'

'Will you two stop shitting yourselves,' said Curvis. 'We'll be alright. This is the last place they'll look. And even if they did, Mr Williams would get lost. He doesn't know up here like I do.'

'Come on!' urged Carlton, not wanting anyone to question his courage.

They crossed the road quickly. They hesitated for a long second before climbing fifty yards into the undergrowth. Curvis switched on his powerful torch and found the path that snaked deeper into the perfect gloom. They all kept close together, almost walking on each other's heels. Owls heralded their entrance as if they knew in advance the boys' destination. Something flapped above their heads.

Carlton looked up and saw only a black roof hanging over him at an unguessable height. He sensed that the trees knew of his fear. He had felt it first back at the cul-de-sac where the rich people live; a strange feeling of helplessness in the presence of the forest's power. Don't be stupid, he tried to convince himself. They're just harmless trees. Why should I be scared of 'em? Fingertips of branches tickled his hands and cheeks as he trudged on.

They seemed to be forever climbing dusty escarpments where the soil crumbled under each step or descending steep hillocks. As they went further into the depths, the path petered out and they all felt their feet crunching through the scrub needle and pine cones. Their shoes and clothing soon changed colour, turning brown and green.

They reached the summit of another steep mound. Curvis could make out in the near distance a small glade, surrounded by impossibly tangled bramble and bending pine trees, whose upper reaches seemed to kiss the stars. 'We'll stop here for the night,' he said, hearing the sighs of relief. 'Bullet, take out the blankets, and Glenroy, I hope you've got those pillows in your laundry bags.'

'Yeah, course I have.'

Bullet proceeded to spread the blankets. Curvis stood the two torches at each end of the glade, beaming skywards, like the headlights of a jack-knifed lorry. Despite this they couldn't see much of the heavens. Instead they saw a green-leaf ceiling, gnarled boughs and deep-ridged bark that were aged beyond the boys' comprehension. The thick smell of parched earth engulfed them. In the eastern sky, rising over the Kent Hills, was the halo of a pale sun. Glenroy studied his new environment. 'I'm knackered,' he moaned. 'So many hills! I'm sure I saw a fox a while ago. While I'm up here I'm gonna catch one of them fuckers.'

'You couldn't catch one if it was a hundred and six-years-old and had two broken legs,' laughed Carlton. 'You're unfit. I keep on telling you to do some kinda sport.'

'I do wrestling,' argued Glenroy.

'Badly,' put in Bullet.

Sitting down on the blankets, Curvis made himself comfortable. 'Yeah, there are many hills around here. There are seven big ones called the Seven Sisters. They're made out of stones and pebbles.'

'No, you don't say,' chuckled Carlton. 'And I thought they were made out of lemon meringue and custard.'

Glenroy and Bullet giggled. Curvis wasn't amused. 'Carlton, take out your food,' he instructed. 'I've got some Jamaican ginger cake and a load of French rolls that I nicked. All that walking has made me hungry.'

'Why are they called the Seven Sisters?' Glenroy wanted to know. 'Seriously. I won't take the piss.'

'Nor will I,' promised Carlton.

Curvis handed out slices of cake as they sat together in a tight circle. Satisfied he wouldn't be mocked, Curvis began his story. 'When I was about seven or eight, my housemother used to take us up here for picnics in the summer,' he began. 'You know, to run about and stuff.'

'Uncle Rodney doesn't do picnics,' said Bullet. 'He might do if it involved marching with a kit bag strapped to your back, a grenade tucked into your belt and a rifle in your hand.'

They all laughed.

'One day,' Curvis resumed, 'me and Stanton were messing about, playing tag or something. Auntie Rebecca told us off and she ordered us to sit on a bench and keep our traps quiet. There was this old man sitting there; he looked old enough to fight at Waterloo never mind the First World War.'

'Where's Waterloo?' Glenroy asked. 'Do they make toilets there?'

Curvis ignored the question and continued. 'I asked this old man why the hills were called the Seven Sisters. He told us a story.' Curvis paused, checking to see who was listening.

Carlton handed out his fairy cakes. Glenroy snatched two. 'Tell the story then!' urged Carlton.

Curvis spoke in a near whisper. The beams of light shone into the sky. 'He told us that many years ago, you know, even before someone made electricity, a little girl used to live here beside the woods. This girl came from a big family; she had six older sisters. But the little girl was the youngest by ten years. I s'pose she wasn't planned, if you know what I mean.'

'What do you mean?' asked Glenroy.

Curvis ignored Glenroy again. 'Anyway, as the youngest got a bit older, her sisters left home one by one. This upset the youngest cos she loved playing in the woods with her sisters all the time, going on adventures and stuff. They used to spoil her a bit. When the second youngest sister left home, marrying someone at just seventeen, the little girl got lonely. She had no one to play with. And there was no television and stuff then. She didn't have any friends so she just kept her own company, playing in the woods, pretending that her sisters were there with her.'

'What happened next,' Bullet wanted to know.

'One afternoon,' continued Curvis, 'she went out to play in the woods, like she usually did before having her tea. But she never came home. Her parents got worried and everything, and when night came, they called the police. There was a massive search for her, with people of the village helping out. They searched the dykes, the bushes, the valleys. But no one ever saw her again. It was like she vanished into thin air. They thought she got kidnapped cos her family were kinda rich, but her family never got a ransom note. Cos of the stress, the mum went mad and ended up in some nut house. One of the sisters reckoned she knew what happened to her, but said no one would believe her.'

'Glenroy peered into the trees. Curvis went on. 'Because she used to play in the woods and up and down the stony hills, locals called the seven big ones the Seven Sisters. The girl's dad sold the house and moved far away. No one ever saw the family again.'

'Mouldy conkers!' Glenroy exclaimed. 'Curvis! You brought us to a place where there's a dead girl! Jesus creeps! We should take you to the nut house. I'm going home.'

'It's just an old man's story,' stressed Curvis. 'What he told to two brats. Me and Stanton. He told it just to keep us quiet. Stop shitting yourself.'

Carlton looked up at the trees. 'So how did you remember that after all this time?' he asked.

Curvis shrugged. 'I always remember stories that people tell me.'

'It seems real enough for me,' feared Bullet. 'Say we fall on the dead girl's body while we're messing around up here. And she's not gonna look like a normal little girl. Over the years her face woulda peeled off. What do they call it? Decomposting or something? And she'll be half skeleton with maggots crawling through her ribs and worms eating her toes.'

'Whassamatter with you lot?' laughed Curvis. 'It's just a story, for fuck's sake. This *is* the best place for us. Who's gonna find us here? This is just a bigger version of Pinewood Oaks.'

Carlton chewed a blade of grass after his meal. 'If I find the girl's body – or it could be bones by now – I'll just tell the police where she is and hope some relatives of the girl's family are around so I can get a reward. They were rich, weren't they?'

'Yeah,' Bullet said. 'I wonder how rich? Maybe they still own most of this land.'

'Stop going on about it!' said Curvis. 'The story isn't true. It was s'posed to have happened ages ago – like when posh women wore about four long skirts – when everyone poor had to work in the fields.'

'How do you know?' asked Carlton. 'The old man could've been the killer. He might have killed loads of kids. Maybe his ghost is still around, looking for young uns.'

Carlton's friends all glared at him in silent condemnation. 'Whassamatter with you lot?' he said, trying to laugh off his embarrassment. 'Can't you take a joke?'

'That wasn't a joke,' replied Bullet. 'You're trying to give us the shits.'

'How do you know the girl weren't murdered?' Carlton sniped, spitting out the blade of grass and picking up a leaf of bracken fern.

'Don't chew that,' warned Curvis. 'It's poisonous.'

Carlton threw the leaf away, annoyed that he couldn't find any lengthy blades of grass. 'Curvis, you could've taken us somewhere I can get chews.' He looked up at the trees. 'They're tall, aren't they? You don't really realise till you're up close.'

'The girl might've got carried away by ghosts and spirits,' suggested Glenroy. 'Or Jesus might've come down and taken her. Or a UFO might have landed and got her.'

'Fucking ghosts and spirits?' chuckled Carlton. 'Jesus? UF fucking Os? How many times do I have to tell you not to eat the funny mushrooms?'

'Or toadstools,' added Bullet. 'And tree bark, grass and anything else that grows under the sun. Slugs and shit, even.'

'No, I haven't eaten anything funny!' Glenroy raised his voice. 'You lot think I'm stupid cos I believe in UFOs, but I read a comic once, and all professors and eggheads were saying that they're possible. So stick that up your arse and eat it!'

'Keep your Afro on,' said Curvis.

Fifteen minutes later, they lay down on the blankets, the four of them sharing two pillows. The moonlight was fading but a hint of sunlight was creeping towards the tips of the pines, creating an amber glow covering half the sky. No one spoke. Each of them was immersed in his own waking dreams, wondering what fate had in store for them.

Glenroy peered through the gaps in the canopy. He dearly wished for a UFO to suddenly appear. He hoped to see little Martians parachuting into the forest with black bug eyes and seven fingers on each hand. His thoughts then drifted to the girl in Curvis's story. He looked around and noticed that Bullet's eyes were closed. He glanced upwards again, willing the extra terrestrials to arrive, to hover over the forest and shadow the sun. They won't say I'm stupid if that happens, Glenroy thought.

One hour later, when the birds had started to sing in the new day, Glenroy lay uneasily with his eyes open. He turned to look at Carlton, who seemed to be enjoying a deep sleep. He searched the wood around him and decided there was nothing to be scared of. 'Bullet,' he whispered. 'Bullet.'

Carlton stirred. 'Glenroy! Can't you sleep? Give it a rest, will ya. Let Bullet sleep.'

'I can't sleep either,' mumbled Bullet. 'We should've taken our beds with us.'

'And how would we carry the beds up here,' asked Glenroy.

'It was a joke,' chuckled Bullet.

Glenroy foraged in Bullet's bag and found his torch. He switched it on and shone it into Bullet's face. Curvis sat up. 'Turn that torch off! We've got to save our batteries when it's light. Just because you lot can't sleep doesn't mean I don't want to.'

Lying down once more, Glenroy refused to close his eyes.

Emancipation
Sunday, 13 June 1976, 7.45 a.m.

The sun threaded its rays through the tangled woodland, spreading its light to every crook and hollow, illuminating emerald greens, pale yellows and dusty browns. The birds had awoken early and welcomed the morning. The leaves whispered in the fragile breeze and the owls stilled their tongues. All seemed quiet as the world began to wake.

Unable to sleep one wink during the early hours, Glenroy rose to his feet, stretched his arms and performed an extravagant yawn. He couldn't remember feeling so relaxed. He looked at his three friends, who were still at rest on the dew-dampened blankets. Bullet stirred and looked around in blurry wonder, not believing he had spent the night under the one-eyed glare of the moon. He caught Glenroy's eyes, and for a moment the two friends smiled warmly at each other, both thinking how good it was to be free. The first day of their freedom had begun.

Carlton was staring at the bush, seemingly mesmerised by a ladybird plodding along a broad leaf. He was thinking of Josephine and her reaction to the night's events. He wouldn't have liked to have seen her face when she entered his dorm offering a mug of coffee. She might've rung his mum about his disappearance, he thought.

Curvis was still fast asleep.

'What's the time?' Bullet asked.

Carlton reached for his bag and unzipped it to find his watch. 'Nearly eight o'clock.'

Carlton studied his surroundings. 'It's like a different place from the one we came to last night,' he remarked. 'Sort of … more welcoming.'

'Look!' Glenroy exclaimed. He pointed north. 'There's a windmill down there.'

Bullet stood up and joined Glenroy.

'Does it work?' Glenroy wondered. 'Do the blades go round? We should check it out tonight.'

'Nah, I don't think so,' Bullet replied. 'Probably hasn't worked for years.'

'We should've slept there,' said Glenroy. 'Least we'd have a roof over our heads.'

Carlton shook his head. 'Too risky.'

Glenroy eyed Carlton's bag. 'Any more biscuits? What're we gonna have for breakfast?'

Carlton offered his bag. Glenroy helped himself to a handful of digestives, giving some to Bullet. Carlton peered once more into the bush. 'Auntie Josephine's gonna kill me. Those biscuits were for the kids.'

'She's gonna kill ya anyway,' laughed Bullet. 'You've run away. Can you believe it? We're really *here*.'

Carlton shook his head. 'I can't believe it.'

Curvis stirred.

'She'll be worried sick,' added Carlton.

'Uncle Thomas will be going nuts,' grinned Glenroy. 'I can just imagine him shouting all over the place. *Where's that fat charcoal bandit! Where the fuck is he?* He's probably gone to Elvin's house to ask him if he knows where we are. Ha ha! Can you imagine the look on his face? His beard will probably fall off!'

'Uncle Rodney's probably going mental an' all,' chuckled Bullet. 'He'll say that you lot forced me into it. I bet he didn't listen to the radio and do his exercises this morning.'

Curvis squinted as he roused himself from sleep. He sat up and looked at Glenroy. 'So you still here then?'

'Yeah, thought I'd go back, eh?'

Curvis stood up and shook the blanket he had slept on. 'We'll go up to the café and get breakfast – it's not too far from here. But first, we've got to find a good place to hide our stuff. Oh, by the way, don't go near the windmill – scouts are always nosing around it.'

'What?' Glenroy exclaimed. 'There's a café up here. In the woods! This is gonna be better that I thought. What do they serve? Fried egg on toast? I could kill a knickerbocker glory.'

'Glenroy, it's a café in the woods, not a Wimpy,' laughed Curvis. 'Be careful when we get there.'

'The café's near to the road that goes through the hills, isn't it?' asked Carlton.

'That's right,' said Curvis. 'Old people drink tea and eat scones there before they go on a ramble.'

'What's a ramble?' asked Glenroy.

'Old-people talk for a long walk,' replied Bullet.

'But you never know who might be up there,' warned Curvis. 'We'll just go there, eat sharpish and disappear.'

'Not a problem for Glenroy to eat sharpish,' laughed Carlton.

Bullet folded the blankets. He wondered where to put them. Glenroy picked up the two pillows and placed them in the black bin bag and waited for directions.

'Put them down at the bottom of the hill and then put ferns over 'em,' instructed Curvis. 'No one goes down there – too many bushes. Oh, one more thing. Don't sleep with your heads too close to the trees and bushes. If you do you might wake up with earwigs crawling through your brains.'

'Seems like they've got to Bullet already,' Carlton quipped.

'Why didn't you tell us last night?' asked Glenroy, checking his Afro.

Bullet treaded carefully down the slippery slope, wondering how they had all managed to climb it in the dark. He crunched pine cones on the way as Glenroy followed him. Carlton and Curvis kicked away cake and biscuit wrappers towards the bushes. 'So what are we gonna do today?' asked Carlton.

'To tell the truth,' replied Curvis. 'I don't really know. Maybe later on, we'll check out what the scouts are doing – they have some sort of adventure playground in their area – it should be a laugh. But we should keep our heads down during the day. Keep away from the road.'

'Haven't the scouts built those tree houses?' asked Glenroy. 'Bullet! You've finally got your wish! You can pretend to be Tarzan for the night.'

'Will you *stop* bringing that up! I haven't read a Tarzan comic for years.'

Glenroy and Bullet had concealed the bags and climbed the steep mound once again. 'Where're we gonna get our wash?' asked Glenroy.

'Just round the corner,' laughed Carlton. 'There's a mud sink by the next tree and it's got mud soap in it. Don't be long cos I want my turn.'

'Ha, ha, very funny,' replied Glenroy.

'Tomorrow we'll go to the Spurleigh Way open-air swimming pool,' announced Curvis. 'It's about three miles away.' Curvis pointed in a north-west direction. 'You can swim and bathe all you like there.'

Carlton delved into his bag again and took out the petty cash tin. He spilled all the money onto the ground. 'Bloody thing weighs my bag down.'

Curvis shook his head. 'Make sure you hide the box before we go. Remember, it's evidence.'

Ten minutes later, satisfied that the camp was well hidden, Curvis started out, leading his friends down into a hollow with fiery nettles on each side. They were relieved to escape the fierce sun for a while. The thicket here seemed untrodden by foot, but Curvis appeared to have a compass in his brain. Glenroy was close behind him, already sweating.

'That girl?' Glenroy asked. 'What's her name?'

'What girl?' replied Curvis.

'That girl in your story. What's her name?'

'Oh, her. The old man said it was Gemmele.'

'Weird name – wasn't it Gemma?'

'No, definitely Gemmele,' confirmed Curvis.

After twenty minutes of climbing, slipping and sliding down

hollows and stony barrows, they came to a dusty path twisting its way through the woods. Only the roots of the pines hampered its progress. Arrows of light penetrated the canopy, creating a golden kaleidoscope. Glenroy, Carlton and Bullet watched Curvis, wondering if he would veer right or left. Without hesitation, he turned left.

Now in the open, they were at the mercy of the June sun, forcing them to leave the path to seek shelter under the trees. Seven hundred paces later, the trail forked off into three directions, as if to purposefully confuse Sunday ramblers. But Curvis, confident, led the way, picking up the pace. As they went on, the wispy pale grass broadened before them and the pines became further apart. They spotted a middle-aged man, sporting a flat cap and smoking a pipe that looked like a miniature saxophone. His Labrador dog bounded around him keenly. Bullet felt a tension in his throat. 'What do we do? Leg it?'

'No,' answered Carlton. 'Just walk normally.'

They passed the man, checking behind them to see if he had turned around. Ten minutes later, Curvis had led them to a gravel car park that fronted a café, built on a plateau. 'Great spectations!' gasped Glenroy. 'You can see for miles.'

Four cars were parked in front of the café. Young children were sitting down outside licking lollies and ice-cream cones. The building seemed old, its windows bearing the dust and grime of countless summers. At the prospect of ice cream, Glenroy hared into the diner, leaving his friends standing. They treated themselves to scones, crisps and ice-cream cones, sitting at a table near the front door. They were laughing and joking, forgetting the seriousness of their deed. Freedom tasted good.

After downing cans of fizzy drink, Curvis led his friends a short distance to a viewpoint. Forged in a platform of concrete in the floor was a bronze-coloured compass the size of a beer barrel's base. A waist-high brick wall, set in a semi-circle, prevented viewers from falling into a steep ravine. The view was magnificent. Under the crystalline blue sky, they could see far-off isolated hamlets. Fields looked like a sliced green-iced cake and distant forests like servings of broccoli. Streams and small rivers glistened and there were sheep in the hills. Curvis studied the compass in the floor. He pointed west. 'Me and Stanton would come up here when the Biggin Hill air show was on. We got a really good view of the Red Arrows and saw all the coloured smoke.'

'Coloured smoke?' Glenroy asked. 'They weren't on fire, were they?'

'No, you divo,' Carlton corrected. 'The smoke's for show – to make it look good.' He looked up at the vast expanse of blue sky. He felt a strange sense of freedom and realised that now he could do anything he liked. 'It kinda makes you giddy looking out from up here,' he commented.

'Yeah,' Bullet answered. 'Back at Pinewood Oaks, I was always jealous of the birds, flying anywhere they like. Now, *we* can go anywhere we like.'

Curvis allowed his friends to enjoy the scenery for another ten minutes before heading south-west. They raced each other down a steep dell. They ended up plunging head over heels into the bottom of the valley, laughing, joking and teasing each other.

As soon as they had regrouped, Glenroy and Bullet started a game of tag, bolting around bending trees and hurdling over fallen branches. Carlton and Curvis joined the fun. Passers-by smiled at their antics. The friends were oblivious as they karate-chopped, wrestled and leaped on each other without a care in the world.

Auntie Josephine gazed at the clock in her kitchen. Half past nine. Pulling tensely on her cigarette, her face contorted with worry. The children in her charge had already left to go to church and Sunday school. She had two members of staff who came in to work at nine o'clock. Both women were shocked to learn that Carlton had run away.

There was worse news. Josephine had been on the phone continuously since seven thirty a.m. She had spoken to irate housemothers, housefathers and the duty social worker from the council. Still watching the clock, Josephine heard her front door being impatiently tapped. She sucked hard on her cigarette before opening. She was confronted with the bald-headed figure of Thomas. Josephine could smell his body odour. He picked nervously at his ginger beard and didn't meet Josephine's eyes. He looked over her shoulder into the house. 'Any news?' he asked. 'I can't believe it.'

'No,' Josephine replied, barely audible. 'Mr Williams searched around the grounds this morning but there's no sign of them … Come in, I'll put the kettle on.'

'Thank you, Josephine. I think I need it. I've been worried sick.'

Thomas entered the house. He followed Josephine into the kitchen. He seated himself down at the table next to the fridge. 'Is Brian's housefather on his way?'

'Yes. Rodney called me about an hour ago. He said he'll try and contact Brian's social worker, although it's a Sunday, and then he'll come down for the meeting. The duty social worker from the council might be coming down, but you know what they're like on Sundays.'

Thomas's temples were smeared with perspiration. He took out a tobacco tin from his shirt pocket and started to build a cigarette. 'Why on earth would they run away?' he asked. He looked up and held Josephine's gaze. 'I haven't done anything to Glenroy for him to do anything this drastic.'

Josephine inspected her fingernails. 'Carlton left a message,' she admitted. 'He wrote that the reason he ran away wasn't *my* fault.'

'Yes. But he might be just saying that. I mean … There's no way that Glenroy would have run away on his own steam. I *won't* believe that. You see, he's a follower, too easily influenced. He's quite a simple lad really.'

Josephine took in a deep breath. She placed her hands on her hips. Her eyes betrayed her disagreement. 'So you're saying that Carlton led him to it?'

'No, no. Just that Glenroy wouldn't have thought of it on his own.' He licked the length of his roll-up and glued the paper down. Josephine watched him as he placed the cigarette between his lips and lit it. Another knock on the door cut into the rising tension. 'I'll answer it,' offered Thomas, glad to be free of Josephine's glare.

Thomas opened the door. His cheeks flushed and his lips stern, Rodney blustered into the hallway. Dressed in shirt and throat-gripping tie, his neck was as reddened as his face. Beside Rodney was a tall middle-aged woman. She held her head high and the lens of her glasses half-covered her oval-shaped face. Her hair was scrunched up into a tight bun with countless clips. She glared at Thomas.

'Heard anything, Thomas?' Rodney asked.

Thomas beckoned the couple inside. 'Afraid not. I'm sure they'll come back today.'

Thomas switched his gaze to the woman and dipped his head ever so slightly. 'Morning, Miss Gallagher – Josephine's just making a pot of tea.'

Miss Gallagher acknowledged Thomas with a nod. She entered the house with the disdain of an owner of a stately home setting foot into the gardener's hut. 'There was supposed to be a case meeting tomorrow morning for Curvis,' she mentioned. 'He has known about it since last week and he's been intolerable lately. Of all things, he wanted to attend. The cheek of that boy! How will my staff talk freely if he attends? He refuses to talk with his social worker and I just don't know what to do with him. Now *this*.'

Josephine led her peers into her study. Thomas and Miss Gallagher dropped themselves into a sofa. Josephine sat down at her desk. She glanced at Rodney who chose to stand with his hands clasped behind his back. 'Carlton's social worker will be down here in an hour,' Josephine said. 'It's a good thing he gave me his home number. He said I'll have to make a report for his supervisor.'

'I've spoken to the supervisor this morning,' Rodney said. 'Mr Holmes swore down the phone to me that this must *not* get out – especially to the press.'

'These kids just don't realise the trouble they have caused,' Rodney continued. 'All this paperwork we're going to have to do, and with the social services looking over our shoulders. In *twenty* years of childcare, not one of the children in my charge has ever done this. *Brazen* they are! *Brazen!* The others must've egged on Brian. He's a sensible boy. He knows what's right and wrong. But he picks the wrong friends – friends that are not as bright as he is.'

'Now hold on a minute!' argued Josephine. 'He's got a mind of his own and I say all four are equally to blame.'

'There's no sense in rowing about who is to blame for all this,' cut in Thomas. 'The fact is we have four runaways on our hands, and the council are going to want to know why they did it.'

'It seems kids today think they can get away with anything,' said Miss Gallagher, not enjoying her tea. 'I'm sick and tired of all the memos I receive from the council telling me how to raise the children in my care. They don't know what it's like to look after ten screaming kids. I'd like to see them bloody well try! I've been going on for ages that I need more staff. Do they listen? No, they bloody well don't!'

'I'm with you there,' said Rodney. 'If we could discipline the children the way we want to, you wouldn't get kids running away. A bit of a whack never did a child any harm; Brian will have a lot to answer for when he returns. You help these kids all you can and they throw it back in your face.'

Deciding not to comment, Josephine sipped her tea. Thomas took a chocolate biscuit. 'So any of you have any idea where they might've gone?' he asked.

'They probably took the first train to London,' offered Miss Gallagher, pushing away her cup of tea. 'I blame these television programmes and films myself. I won't let the under elevens watch *Oliver!* What were they thinking? They'll be walking the streets of London begging for meals and pretending to be the Artful Dodger before your back is turned. And the Artful Dodger *was* a thief.'

'They'll come scurrying home when they're hungry,' said Rodney. 'They always do.'

'Carlton stole the petty cash,' admitted Josephine. She lit her cigarette and pulled on it hard. She closed her eyes for a long second before speaking again. 'There was about twenty pounds in the box.'

'That doesn't surprise me,' sniped Miss Gallagher, refusing the offer of biscuits from Thomas. 'He appears the type.'

Josephine couldn't hide her rising anger but said nothing. Rodney nodded. 'When they come back,' he announced, 'they deserve a harsh lesson. A spell of juvenile detention will do them no harm. They'll realise how lucky they are to be living in Pinewood Oaks. Poor children in the slums of London don't have the facilities and grounds we have here. They have more food than was available during rationing. Those kids didn't scarper off when they felt like it.'

'Too right,' agreed Miss Gallagher. 'Kids here are so lucky.'

Josephine bit her top lip.

'Brian should know better than most why he's so lucky,' Rodney continued. 'If it wasn't for social services, who knows what would've happened to him after his mother left him on the doorstep at Area 3 offices – I told him all the details, how he was left with only a bottle of milk. And we have to pick up the pieces.'

Thomas stood up. 'I think I left my tobacco in the kitchen – I won't be a minute.'

Thomas departed, closing the door behind him. Miss Gallagher looked at Rodney. 'That Glenroy's always acting the buffoon.'

'That's not fair, Ruth,' countered Josephine. 'They've all been stupid.'

Rodney took an interest in the book selection on the shelf. 'The police told me that if the boys have been missing for more than twenty-four hours, we'd have to provide recent photographs of them,' he said. 'The sergeant promised he'll send two officers down from New Craddington by the afternoon. I didn't want the police to get involved but Mr Holmes made it clear we have no choice. And you know what that means! They're always suspicious of us.'

Thomas returned with a rolled-up cigarette between his fingers. Josephine tried to digest Rodney's news about the police. Miss Gallagher inspected the decor. 'Did Mr Williams question Elvin?' she asked.

'Yes, but he says he knows nothing,' replied Josephine.

'He's not going to grass on his friends, is he?' suspected Rodney. 'Of course he knows something! If the police come down I hope they get it out of him. Give me a few minutes with him and I'll get it out of him!'

'No, I don't think so,' said Thomas. The sweat returned to his temples and forehead. 'I've heard the kids call him big mouth and other things so I don't think the boys would've told him of their plans. Besides, Elvin's a good lad and if he did know of something, he would've told me. Since I taught him to swim he looks on me like a father.'

'I don't care how he looks on you,' interrupted Rodney. 'Someone should question him properly. He must know where they're hiding out or he has an idea.'

'I just want them home,' said Josephine. 'Who knows what they're getting up to? If they did take the first train to London, they'll be in all sorts of danger.'

'I don't know about the danger,' said Miss Gallagher. 'Definitely embarrassing. Can you imagine it? Kids in our care walking the streets of London begging and stealing.'

1.30 p.m.

The sun had reached its pinnacle and there was no escaping its heat. Carlton, Curvis, Bullet and Glenroy, the forest in their wake, had made their way to the summit of Cravell Hill, overlooking the New Craddington golf course and the hamlet itself surrounded by trees and endless heath, six miles south of Pinewood Oaks. Twice the size of Pinewood, New Craddington boasted a police station, a fire station, a library, a gardener's shop, an undertaker's and the New Craddington Arms that offered a backroom snooker table as well as beers and fine ales. Carlton remembered the place well, once playing cricket for his school there on the neatest pitch he had ever seen. A few boys from Pinewood Oaks, who had saved their pocket money, took a green bus to the summer fair at New Craddington heath. They returned with half-coconuts, handfuls of candy floss and gold-fish swimming in circles in polythene plastic bags.

'Didn't realise we're so high up,' said Glenroy. 'Those stacks of hay look like lumps of brown sugar.'

They sat down in the shelter of the forest, forty yards away from the corkscrewing Cravell Hill road, weary from their exertions in the morning. They peered into the valley.

'If it snows, a lot of those people who live down there get cut off,' said Curvis.

'Why? Is that the only way in?' asked Carlton, pointing to the hill. 'Never been to the other side.'

'It's alright going downhill but trying to go up is almost impos-sible,' explained Curvis. 'Stanton used to nick stuff from abandoned cars down there. He once got a toolbox. Where d'you think I got my spanners from?'

'You two come all this way in the snow?' asked Bullet.

'Yep, in our wellington boots.'

Bullet noticed something coming up the hill. 'The Old Bill!' he shouted, pointing a frightened finger.

They quickly retreated into the forest, Glenroy the last to make it. From under cover they watched the patrol car skirting the bend.

'You think they saw us?' panted Bullet.

'Nah, they would've stopped if they did,' replied Carlton. 'They probably don't even know we done a runner yet.'

'Who knows?' said Curvis. 'I bet Uncle Rodney has called them already. He's probably called the SAS an' the Gestapo an' all. Let's get back to base.'

Pacing ahead with stick in hand, Bullet sang.

'Four of us mighty are we
Three'll be like cutting off our knees

Two'll be like the sinking of a crew.'

His friends joined him in song for the last line.

'And one'll be like killing us with a gun!'

10.30 p.m.

Bullet shone his torch forward as he and his friends stealthily made their way through the scouting complex in the woods. The sun had quit half an hour ago and the owls stirred. In single file, they threaded through the trees and bushes. A still blackness surrounded them. From the tree trunks, they could hear the mating songs of the cicadas, a repetitive, rasping sound. Glenroy spoke in a whisper. 'Where do these bum chums camp out? We've been walking for ages.'

'We're in the scouting grounds already,' replied Curvis. 'Sometimes they sleep in huts and sometimes they bed down in tents. Look out for any camp fires; they love to have one of their wanky sing-songs before they fuck off to bed.'

'I bet they don't sing any sweary rugby songs,' said Bullet.

'They probably go through *The Sound Of Music* songbook,' laughed Carlton.

'*The forest is alive with the sound of scout shit,'* Glenroy sang.

'Shut up and put a gobstopper in it!' Curvis scolded.

They approached a still lake, its oval length the size of an ice rink. With the eye of a single torch, they could just make out the shapes of one-man canoes, bobbing gently on the water, attached to ropes that were tied to small, wooden moorings speared into the firm ground. On the other side of the lake was a tiny estate of pre-fabricated huts, no higher than seven feet tall. The buildings were moon-shadowed by giant pines. They noticed an array of dim, yellow lights, shining like giant fireflies from the wooden structures. 'Let's cut the ropes,' Carlton prompted. 'Bullet, got your penknife?'

'Yeah, it's in my pocket.'

Crawling on his hands and knees, Carlton reached the nearest boat. Bullet passed on his penknife. Curvis remained under the cover of trees acting as lookout. Glenroy looked dreamily at the water.

Carlton began to saw the rope. Thirty seconds later, Carlton and Bullet cackled as they watched the boat float away towards the middle of the lake. Glenroy crept to another boat and Carlton threw the penknife to him. He wasted no time in sending out the boat to join its sister in the murky waters. Curvis peered nervously from his position as his three friends giggled at their own mischief.

Carlton freed another boat, but got his feet wet as he slipped on the soft mud that ringed the lake. 'Shit!'

'Let's go for a skinny dip,' suggested Glenroy.

Before anyone had a chance to answer, Glenroy had already taken off his T-shirt and pulled off his trainers.

'You perv!' mocked Bullet. 'I'm not taking off my clothes for you!'

'You're just saying that cos you haven't grown any pubes yet,' returned Glenroy. He pointed to his genitals. 'You're as bald around your bollocks as Kojak is on his head.'

'Fuck you!'

'And fuck you too!'

Carlton watched Glenroy take off his socks and pull off his jeans. 'I'm not one for taking up Glenroy's mad ideas,' he said. 'But this is a good one. I've been sweating hoses all day.'

'I'm not taking off my pants so that perv can have a look,' protested Bullet.

'Sometimes I wonder if Bullet's got a real willy,' laughed Glenroy. 'Maybe he's got a worm or a slug or something.'

They collapsed into giggles.

Curvis walked down to the edge of the lake, breaking his concentration on the huts. 'I'm going for a swim!'

Soon they were all neck high in the water, enjoying the cool sensation on their bodies. The lake bed was soft and muddy and it was a relief for their feet to be free of trainers and socks. They could smell the reeds that were clustered together around the rim of the lake and they had an excellent view of the three-quarter moon, dark spots and craters spotting its yellow-white surface. From lake level, the pines looked magnificent in their size and stature, as if they were giant landlords watching over their property. For half an hour the boys swam, played water tag and marvelled at their environment, blissfully washing away the day.

Regretting that they hadn't brought any towels with them, they donned their clothes over wet bodies. Curvis was the last one to pull on his trainers. Suddenly, a figure emerged from the bushes behind him.

'Oi! What the fuck are you lot doing here?' bellowed an adult voice.

Curvis turned around in panic, one shoe not yet tied. He was stilled into shock, his mouth wide open.

The man, late teens or early twenties, wearing a venture scout outfit, lunged at him. 'Come here, you little runt!' The man grabbed Curvis and held him by the neck, pulling him to the ground. 'Lawrence, Frank! I've found trespassers! Come quick.'

Glenroy, Bullet and Carlton scampered to Curvis's aid, clenching their fists. They launched themselves at the man, throwing punches and wild kicks. Running steps resonated in the distance. Birds flew out of trees. Something four-legged ran into a hole in the ground. Carlton put together a rapid combination of punches. Bullet held the man down. Glenroy was kicking the man's legs. Curvis fought for his breath. The footsteps were getting closer. 'Lawrence, Frank! I'm over here!'

'Where?'

Bullet pulled Curvis away. Glenroy offered one more kick before wondering which way to go. Carlton kept on punching. 'Shut up!' he yelled.

'There's more of 'em,' panicked Bullet. 'Curvis, which way?'

Curvis didn't reply; he was still in shock. Bullet slapped his face. 'Which fucking *way?*'

Curvis pointed an unsteady finger. 'Glenroy, stay close,' Bullet told Glenroy. 'Carlton, *come on!*'

'Don't put your hands on any of my mates again!' screamed Carlton. The sound of crunching pine cones came closer.

'Carlton, leave him!' implored Bullet. 'Leave him!'

Carlton finally left his bruised and battered victim and joined his friends. Regaining his composure, Curvis switched on his internal compass and led the way, scampering around bushes, under branches and up and down slippery hollows. They heard voices behind them.

'Matthew's hurt! He's hurt bad. Get the first aider!'

'Look at the state of him!'

'*Don't move him.* He's concussed.'

'Lawrence, go back and call the police. I won't sleep easily till the bastards that did this are caught. Look at the state of his face!'

The four runaways weaved their way through the forest. They frantically climbed a fence. 'Bullet, shine your torch,' ordered Carlton. 'I nearly ruptured myself on that bloody fence.'

'What if the venture scouts see it?'

'Just shine your fucking torch!' raged Carlton, aggressive adrenaline still running through his veins.

'Calm down,' said Curvis. 'They're not following us.'

'Yeah, but you have to be safe,' replied Bullet.

'You alright, Curvis?' asked Glenroy. 'That guy looked like he wanted to choke you to death.'

'Yeah, I'm alright,' replied Curvis. 'Neck's a bit sore though.'

'Fucking scout wanker,' cursed Carlton. 'We should've choked him. See how he'd like it.'

'I thought you weren't gonna stop punching him,' remarked Bullet.

'I didn't want to,' said Carlton. He took a couple of breaths. 'I'll do *anything* to protect you lot.'

They made their way to the other side of the forest, an hour's trek. In the distance they could hear police sirens. 'The whole of the Surrey plod are gonna be looking for us now,' warned Curvis. He grinned. 'But they still won't find us.'

His friends didn't share his confidence.

When they reached their base camp, Bullet laid out the blankets. Aided by the light of their torches, they started a card game. They feasted on crisps and chocolate bars. Glenroy peered into the blackness. 'This place is weird,' he commented. 'It's like at night we're somewhere else – not in the same place as during the day.'

'Of course it's the same place,' replied Bullet.

'Glenroy's right for once,' said Carlton. He studied the cards in his hand. 'It's like ... the place is alive.' He looked up at the trees. 'It's like the whole place is alive during the day and it's ... nice. But at night ... it's not so nice. What d'you reckon, Curvis?'

Curvis took his time to answer. 'It's alive,' he finally replied. 'Everything around us is alive. The trees, bushes, everything. I've been up here loads of times, and at night, the whole thing kinda changes.'

'That girl,' Glenroy said. 'In your story. If she's still alive she'll be an old woman by now, innit. She might be a witch! Who knows? She might be still walking around in the woods today, or even tonight?'

'Will you stop going on about her,' snapped Curvis. 'She's *dead*. Dead as that spider you stomped on this morning.'

'If nobody found her body,' added Carlton, 'Glenroy might be right.'

Bullet shook his head. 'You two are letting your imaginations leg it away from you. If the story's true, she would've been walking around here for about a hundred years. What's she gonna live on? Pine cones and nettles?'

'She might nick some chickens and stuff from the farms around here,' suggested Carlton. 'When you think about it, it wouldn't matter how long ago it was if she was a witch. She might still be alive. Witches live long, don't they? You don't get hunchbacks, fat warts and bent noses when you're twenty-one.'

'Who knows?' Glenroy nodded. 'She might've made her camp where no one could ever find it. Remember when we were kids. No one ever found our hideout.'

'Yeah, but you always told someone where it was,' scolded Curvis.

'Wherever she is, she might come out at night looking for something to eat,' Glenroy continued. 'If we stay up, we might see her.'

'You're a nutter,' dismissed Bullet, shaking his head.

'Even if she did,' laughed Curvis, 'are you gonna be scared of a woman who's over a hundred years old? Gorillas on a twig! You lot crack me up!'

Carlton glanced warily at the trees.

Half an hour later, they took to their sleeping positions. Even Glenroy was confident enough to close his eyes. He thought of the little girl in Curvis's story, wondering what she looked like and what games she played in the woods. He wished he could have met her. Maybe they could've been great friends. Maybe they could've run about in the woods playing tim-tam-tommy.

Bold Like Nimrod

Curvis had woken early and set off with purpose deep into the woods. Glenroy watched him disappear. Curvis went on, glancing upwards to see if he could catch sight of the singing larks. He spotted a nest with tiny, eager beaks protruding from it, awaiting their first meal of the day. Curvis thought of Glenroy and smiled.

Two minutes later, he came to a particularly tall pine, its needles growing in clumps of four and five, almost concealing the trunk and branches. He stooped, lifted a branch and sat down facing the trunk. Inscribed in the bark were two letters that Curvis had penknifed out six years ago; C for Curvis and S for Stanton. Below it was the figure 4 and underneath that the word *Ever*. He looked up to the heavens and then closed his eyes. In his inner vision, he saw painful bloodshot-brown eyes set in a heart-shaped face with a long, aquiline nose. Chaotic, auburn hair framed the picture.

'Morning, Mum,' Curvis whispered. 'I dunno if you agree with what I've done. I just had to get away. Nearer to you. Maybe I should've come on my own.' He gently placed his hand on the tree, caressing it, feeling its rough texture. 'But they'd never let me go on my own and they would've never forgiven me if I didn't tell 'em I was doing a runner.'

He paused for a few seconds as his mind brought up an image of his brother Stanton. 'I know you want me to find Stanton and see how he is. And I will. Those cunts won't keep me from him. I'm not gonna lie. I feel scared without him. That's why I've come here, Mum. Be near to you. As long as I'm up here I know you're looking over me. If the others go, I might stay. I can look after myself. I can't live in that place any more. Not without Stanton. It'll do my head in.'

Curvis took his hand off the tree and wiped away the tears falling over his lips. 'I'll talk to ya tomorrow, Mum. Gotta go, the others will be wondering where I am. Somehow I've gotta teach 'em to respect this place – *your* place.'

Five minutes later, Curvis returned to the camp to find Glenroy moaning about food. Bullet was folding the blankets while Carlton searched for something. No one wanted to admit it, but they all felt more at ease now the sun had risen.

'Anybody seen my watch?' Carlton asked.

'I've got it,' answered Curvis, delving into his back pocket. 'It was under your pillow and I took it up cos you looked like you was gonna roll over it. Did you have a bad dream?'

'Yeah, I did, as it goes,' Carlton admitted. 'Toss it over.'

Curvis lobbed the watch over to Carlton, who caught it and strapped it to his wrist. 'Bullet, d'you have to snore all night? It's like sleeping next to a combine harvester.'

'Who put earwigs up your nostril?' returned Bullet.

'*Your* snoring did!' laughed Carlton.

'What's that song about a combine harvester that's number one?' Curvis wanted to know.

'It's them trampish bumpkin people who talk weird,' said Glenroy. 'They're called the Weezils or something. When they talk, they go oooaarh, oooaarh.'

'They don't sound like that,' laughed Bullet. He stood up and burst into song. '*Well oive got a brand new combine harvester, you've got an old donkey. C'mon now let's get together in perfect harmony.*' Everyone collapsed in giggles.

'We going back to the scouts' place tonight?' asked Glenroy.

'Oh yeah, and have every bob-a-job and scout in the country sniffing our tracks?' said Bullet. 'They'll take to the skies and drop smoke bombs to make us come out from hiding. You're a nutter to even think of going back.'

Carlton and Curvis chuckled. Glenroy wasn't deterred. 'It was a laugh, though,' he said. 'You gave that scout a few George Foremans and a couple of Muhammad Alis. Reminded me of the time you beat up that greaser last year. Remember that? You tore the ring from his ear.'

Carlton didn't want to be reminded of that incident. 'Auntie Josephine's probably getting the kids ready for school and nursery,' he said. 'She'll be making their toast and cereal. Phillip is probably having a fight with Donna.'

'I don't give a flying cornflake what's going on in my house,' said Curvis.

Bullet decided not to comment and Glenroy didn't want to think about what Uncle Thomas was saying about him.

Curvis looked at Carlton. 'Kids in your house are lucky,' he said. 'In my house the teenagers have to make the little ones their breakfast. My housemother says it teaches us responsibility. I said to her face she's a lazy witch. When I was talking to her, I'd call her Ruth. She *hated* that so I did it even more. The bitch complained to my social worker.'

'You're right,' nodded Glenroy. 'Carlton's a lucky git to be in Auntie Josephine's house. Even Uncle Thomas treats him good.'

Carlton visibly winced at the mention of the name. 'When we were little,' Glenroy continued, 'after swimming, he used to buy sweets and give 'em to Carlton.'

'That's cos I used to behave myself,' said Carlton. 'I didn't run up and down by the pool like you used to. It doesn't mean I *liked* him.'

'He used to buy Elvin sweets an' all,' added Bullet. 'He's never even bought me a black-eyed joe or even a gobstopper! I can't even remember him ever saying hello to me.'

'Consider yourself a lucky mutt,' said Glenroy.

'Anyone knows when the cricket starts?' asked Carlton, wanting to change the subject.

He was ignored.

'You're luckier than most,' said Glenroy to Bullet.

'I dunno about that,' countered Bullet. 'Uncle Rodney doesn't believe in a lot of things. Like kids being allowed sweets. He says its bad for the teeth and gums. He searches under your pillow in case you're hiding 'em.'

'Whatever made him wanna be a housefather?' wondered Carlton. 'He's more suited to being a screw in a prison.'

'So he can still be in charge,' replied Bullet. 'That's what he's all about. As long as he can order people and kids about and tell 'em what to do, he's happy and smiling.'

'Uncle Rodney doesn't believe in kids smiling,' chuckled Curvis. 'If he had his own way he'd have us marching up and down in Pinewood Oaks in army uniform singing "Rule Brittania".'

'He probably bursts into tears when he watches *The Dambusters*,' cackled Glenroy. 'He probably fucks an Action Man instead of his wife – that's why he hasn't got any kids.'

Everyone collapsed into giggles.

Still laughing, Glenroy approached Bullet, wanting his turn with the penknife to etch his name in the tree. Bullet gave him the blade. 'He's not that bad,' Bullet said. 'It's just that sometimes he think he's still in the air force. When I first came to Pinewood Oaks, he'd line us up and inspect our fingernails and check behind our ears. If anything was dirty, he'd send us to have a bath, giving us a mangy scrubbing brush on the way. He doesn't do that now.'

'I think he heard too many bombs in the war,' laughed Curvis. 'Maybe some nerve gas is still inside his brain and he thinks that all kids are Germans.'

'Nerve gas wasn't used in the Second World War,' corrected Bullet. 'Besides, how could he hear bombs when he's dropping 'em from a plane?'

'Sorry, Mr Encyclopaedia,' mocked Curvis.

Curvis dug into his holdall and pulled out a crumpled white T-shirt. He took off the top he was wearing and donned the fresh one. 'I hope you lot got your swimming stuff,' he said. 'I did tell ya all before we left.'

'Yeah,' answered Bullet. 'Got mine.'

Curvis and Bullet stared at Glenroy. 'On the night we done a runner,' Glenroy stuttered, staring into the ground, 'I was all nervous and all that … I forgot my trunks.'

'I knew you'd forget something!' snapped Curvis. 'To be honest I'm surprised you remembered the pillows.'

'Anybody got a spare pair of shorts?' Bullet asked.

'I have,' answered Carlton. 'He can use my football shorts. Try not to stretch 'em out.'

Glenroy stood up, pushed the penknife into his back pocket and walked away from the others.

'Stop sulking, you baby!' Bullet called after Glenroy. 'Carlton's got a spare pair of shorts.'

Curvis turned to Carlton and Bullet. 'Take it easy on him. I don't want him on one of his mega strops while we're up here. You know what he's like.'

'Yeah, but sometimes he does stupid things,' Carlton said. 'Last night he started to wander about, telling me he heard voices. He reckoned that the scouts followed us up here. Then he was going on about that girl in your story, telling me that at night she becomes a witch. I wish you never told the tale. It's given him the creeps.'

'He's more shit scared of the dark than I realised,' admitted Curvis. 'Maybe we should move to clearer ground.'

'Then we'll get caught,' said Bullet. 'Someone's bound to see us.'

'Not if we find a good spot,' replied Curvis.

'There isn't any good spot!' Carlton raised his voice. 'If we're in the open we'll be in danger. No! We'll stay here. It's only Glenroy who's scared of the dark. We can't change our plans just cos of him.'

Curvis held his hands up. 'If you say so.'

Ten minutes later, Carlton and Curvis grinned as they watched Glenroy and Bullet begin round 972 of their eternal wrestling bout. 'That story about the girl,' Carlton wondered. 'Is it true?'

'It's true alright,' said Curvis. 'I was up here one day and asked a woman why the stony hills are called the Seven Sisters. She told me the exact same story as the old man. She said it happened a *long* time ago.'

'That's spooky,' said Carlton. 'Better not tell Glenroy any more about it.'

'Better not,' Curvis agreed.

'So we really could find a dead body up here?' Carlton wanted confirmation.

'Who knows?' replied Curvis.

'Who knows? Is that all you can say? Maybe Glenroy's right when he reckons there was a witch up here last night.'

'It's hard enough trying to deal with Glenroy's imagination, but you? A witch? Are you serious? We're not in the land of Oz.'

'No, course not. When we were younger, Glenroy even hated the orchard. He believed the story of the invisible bogeyman.'

'Didn't we all?' chuckled Curvis. 'Older kids were always trying to give us the shits with that one.'

They watched Glenroy lifting Bullet up and body-slamming him into the ground. Bullet got up and executed a flying kick into Glenroy's chest.

'Let's get off to Spurleigh Way before them two kill each other,' said Curvis.

'How do we get to Spurleigh Way from here?' asked Carlton.

'It's about three miles,' replied Curvis. He pointed the way. 'We head north-west, go over the hills. And Spurleigh Way is on the other side of Pig Folly's Shaw.'

'Pig Folly's what? What's a shaw?'

'A small wood.' Curvis explained. He ferreted into his bag and drew out a weather-beaten compass. 'This will come in handy now.'

'How much is it to get in at Spurleigh Way pool?' Carlton wanted to know.

'Last time I went it was forty pence for kids.'

'Forty pence!' cried Carlton. 'That's a pound sixty for all of us. Isn't there any fence we can climb over?'

'Er, yeah, but we're in enough trouble already. It'll be worth paying the price. I dunno about you but I feel like I've got ladybirds crawling about in my pants and I'm itching all over. And I'm *not* going back to the scout lake!'

Curvis waved to Bullet and Glenroy. 'Hey! You two! We're going in a minute. Come and help us tidy up.'

Ten minutes later, they set off, carrying their swimwear and towels in their holdalls. They paced themselves sensibly, emerging out of the forest after twenty minutes into a valley. Curvis led them through copses, across two streams and over a steep hill until they gazed down on the hamlet of Spurleigh. Bullet imagined commandos going beyond enemy lines during the trek.

Encircled by a ring road, the small town had straight avenues and detached houses with tidy front gardens. It was backdropped by a golf course. Bullet imagined the sand bunkers were bomb craters. All the kids they spotted seemed to have Chopper bikes. There was a toy shop in the High Street called For Little Guys and Princesses.

'Come,' said Curvis. 'Not far to go now.' He pointed to a highway. 'The pool's at the end of that road.'

Despite it being a school day, the open-air pool was packed with young bathers and toddlers, running about on the grassy areas around the swimming area, shrieking with glee. Adults sunned themselves on long towels. Pool attendants, dressed in brightly coloured sleeveless shirts and white shorts with whistles hanging around their necks, sat alert on wooden stools.

The friends swam away their fear and troubles, playing tag in and out of the water. They were all accomplished swimmers. Glenroy floated on the water with minimal effort. Bullet was a busy swimmer, all arms and legs, making large splashes. By contrast, Curvis, owning the physique of a long-distance runner, hardly disturbed the pool with long, elegant strokes. They remained at Spurleigh for the rest of the morning and early afternoon until Carlton suggested they'd better move on before schools were out in case any pupil on their way home recognised him.

Returning to camp at four thirty, Glenroy took out a notepad and pencils from his bag. He sat cross-legged, supporting the paper on his lap, and started to sketch. Carlton, carrying three empty Coca-Cola bottles, set off to the café to get drinking water. Curvis picked the leaves off nearby shrubs; he wanted to improve his friends' bedding as well as adding camouflage. Bullet collected all the rubbish and in a spot twenty yards away he cleared an area the size of a discus circle. He had matches in his pocket, but decided for a reason he didn't know, to try and start a fire with two sturdy twigs, gouging out a small hole in one of them.

'Bullet, what're you doing?' Curvis asked.

'Trying to start a fire, innit. Get rid of the rubbish – it has really built up.'

Curvis dropped the leaves in his arms and rushed over to Bullet. 'Are you mad? We'll all burn! The heatwave has left everything really dry. If something catches alight it'll burn half the forest before we can say tim-tam-tommy. They won't recognise our bodies.'

'Sorry,' said Bullet. 'I was just trying to see if I could do it. Like say the batteries run out and I didn't bring my matches, we'd have to learn how to build a fire.'

'If you want something to do,' said Curvis, almost jabbing his finger into Bullet's face, 'give me a hand picking those dock leaves; they're better to sleep on than the hard earth.'

Oblivious of what was going on around him, Glenroy concentrated on the figure he was sketching, rubber in his left hand and pencil in his right.

An hour later, Carlton returned, his bottles now filled with water. 'Next time we need water, I think I'd better go somewhere else and get it. The woman at the counter looked at me funny like she knows something. She didn't charge me for the water though.'

'You're right,' agreed Curvis. 'Must be somewhere else we can get water around here.'

Carlton spotted dock leaves covering the ground. 'You've been busy. I'll look forward to sleeping tonight.'

'It's alright, innit,' offered Bullet. 'Me and Curvis did it. Glenroy just sat down and started to draw – lazy sod.'

Glenroy looked up. 'Wotcha, Carlton. Give us one of them bottles.'

Carlton grinned a mischievous grin. 'Not until you show me what you've done.'

'Yeah! Let's have a look,' urged Bullet.

'No!' Glenroy refused. 'You can keep your water.'

'Oh, stop being childish,' chuckled Curvis. 'We won't laugh.'

Bullet collapsed into giggles.

Glenroy turned his pad upside down as Carlton approached. 'I want Bullet to promise. *Look* at him! He's taking the piss.'

'Promise, Bullet,' ordered Carlton, placing the bottles on the ground.

'Alright, alright,' Bullet relented. '*I promise.*'

Glenroy turned over his pad. His friends ran to look. Their eyes widened and their mouths opened.

'That's, that's,' Carlton stuttered, 'it's pretty good. It's *really* good.'

Bullet nodded, not knowing what to say. Curvis looked at Glenroy in astonishment.

'So much detail,' Bullet remarked. 'Why didn't you tell us you're good at art? And who is it?'

Glenroy smiled. 'It's Gemmele. The girl from Curvis's story. I don't show my drawings to anybody, not even Uncle Thomas. He's bound to say they're rubbish.'

'If we ever get back,' said Carlton, 'you should show him. He can't think of you as a nut job if you show him what you can do. He'll have to talk to you different, treat you better.'

'Carlton's right,' added Curvis. 'You can go to college or something drawing like that.'

'You can go to college and draw all day?' wondered Bullet.

'Yep, you can,' replied Curvis. 'If you behave yourself they might even let you paint.'

'*Funny!*' snapped Bullet.

Glenroy's art caught the despair of a young girl. Her eyes were intense. Her innocent expression was framed by long hair that parted in the middle and reached down to her hips. She was frightened by something. She was barefoot, wearing a simple dres. In the background, even the contours of the bark were visible on the tree trunks.

Carlton couldn't remove his eyes from the image. The girl of Curvis's story was now made real.

9.30 p.m.

Miss Gallagher peered through her kitchen window and watched a light-blue Panda car pull up outside her cottage. A policeman and a female officer climbed out of the car. They paused to watch the sun disappearing over the forking branches of the oak trees, creating a light green, reddish glow. The policeman rattled the letter box impatiently. Miss Gallagher's silhouette came into sight through the frosted glass.

'Good evening,' she greeted, smiling pleasantly. 'I was expecting you at nine o' clock. But you're here now. Can I get one of the children to make you a cup of tea or a cool drink? When will this heatwave end?'

'No, thank you,' replied the policeman. 'Just had cold drinks at the last house.'

Miss Gallagher led the officers into the recently hoovered sitting room; usually the children would watch television here but Miss Gallagher had emptied the room two hours ago, then ordered one of her teenage charges to make 'the dust disappear'. There was a large black-and-white television in the corner and a brown-buttoned three-piece suite facing it. There weren't any pictures hanging from the straw-coloured wallpaper and no plants. The policeman sat down on the sofa and his colleague joined him. He pulled out a small notebook from his breast pocket and waited for Miss Gallagher to take her seat in an armchair before he spoke.

'Are you Miss Gallagher?' he asked.

'That's me for all my sins.' Miss Gallagher tried to be humorous. It didn't work. 'Correct. I'm the officer in charge of this house.'

'It's Curvis who resides here, isn't it,' began the policeman. 'We are just calling to get some background information about the boys who have run away. I want to make that clear, because when we called at the previous house, the man in charge there seemed to think we're on a witch hunt. So is there anything you can tell us to help with our search?'

'Curvis was treated really well here,' Miss Gallagher replied quickly. 'The staff treated him just like a son. I think the reason he scarpered was because of his friends – they're a bad influence on him.'

The policewoman scribbled down notes. Miss Gallagher stole a glance at her. Reading his own notes, the policeman continued. 'Can you tell me the reason why Curvis was not told of his brother's whereabouts? The social worker was a bit vague on this.'

Miss Gallagher folded her arms. 'After a case meeting – I think it was about seven weeks ago – it was clear that Stanton was having a bad effect on his brother. So we had to move him. The decision *wasn't* just mine. All of my staff agreed with it and it *was* approved by the social worker *and* his supervisor. You see, Constable, life has been hard enough for Curvis, and we thought he could do without seeing his brother in a detention centre – he's got mental problems, don't you know. When Stanton was only little the doctors said he was maladjusted. You wouldn't know the harm it would've done to Curvis to have Stanton still around.'

The female officer leaned forward. 'Don't you think that this decision had something to do with him running away?'

'*No*, I do not!' Miss Gallagher inhaled sharply. She sat up straight. She composed herself and lowered her voice. 'Curvis knew that the decision was made for his own good. I'm sure he understood it.'

'Did Curvis say he understood the decision?' probed the policeman.

'Yes. I put it to him and he was calm about it. He didn't play up about it afterwards, if that's what you want to know.'

Miss Gallagher scratched her nose and put her hand to her mouth as if to stifle a cough. The female officer tried to read her body language. 'We understand that Curvis and his brother were very close,' she said. 'And didn't want to be separated.'

'The decision was taken to *protect* Curvis,' insisted Miss Gallagher. Her hands were now clasped together. The flesh beneath her fingernails turned pink.

'But hasn't Curvis a right to know where his brother is?' asked the policewoman.

'With respect! I know a lot more about teenagers than *you* do! I've raised scores of them.'

'We are straying from our point,' said the male officer. 'Our job is to bring the boys back safe.'

'As I said before,' Miss Gallagher interrupted. 'The decision was made for Curvis's well-being. You see, Stanton is nothing like Curvis. Stanton is violent – a danger to himself and anybody around him. He always got into fights. Curvis is quiet and very polite. You wouldn't believe they're related.'

'I'm sure that's true,' the policeman said, reading his notes. 'Now let's get back on track … We have checked with the local bus depots and no one can remember seeing four boys board a bus in the Pinewoods area on the night or morning that they ran away. We thought we had a lead after hearing there was some trouble at the scout complex in the Pinewood Hills, but apparently the troublemakers were all adults. Sometimes, after young men drink too much in the Pinewood Inn, they wander off into the Hills, causing all sorts of strife.'

Miss Gallagher tutted.

'We're assuming that the boys must have gone on foot to wherever they're heading,' the policeman said. 'And in most cases, runaways head for London. Yesterday, we spoke to Curvis's uncle and he says he hasn't seen him. He's very worried. Do you know if Curvis has any friends in the Lambeth area?'

'Not that I know of,' replied Miss Gallagher. 'I wouldn't have thought so. He only has friends in Pinewood Oaks, none at school. His teachers say he's a loner.'

'Yes, we heard,' said the policewoman.

'Is there anybody else he knows outside Pinewood Oaks?' asked the policeman. 'Any girlfriends?'

'Good lord, no. He's shy that way. After school he comes straight home. He's not interested in sports, not like that Carlton boy. He doesn't even watch television that often. The only programmes he watches are those nature documentaries – wildlife stuff. He likes birds.'

The policewoman scribbled down notes as Miss Gallagher looked on suspiciously. She glared at the policeman. 'So what *else* have you done to find them? Have you *actually* searched for them yet?'

'We have alerted most of the police stations in the Surrey, Kent border area and also informed the Met stations in London. We gave full descriptions of the boys. I can tell you we're doing everything we can.'

Miss Gallagher narrowed her eyes.

'We are due to check the local railway stations in the morning,' the policeman added. 'Perhaps someone who sold tickets on that morning or the night before will remember four teenagers fitting our descriptions – they did have money to travel.'

The policeman inspected his watch. 'If you remember anything else that might help us, feel free to call us at the station. We're taking this very seriously.'

'I should think so,' replied Miss Gallagher.

The officers stood up and made their way to the hallway. Miss Gallagher cursed under her breath as she followed them to the front door. The policewoman turned around. 'Miss Gallagher, I know that the kids in this place aren't easy to care for with the backgrounds most of them come from. So with that in mind, unless they do something really stupid, as soon as we find them we'll hand them over to social services. After that you can do what you like with them.'

'That's good to hear,' Miss Gallagher nodded. 'They might decide to send them to a secure unit. They won't be so ready to run off again.'

'Goodbye, Miss Gallagher,' the policewoman said. 'We'll be in touch as soon as we hear something.' She closed the door behind her.

Once they reached their car, the policewoman leaned on the bonnet and turned to her colleague. 'What do you think?'

'I don't know,' the policeman replied, looking at the cottage. 'It seems everyone we've talked to tonight is hiding something. We know Curvis's motive, but there must be something more. Something's not quite right.'

The policewoman nodded. She fished in her pockets for her car keys. 'That Mr Thomas Pearson, he was very nervous.'

'Yeah, I noticed that. He was going through his fags a bit lively. And he was speaking through his fingers when he was answering our questions. *Dodgy.* He was a bit *over*-nice. You notice?'

'Yeah, he was. He would have cooked us an early Christmas dinner if we'd asked him to.'

They both chuckled, taking in their surroundings and drawn by the twilight beauty of the orchard. 'But there's something strange about him,' added the policewoman. 'I can't quite put my finger on it.'

'They're all a bit strange,' said the policeman. 'That Rodney bloke who lined up the kids in his house to give us a formal greeting. He's another one, but I suppose to care for the kids in this place, you have to be a bit mad. I tell you, I couldn't do it.'

'But it's that Mr Pearson,' the policewoman said, shaking her head. 'Creepy. Glenroy's the boy in that house, isn't he? The way he kissed that little boy on the forehead before he went to bed. It didn't seem right. Not what Mr Pearson did but the way the boy reacted. He flinched.'

'That's normal. No boys I know like to be kissed goodnight. It's embarrassing. My dad kissed me at my wedding. I didn't know where to put my face.'

'Yeah, I suppose you're right.'

She climbed into the car and turned the ignition. The policeman filled the passenger seat. 'Who knows what really happens in these places,' he said. 'The social workers wouldn't let us read the boys' files; they had a meeting we weren't invited to and they are scared to death of the press hearing about all this. It's like investigating a cult.'

'I just feel sorry for the boys,' the policewoman said, hitting first gear and feeling the roll of a road ramp. 'It's obvious from what we heard today that once they're caught, they'll be separated and placed God knows where … I wonder where they are now.'

The temperature had only dropped a few degrees lower than it had been in the afternoon sun. The leaves on the bushes and trees were moistened by the humidity, producing a thick scent that hung in the air; the four runaways could taste it on their lips and feel it in their armpits. They moved stealthily through the tangled wood; even Glenroy was sure of his footing now.

They had made their way from their base to the eastern side of the forest, crossing from Surrey into Kent, beyond the Pinewood Hills and near to a bush-lined road with cats' eyes peering brightly from the asphalt. Shining his torch in front of him, Curvis led the way. Carlton was at the rear. 'Can't be much further to the big house?'

'I can't see it yet,' replied Curvis. 'It must be soon though.'

Glenroy was behind Curvis. 'What are we gonna do when we get there?'

'Play cricket on their front garden,' replied Bullet. 'Or tim-tam-tommy at the back. It's massive.'

Late in the afternoon, after spying on the scouts, Carlton had offered to take his friends 'for a long walk and see what they come across'. Curvis made sure he used his compass so they could return safely. They had stumbled on the mansion while on their trek. None of them had ever seen a house quite like it. It was a ranch-type building that seemed as long as a playground. Carlton was fascinated by the French shutters and the huge windows. They all wondered who lived in such a house, and decided to come back again at night.

Curvis stood in front of a seven-foot-high green-meshed fence that was fronted by nettles. 'Glenroy, Bullet! Help me clear away the stingers,' he ordered. 'It's well camouflaged – I didn't see the fence till I was right in front of it.'

Curvis pointed. 'It's over there.'

Bullet shone his torch.

In front of the mansion was a manicured garden criss-crossed by narrow pathways. Garden chairs were placed around white tables with yellow-and-white striped umbrellas sprouting from them. A pond was rimmed with a rockery, its stones knee high. A large greenhouse, reflecting the moon and stars, was beside a wooden hut. A paved path curled its way from the back of the garden to the wooden-panelled main back door of the house. There were no lights on inside the house.

'Some film star must live here,' said Glenroy, kicking away the nettles. 'The pond's about as big as the swimming pool at Pinewood Oaks.'

'Who's coming over then?' challenged Carlton. 'To have a look round. Might find some food.'

Glenroy started climbing. 'Last one over is a tosspot!'

Seconds later, all four were on the other side of the green fence, adrenaline surging through them. They stood before an immaculately kept flower bed. Glenroy simply walked across it. Curvis shook his head as he and the others stepped around it. They headed for the greenhouse. 'Glenroy,' Carlton whispered. '*Don't* wander off.'

Carlton opened the greenhouse door as if there was a bomb attached to the handle. They crept in. Various potted plants hung from twined baskets, the colours forming a kaleidoscope. Strange-looking buds were forming in trays upon shelves. Bags of peat and earth were resting on the floor. A garden manual was open on a small wooden table. Curvis noticed something. '*Tomatoes!*'

The other three joined Curvis. Without hesitation, Glenroy plucked a tomato and tasted it. Carlton trained his eyes on the windows of the house. 'Not bad,' Glenroy remarked. 'Juicy. They're better than the ones that grow in Pinewood Oaks – try one.'

They sat down on the dusty floor and sampled the fruit. After eating his tomato in three bites, Bullet slipped out of the greenhouse and stood outside, eyeing the hut. Curiosity getting the better of him, he lifted the latch. He pushed the door ajar and, to his dismay, watched as a garden fork fell to the ground. It hit the concrete floor with a resounding crack. 'Shit!'

'Bullet! What're you doing?' snapped Carlton.

'I just pushed the door and the thing fell down.'

Curvis scanned the windows of the mansion. Glenroy bit into another tomato as Carlton glared at Bullet. Bullet returned to the greenhouse. A light came on in a bedroom. The sound of hurrying feet descending stairs was audible. Curvis saw the light. 'I don't think whoever's coming down is gonna give us scones and cups of tea. *Move!*'

Something four-legged approached from the side of the house.

'Dogs! Leg it!' screamed Curvis.

Glenroy spat out his tomato and bolted out of the greenhouse, heading for the fence. Bullet and Carlton sprinted with him. Momentarily in shock, Curvis was left behind for a crucial three seconds before he started running. Glenroy performed an almighty leap on the fence. Bullet and Carlton soon realised that Curvis might not make it. Carlton grabbed his arm. 'Come on!' The Dobermans bared their teeth, getting closer. The barking disturbed the quiet of the night. Birds fluttered in trees. A figure appeared by the back door of the mansion. The dogs neared their prey. Having no time to jump on the fence and climb high enough, Bullet picked up a plant pot. Carlton collected a smiling gnome with a fishing rod in his hand from beside the pond. Curvis stood perfectly still once more, rooted in fear. Canine jaws slavered. Bullet flung the pot, missing a Doberman's head. Glenroy was up and over the fence, his body leaving a dent in the mesh. Carlton scored a hit with the happy gnome, striking a dog in its side. The creatures halted their advance and resorted to barking. The figure by the door moved. Regaining his composure, Curvis ran to the fence. 'Give us your hand!' yelled Glenroy. 'I'll pull you over.'

Bullet and Carlton soon joined Curvis clambering over the fence. Bullet's T-shirt caught on a stray piece of mesh. One of the dogs hotpawed towards Bullet.

'Pull him! Just pull him!' screamed Curvis.

'Swing your fucking legs!' yelled Glenroy.

Somehow, Bullet scrambled over the barrier.

'*This is private property,*' a man bellowed. '*Get off my land or I'll call the police!*'

'Shut your mouth and suck your dogs!' Glenroy returned. He picked up a stone and threw it at the greenhouse. A loud smash distracted the barking dogs and they went to investigate. Another bedroom light came on.

'That wasn't too helpful,' said Carlton.

'What you do that for?' demanded Curvis. 'The place is gonna be crawling with the police and we've still got to cross the road to get back to our camp!'

'Fucking snob!' Glenroy cursed. 'I should've put the stone through one of his upstairs windows.'

'Do something like that again and I'll chuck a stone through your head,' threatened Bullet.

Ignoring Bullet, Glenroy picked up another stone and threw it over the fence. Curvis didn't wait to see if the missile hit its target. For half a second Bullet glared at Glenroy, primed to rebuke him but thought better of it. He turned and ran. Glenroy stood still, staring ahead.

'Move it, Friar Tuck!' urged Carlton. 'That fence might have a hatch for the dogs.'

The intruders quickly weaved their way through the coppice. Curvis took the lead, shining his torch in front of him. 'This reminds me of the time Uncle Rodney told us about the war in the Burma and Malaysian jungle,' panted Bullet.

'Oh God! Here he goes again,' sighed Carlton. 'Telling us one of Uncle Rodney's war stories.'

Bullet was undeterred. 'There were about a thousand Allies in the jungle surrounded by about a million Japs,' Bullet began.

'More like ten thousand Allies being chased by a thousand Japs,' chuckled Carlton. 'Those Japs were nut jobs.'

'Them tomatoes were alright,' said Glenroy. 'We should go back for more on another night.'

'Yeah, but we're lucky we're not a dog's supper,' said Curvis.

'Don't you wanna hear the story?' moaned Bullet.

'I know the story,' said Carlton. 'Tarzan came to the rescue with his chimp and killed five thousand Japs on his own. Two thousand got killed in quicksand and the others shot themselves out of frustration cos they couldn't find a ripe tomato.'

'And their compasses didn't work,' mocked Curvis.

'And they ran out of toilet paper,' laughed Carlton.

Bullet raised his voice. 'So you don't wanna hear how a lot of the Allied soldiers got awarded their Victoria Crosses?'

'For fuck's sake!' Carlton swore. 'Go on then if it's gonna kill ya.'

They slowed down to a swift march. An owl watched their progress as an unseen beak hammered against a tree trunk. 'You're right, Carlton, when you say there was quicksand,' resumed Bullet. 'But also there was those vampire leeches, bigger than Glenroy's feet. You know those things got fangs.'

'Bigger than Glenroy's feet!' laughed Carlton. 'That's gruesome enough.'

'Fuck you,' replied Glenroy. 'My feet ain't gruesome.'

Bullet continued. 'The Allies were running out of food and stuff and the zillion Japs were closing in.'

'And then they ran out of toilet paper,' laughed Carlton. 'We've run out too. I scratched up my arse this morning with those dock leaves. It's rough. I'm gonna look for something softer in the morning.'

'If you're not gonna listen then fuck off,' complained Bullet.

'And Bullet,' Curvis scolded. 'Stop doing your shitting near the camp! I nearly walked in your crap this morning.'

'*That* was a brush with death,' chuckled Carlton. 'Probably the most dangerous thing that's happened to us up here.'

As they neared the Pinewood Hills road, they lay flat on the ground, camouflaging themselves in the long grass. The odd car went by, headlights showering light upon bark and leaf and the sound of engines fading into the night. When Curvis decided it was safe, they continued their trek back to their base, the mounds and hillocks becoming more difficult to negotiate as they grew weary. They settled for the night on the now dirt-and-grass-stained blankets. They feasted on Carlton's cakes and biscuits.

Curvis knew the food wouldn't last for longer than two days and thought of seeking out allotments near the farms for a source. He was annoyed with himself for allowing their night excursion to the mansion. We're starting to do stupid things, he thought. Carlton's getting more adventurous by the hour. What would've happened if he had hit that guy in the head? He thinks he can do anything and get away with it. Glenroy's not much better. It was a crazy risk. He looked around at his surroundings. 'Yeah,' he whispered. 'You're daring us.'

Bullet sat up, peeling a stick with his penknife. His strokes were brutal.

Carlton looked up to the stars, noticing how some shone brilliantly while others were barely visible. He watched the trees' fingertips move gently above his head, before switching his gaze to Glenroy. He can draw, he thought. That makes him something. I could never do anything like that.

Glenroy searched the darkness around him before he settled his gaze on Curvis. 'That girl, did she play in the woods when it was dark?'

Curvis sat up and grabbed his torch. He beamed it into the hollow. 'Probably. Can't see how she could've been scared of the dark when she lived all her life near the forest.'

'She might've run away just like us,' Glenroy suggested. 'Maybe her mum and dad used to hit her all the time. Just like what happened to me when I was younger. D'you think real parents hit their children like the housemothers and housefathers do? Maybe they get hit once a week instead of every day? Maybe once a month?'

Curvis digested Glenroy's words and tried to think of an answer. He quickly realised that neither he nor any of his friends had any idea of normal family life. None of them had close friends outside

Pinewood Oaks and typical family interaction was as far away as the stars. He thought of his mother and what life would have been like if his father hadn't killed her.

Carlton interrupted his thoughts. 'Will you two ever shut up about this girl? Glenroy, you've gone on about Curvis's story *every* night since we've been here. It's getting on my nerves! Anyway, I don't give a fuck what happened to her.'

'Would you say that if one of us went missing?' asked Curvis.

'Course not!'

Bullet pushed his stick into the earth. 'Maybe she was eaten by mad, nutter hounds. You ever seen that film *The Hound of the Baskervilles*? The dog's about as big as a horse.'

'I saw it once,' said Carlton. 'It was about as big as a pony.'

'It's just a film,' said Curvis. 'You lot really let your imaginations run mad.'

'The story of that little girl wasn't a film,' said Carlton. 'You told me it was definitely true.'

'When this is all over,' cut in Bullet, 'I'm gonna check if she's still officially missing. I'll go to the Town Hall or somewhere. Some old fart must know.'

'What will happen if we go missing?' asked Glenroy. 'D'you think they'll have a big search for us?'

'Glenroy, we are missing,' pointed out Curvis.

'They won't be searching for us,' said Carlton. 'They'll be hunting us down with pitchforks and Frankenstein clubs. We're not normal kids, remember.'

'No, no. Say six months from now,' said Glenroy, his face serious. He looked at his friends one by one. 'Will they just give up? Say we were murdered up here, no one would know. We'd be lying dead somewhere, just like that little girl. And cos she didn't get a proper burial, she's now a ghost in the daytime and a witch at night. No one gave her the last rites. Father Patrick told me that if someone doesn't get the last rites, their soul has trouble getting to heaven. That's why Gemmele's probably haunting this forest.'

For a moment they all looked at each other.

'For fuck's sake!' snapped Carlton, slamming his right fist into the ground. 'Stop bringing her up. Just shut up! Father Patrick talks out of his arse!'

Sweat appeared on Carlton's forehead. To him, it smelt like chlorine. The chlorine of the swimming pool back in Pinewood Oaks … In *that* cubicle … Uncle Thomas. His insides shook. He desperately tried to rid himself of the image.

'They'll soon realise that we're up here,' said Curvis. 'Especially after last night and what happened with the scouts. The police might've already looked for us in the daytime. Let 'em search till we're ready to go back. Who knows, our names might be in the local papers. That'll be something.'

'Uncle Thomas is gonna kill me,' said Glenroy. 'He's gonna fucking kill me.'

'Only if the witch doesn't get you first,' laughed Bullet.

'No, he's not!' Carlton spat. 'He's *not* going to touch anyone!'

Curvis watched Carlton with alarm. Maybe I should take them to clearer ground, he considered.

An hour and a half later, Curvis, Bullet and Glenroy were asleep. Carlton was drifting in the surreal chasm between slumber and insomnia. His mind recalled an incident in his past.

He was five years old, lying in his bed. Awake. Two hours earlier his mother had kissed him goodnight, the lipstick still remained on his forehead. The fragrance she wore was unknown to him but it was nice. Comforting. He liked the way she tucked him in and ruffled his hair, her hands so soft. But now she was gone. Left the house for a place he didn't know, leaving him alone. In the dark. All he had for company was a dummy. His mother had tried to wean him off it but he cried the house down in protest. He sucked on the dummy feverishly and he'd keep on sucking until she returned. A few more hours he would have to wait. In the dark. Not daring to get up and turn on a light or to peer out the window for his mother's return. The room was cold. Blackness surrounded him. He felt bound to his bed. He refused to answer a call of nature, preferring to wet his bed. She'll have to see to me as soon as she gets in, he thought. She'll have to wash me. She knows I never wet my bed if she's here. But she's not. She's gone.

Dancing in the Dark
16 June 1976, 10.15 a.m.

Sitting up from his distracted sleep, Carlton felt a multitude of emotions swirling inside him. He plucked a blade of grass, placed it in his mouth and sucked on it. The morning song of a skylark soothed his mind and he could smell the dew mingling with the strong scent of the pines. He squinted as he looked up at the bright June sky. He was in his rightful place, he thought to himself – beside his friends. They wouldn't leave him. He smiled as he watched his mates resting peacefully. 'Four of us mighty are we,' he whispered.

He was glad that he found a moment to himself, for it gave him time to think. Glenroy wasn't whining, Bullet was not reciting tales from the Allied campaign in Burma, and he didn't have to listen to Curvis going on forever about his housemother. He hadn't dislodged the memory of his mother slapping him for wetting the bed. Her harsh voice still rang inside his head. '*There's a toilet in this place, fucking use it!*'

He rubbed his eyes and delved into his bag, unzipping a small compartment. He counted the cash – seven pound sixty. Guilt struck him again. Auntie Josephine grew large in his mind. He recalled her kindly words of advice and encouragement. They were quickly superimposed with images of his mother's rants. He recalled the last time he saw her – in the spring of 1974. He was already at Pinewood Oaks. That morning he had refused to see his mother and ran away to the orchard where he and his friends had made their hideout, not returning home until past midnight. His mother was distraught. Josephine had to comfort her the best way she could, telling her gently that the last green bus always departed outside Pinewood Oaks at 11.08 p.m. Josephine had walked her to the bus stop, unaware that Carlton was watching from the bush. 'You bitch,' Carlton had whispered.

About thirty yards away, its roots hidden by shrubbery, Carlton approached the tallest of the trees. Once he reached the base of the trunk he looked up to its looming height. 'And good morning to you,' he whispered. He gripped the branches firmly. 'Now, don't snap on me.' He ascended the tree with ease. From his vantage point he could see the vast area of woodland and sprawling plains beyond. The windmill stood lazily a mile away. He could make out the seven barrow hills looping south-west, their stones bleached by the sun. In his mind, he saw Glenroy's sketched creation, Gemmele. She was pretty and carefree. She ran and laughed, careering up and down the hills with her hair trailing in the breeze.

'Hey, monkey,' Glenroy called. 'What're you doing up there?'

'Just looking,' Carlton replied.

'What're we having for breakfast?' asked Glenroy. He held his stomach. 'I'm starving.'

'Then eat the grass!' joked Carlton, descending the tree.

'Give us some money,' asked Glenroy. 'I wanna go up to that café and buy some sandwiches.'

'Will you stop moaning! You're always thinking of your belly.'

The exchange woke Bullet. Bleary-eyed, he hauled himself up and trudged towards the tree that Carlton had jumped from. 'My back,' he wailed. 'I can't take sleeping on the ground any more – the leaves don't make much difference.'

'Then go home,' suggested Glenroy.

'Why don't you go home,' returned Bullet. 'You're the one who's shit scared of the dark.'

'Scared of what dark,' argued Glenroy. 'You see me crying about it?'

'Who got up in the middle of the night and shouted '*what the fuck was that!*' when some squirrel was running about,' mocked Bullet.

'It could've been one of them scouts creeping up on us,' reasoned Glenroy.

'At three o'clock in the morning?' Bullet teased. 'You thought it was the bogeyman, innit.'

'Fuck you!' Glenroy dismissed him.

'Will you two shut up!' Carlton cut in. 'Jesus Christ! It's like going on summer camp with ten Georgie Bests and eleven referees.'

'Well, tell him!' sniped Glenroy, pointing an angry finger at Bullet. 'I wished he'd stayed at home!'

'You asked me to come, you divo!' volleyed Bullet.

'I wish I never now,' countered Glenroy.

'Shut up!' yelled Carlton. 'Just *shut up!* I can't take this any more. *Shut up!*'

Bullet and Glenroy stilled their tongues. They stared at Carlton. Carlton took in deep breaths. Glenroy started down the hill.

Curvis stirred. He opened his eyes and watched Glenroy stroll away. 'What's wrong with them two now?' he asked.

'They're arguing again,' answered Carlton. 'And getting on my nerves.'

Entertaining himself by throwing pebbles at a tree, Glenroy turned to Curvis. 'Can you tell Carlton to give me some money so I can get something to eat.'

'How much have we got left?' asked Curvis.

'Seven pound sixty,' Carlton replied. 'I counted it this morning. We're not gonna last too long on that. It'll soon be time for late-night sweet-shop raids and robbing banks.'

'We'll use Glenroy's head to break in,' chuckled Bullet.

'Fuck you and all your toy soldiers!'

Curvis stood up and shook the blanket he slept on; dock leaves and tiny twigs danced in the warm air. Curvis coughed and folded the blanket. 'Bullet,' he called, 'what time does your school have dinner break?'

Bullet was leaning on a tree, twirling a green leaf around his thumb. 'Twelve thirty. Why?'

'One of us should go down Elvin's school and find him,' suggested Curvis.

'See Elvin?' wondered Carlton. 'He'll tell everybody that he saw one of us.'

Glenroy heard the proposal. He returned to the others. 'I'll go,' he offered.

'No!' replied Curvis. He turned to Carlton. 'Carlton, you go. No one in the school knows you.'

'There are only a few boys who know me there,' argued Glenroy.

'Nah,' Curvis shook his head. 'What happens if one of those boys sees you? It's best for Carlton to go cos he knows the back way around Pinewood Oaks to get to the school.'

'For fuck's sake! You don't trust me to do anything,' complained Glenroy.

Curvis ignored Glenroy. 'Carlton, if you get to see Elvin, ask him to get us some food and stuff. He can meet us later on tonight to give us the grub.'

'And what if I don't see him?' asked Carlton.

'Then you'll have to go back after school and see if you can catch him then.'

Carlton took a pound note from his bag. He turned to Glenroy. 'Buy four of those hot pasties, and don't take the scenic route. And *don't* stay there too long.' He handed the cash to Glenroy.

Glenroy banked the money in his back pocket and ran down the hillock, stumbling over pine roots.

Curvis and Bullet tidied the camp area as Carlton looked on, turning something over in his mind. 'How much longer are we gonna be on the run?' he asked. 'It's cool being up here with all them fuckers trying to find us but we can't stay here forever.'

'He's right,' said Bullet. 'Even deserters from the army get caught after a while.'

Curvis dropped his head. Maybe he should remain on his own, he thought. 'I dunno,' he said. He forced a smile. 'I s'pose we'll go back when everyone is sick and tired of shitting in the bushes. I should've brought more crap paper on the night we left.'

'Which way shall I go?' asked Carlton. 'To the other side of the golf course and cut through Badgers Dyke? Then take the Hawthorn path next to Hogspill Wood?'

'Yeah,' Curvis nodded. 'When you come out of Hogspill Wood, follow the road to the Pinewood library and cross at the lights. Go down to the bottom of Grove Avenue, turn left, and you're there.'

'Tell Elvin to keep his trap shut,' warned Bullet. 'You know what he's like. His mouth's bigger than the Dartford Tunnel.'

Curvis nodded. Without another word he set off to his adopted tree where he spoke with his dead mother. Carlton and Bullet paused conversation until Curvis was out of earshot. 'What d'you reckon?' asked Bullet. 'We've made our point. We've got to go back sometime.'

'Yeah, I know,' replied Carlton. 'But are you gonna tell Curvis we should go back? You know what he's like. He'll probably want to stay up here on his own. Best to wait for him to get sick and tired of it an' all. I have to admit though, it's a great feeling to be up here, knowing those cunts don't have a clue where we are. It'll be a shame to go back. We can hold on for a few more days, especially if Elvin can help us out.'

Half an hour later, Glenroy returned, holding four hot pasties in white wrappers. The boys sat down to eat their breakfast. Glenroy was first to finish his food. 'Should've got two each,' he said. 'I'm still hungry.' He threw his wrapper behind him. 'So what are we gonna do while Carlton's seeing Jaws?'

'Watch the snobs playing golf and see if we can nick their balls,' suggested Bullet.

'Might as well,' agreed Glenroy. He looked at Curvis. 'Or we can go to Spurleigh pool again?'

Curvis's eyes were fixed deep into the wood, his thoughts still with his mother.

'Yeah,' Bullet agreed. 'Last time it was a laugh. Coming, Curvis?'

'Nah,' Curvis finally replied, not bothering to turn around. 'I'll stay round here for the day. Don't feel like going anywhere.'

The others looked at each other. 'Something wrong?' asked Bullet.

'Nah, just feeling really tired.'

Carlton checked his watch and began to ready himself for his long trek, combing his hair with an Afro pick. 'Turn left at Grove Avenue?'

'Yeah,' Curvis nodded. 'Be careful when you're crossing roads.'

'I'll be back around half two,' Carlton said. 'So if you lot are going on a mission, don't leave me up here too long on my own.'

'Tell Elvin to get us some apples and oranges and some of those shortbread biscuits that his Auntie makes,' asked Glenroy. 'And tell him to get us some of those Marks and Spencer cakes.'

'Sure you don't want roast lamb with mint sauce and baby spuds?' laughed Carlton, making a start. Before he left, he gave Bullet some cash.

'Sure you don't wanna come?' Bullet asked Curvis again.

'*No!*'

'Alright, keep your Afro on,' said Bullet. 'Let's get ready, Glenroy. We'll leave the king of the sulks on his own.'

Two hours later, Carlton jogged through Ashburden playing field, approaching Elvin's school. Around him were dog-walkers, sunbathers, toddlers crowned with white handkerchiefs and pensioners relaxing on wooden benches beneath a fierce sun.

Carlton swabbed the sweat from his brow. He rested on the grass and checked his watch. Twelve fifteen. 'Only fifteen minutes to go,' he said to himself. He plucked a blade of grass and pushed it into his mouth. 'A jubbly would go down nice after my five-mile trek.'

He lay flat on his back in view of the school buildings a hundred yards away. He remembered the first day he arrived in Pinewood Oaks. He asked the strange man, who was holding his hand on the journey to the children's home, where his mother was. He told him she was on holiday. That night he refused to sleep with the dormitory light switched off. He woke up the whole household with his screams. Auntie Josephine had to take him to her room where she had a lamp. This routine carried on for six weeks. He pined for his mother, not knowing if she would ever come back for him.

Teenage shrieks and shouts came from the school. Pupils streamed out of the buildings. Some decided to remain in the school grounds out of the sun's harsh glare. Carlton spotted a boy about his age and approached him. 'Do you know Elvin? Skinny black boy? He rides a bike.'

'Yeah,' the boy replied. 'I saw him in the playground.'

'Can you take me to him?'

'Yeah. C'mon then.'

Elvin was dressed in black trousers and a white shirt that was unbuttoned to his navel. 'Elvin!' Carlton called. 'Elvin!'

Elvin turned around and saw the dishevelled appearance of Carlton – dried mudstains on his face and his hands. Elvin's eyes brightened and his mouth gaped. 'Fuck the daisies! Where d'you come from?'

Carlton checked around him. 'Come here!' he ordered.

Elvin did as he was told.

'Keep your voice down!' Carlton raged in a loud whisper.

They walked towards the playing field.

'Where've you been?' Elvin wanted to know. 'Pinewood Oaks has been crawling with the Old Bill. Me and Mellor had to go up the station to answer questions. There's a curfew going on. Somebody said you were all dead. Someone else said you were kidnapped. We all thought you did an Oliver Twist and went up to London. There are strange men in suits walking everywhere. Everyone's going nuts, arguing with housemothers and housefathers. Where've you been?'

Elvin stopped for breath.

'Slow down a bit, Elvin, you're gonna bruise your tonsils.'

Elvin exhaled.

'What did you say to the police?' Carlton asked.

'Nothing,' Elvin replied proudly. 'I didn't know where you were anyway. They even interrogated Sonia, asking her if you lot had any girlfriends in Pinewood and nearby.'

'So what did Sonia say?'

'Nothing – she was really cool about it. But Mellor lost his temper with the Old Bill. They were screaming at him and Mellor lost it. He came out with his face duffed up. When we got back to Pinewood Oaks, he smashed Mr Williams's window.'

'He must be on some serious punishment?'

'Yeah, but he's going nuts. He shinnied down the drainpipe last night to see Sonia and he wants her to run away with him.'

'I didn't realise all this shit would've happened to you lot.'

'Like I said there's a curfew,' said Elvin. 'Everyone has to be in by eight o'clock. Friends from outside have to be out of the grounds by seven. The staff are watching us like hawks. At night we hear cars driving up and down.'

Carlton lowered his voice. 'Have you seen Auntie Josephine?'

'No … I heard that she went with the police up to London. But Sonia saw her yesterday. She reckons she's been crying all the time. Her eyes are all puffed up.'

Carlton took a moment to swallow his guilt. 'Elvin, listen to me. We're running out of money and we need food. What d'you reckon? Can you get us some nosh and meet us tonight?'

'I'll try my best. It'll have to be before eight.'

'It'll still be light then,' Carlton replied. 'We'll have to risk it.'

'We'll risk it too. Uncle Thomas followed me up the shops yesterday. He wants to talk to me but I'm keeping away from him. I rode off. He looks like he's got the shits.'

'Don't say anything yet until I come back,' ordered Carlton. 'Then we'll tell everybody, including the social, what a fucking bummer he is. I hope they get rid of him.'

'D'you think they'll listen to us?'

'Not me on my own. That's why you have to back me up and tell 'em what that cunt done to you. I'm depending on you, Elvin. Hopefully, others will say something an' all.'

'So who you gonna tell first?' asked Elvin. 'I thought you'd *never* tell anyone.'

Carlton took his time answering. He stared at the ground. He felt a queasy sensation in his stomach. 'Auntie Josephine,' he said finally. He looked up. 'I know she'll believe me. I've been thinking about it while I've been on the run. I *want* that cunt to pay.'

There was silence as Elvin digested Carlton's words. His heartbeat accelerated. Elvin wondered how it would all end.

Carlton broke the tension. 'Meet us by the fence near the junior school shed just before eight o'clock with all the food you can get. Be careful nicking the stuff.'

'I will. What you get depends on what's in the larder though.'

'We're not too picky. Right now Glenroy would eat a mouldy pasty.'

'Alright then,' chuckled Elvin. 'I won't let you down. Where're you hiding out?'

'You don't need to know.'

Carlton placed his hand on Elvin's left shoulder. He forced a smile. 'Elvin, you're a good mate. You get on everybody's nerves sometimes, but you're a good mate.'

Elvin returned the grin as he watched Carlton about-turn and jog away.

Carlton returned to the camp three hours later. He found Bullet meticulously carving something in a tree. He had a sheet of paper in his hand and glanced at it now and again. Glenroy was sitting down sketching, not yet aware of Carlton's presence. 'Where's Curvis?' Carlton asked.

'Gone to get some water,' Bullet replied. 'We've run out already. Did you see Elvin?'

'Yeah. We're gonna meet him later on today. He's gonna bring us some food.'

Glenroy looked up. 'Brilliant! What time?'

'Before eight.'

Glenroy licked his lips. 'I hope he brings some cakes. Doesn't his Auntie make apple pies?'

'Or jam tarts?' said Bullet. 'God! If I had a lemon jam tart right now I would eat it crumb by crumb.'

'Mr Kipling makes exceedingly good jam tarts,' chuckled Glenroy. 'And choc fairy cakes.'

'We're not meeting Mr fucking Kipling later on,' said Carlton. 'We're meeting Elvin. We'll be lucky to get a few slices of bread and half a jar of jam.'

Bullet and Glenroy dropped their heads and returned their tongues behind their teeth.

Spent from walking in the hot sun, Carlton dropped against a tree. 'So what have you two been up to today?'

'Went swimming,' Bullet answered. 'Couldn't get Curvis to come with us. Then we watched some blokes playing golf.'

Bullet and Glenroy smiled mischievously. Bullet dropped his penknife and took out three golf balls from his pockets. 'And we got these,' he revealed, a grin rippling from his mouth. 'You should've seen their faces when they walked to the green. I had to put my hand over Glenroy's mouth to stop him cracking up. They just didn't know what happened to their balls.'

Glenroy roared with laughter and Carlton joined in. 'What's that you're doing?' Carlton asked Bullet, regaining his composure.

Bullet stepped two paces back. 'Oh, I bet Glenroy that I could do his new drawing on the tree. Not bad, eh?'

'Let me see that,' said Carlton. He stood up and snatched the sheet of paper out of Bullet's hand.

Carlton flinched when he studied the image.

'I've got to give it to him,' said Bullet. 'It's brilliant.'

'Yeah, yeah it is,' Carlton admitted.

Glenroy smiled. Carlton examined the drawing once again. From the neck down, it was more or less the same sketch that Glenroy had drawn previously, but Gemmele's face was replaced by a head with horns dripping blood. 'Where d'you get the idea to do this?'

'In a dream I had last night,' replied Glenroy. 'She changes like that when the night comes.'

Carlton looked at the tree. Bullet had carved out the outline of the head and had already grooved the horns. He had started on the eyes. '*Jesus*,' exclaimed Carlton. 'Ain't you got anything better to do than devil stuff?'

Glenroy and Bullet laughed.

7.55 p.m.

Carlton led his friends swiftly across the browned playing field. The sun was setting, its rays kissing the treetops. Young footballers and teenage sweethearts were in the park. The wooden benches were empty. There was no breeze.

They soon reached the eight-foot-high wooden fence that encircled the northern acres of Pinewood Oaks. The junior school loomed silently beyond it. They grouped near a tree to catch breath. Dread filled their eyes.

'Keep your eyes peeled,' Carlton instructed. 'Who knows who we might come across tonight? Be prepared to leg it.'

'Carlton,' Glenroy called. 'You should've told Elvin to meet us here in the rec.'

'Too risky – they're all being watched and the cunts would know there was something up if they went out of the grounds.'

Carlton leapt onto the fence. He hauled himself up with his strong arms. He balanced on top and scanned the vacant playground. 'Clear,' he whispered. 'But no sign of Elvin. *Where* the fuck is he? If he doesn't turn up I swear I'll bend the forks on his bike and reshape his nostrils.'

'I knew he wouldn't come,' complained Glenroy. 'He probably told someone.'

Carlton jumped down to the asphalt and peered into a flat-roofed shed in a corner of the playground. It was about twelve feet high and supported by wooden pillars. 'Not there,' Carlton muttered. 'I'm gonna *kill* him.'

'What's the time?' asked Bullet as he clambered over the fence.

'About a minute to eight,' replied Carlton. He searched the rest of the playground.

Curvis and Glenroy climbed the fence and dropped to the ground. 'He might've got caught nicking grub,' suggested Carlton. 'We'll give him another ten minutes then we'd better leg it. I'll come back and kill him later.'

'I'll come back with ya,' nodded Glenroy.

'Shhh,' ordered Curvis. 'I can hear something.'

Retreating into a corner of the shed, they crouched low into the shadows. Heartbeats raced. They spotted a silhouette emerge by the corner of the main building, its shadow lengthened threefold by the dropping sun. The runaways inched forward to the fence. A slim figure appeared in the playground looking this way and that. It was Elvin. He was carrying plastic bags. They saw another figure walking behind Elvin. 'I hope that's really him?' said Glenroy. 'Otherwise we're well and truly fucked like a fox with a broken leg surrounded by hounds. Who's with him?'

'It's Sonia!' said Carlton. 'That's all we need. Who else has he told?'

'Probably everyone who lives between Bognor and the Crystal Palace towers,' joked Bullet.

They all met in the middle of the playground. Changing his mind, Curvis ushered everybody back inside the shed. Carlton glared at Sonia. She was wearing a T-shirt and a two-tone skirt that met her calves. Her hair was styled in corn-row plaits. She was holding two plastic bags. 'We weren't too sure if Elvin could get out,' she said. 'So we decided that we'd both try and get here for eight.'

Glenroy licked his lips. 'What've you got?'

'Anything we could lay our hands on,' replied Sonia. 'Even Brenda nicked some food for you earlier.'

'You told Brenda?' snapped Curvis. 'Did you write down our arrival on the Lodge's notice board? Who else knows? The mayor of Spurleigh?'

'Just Mellor, Brenda, Sonia and me,' replied Elvin.

Bullet watched Sonia warily as Glenroy examined the contents of the plastic bags. 'Bourbons!' he exclaimed.

'I thought Mellor was on punishment,' Carlton said.

'He is,' replied Sonia. 'But he sneaked out to see me about seven o'clock.'

Elvin and Carlton wandered off to talk among themselves.

Glenroy plucked an apple from one of the bags – he almost halved the fruit with one bite. Sonia addressed Curvis. 'So you lot alright then?'

'Yeah, we're coping,' Curvis answered. 'Had a couple of scares though.'

'All the police and staff have been on our backs,' explained Sonia. '*Come straight home from school. Don't leave the grounds after seven o'clock.* We can hardly go anywhere now. It's like living in Colditz.'

'We heard,' Curvis nodded. 'Thanks, anyway. You've made a friend for life with Glenroy.'

Sonia laughed.

'I s'pose you know that Brenda is going mad with worry about you lot. Especially Carlton.'

Curvis glanced at Carlton. 'That's news to me,' he replied. 'We don't wanna be worrying about that. None of us need girlfriends right now.'

'Yeah,' agreed Bullet. 'Don't need 'em.'

The hum of a car's engine could be heard in the distance. It approached the school. Carlton and Elvin were the first to move. Glenroy swiped the bags before he darted towards the fence. Sonia ran to a corner of the shed. Elvin joined her. They breathed hard. Curvis almost ran up the fence vertically and somersaulted over. Glenroy threw the bags to the other side. Sheer panic helped him clamber over the top.

A policeman stepped out of a sky-blue Panda. Hands behind his back, he ambled into the school grounds. He looked this way and that. The runaways watched him through a hole in the fence. Elvin and Sonia stooped low in the shed. To them the policeman's footfalls sounded like wrecking balls. The policeman halted. He scanned the length of the playground. Elvin closed his eyes. 'If he sees us … gissa kiss,' Sonia whispered. 'He'll just think that we're a couple snogging.'

Elvin didn't know what to say. He tried to kill the smile spreading from his lips. The officer turned around and returned to his car.

'That's a shame,' Elvin said. 'Mellor would've killed me though!'

As Elvin fretted about Mellor, the four runaways hared across the playing field through the gathering dusk.

3.00 a.m.

The night breeze picked up, tossing the leaves of the pines to and fro. Carlton couldn't sleep. He hated it when Curvis ordered the torches to be switched off. The snoring from his friends comforted him. He groped for a torch. He found one near Bullet's head and switched it on. Inexplicably, the beam found the tree where Bullet had gouged Glenroy's sketched image. Carlton shuddered and felt something cold in his veins. He didn't want to look yet he felt compelled to. He looked up at the height of the tree and then returned his gaze to the image. He imagined it coming alive, ordering him to do something. His hands trembled. He could feel his T-shirt sticking to his chest. It *was* telling him to do something. He switched off the torch, lay back down and willed for the dawn. Suddenly, a scream pierced the night. It was Glenroy. His eyes were wide and his face was covered in sweat. He sat up, his back as straight as a board, his head still but his lips quivering.

'Whassamatter?' Curvis asked, reaching for his torch. He switched it on.

'I … I had a nightmare,' stuttered Glenroy. 'A … A bad one.'

'You shit the life out of me,' said Bullet. 'Your scream went right through my brain.'

Carlton tried desperately to control his own fear. He stood up. 'We … we should leave one of the torches on … for Glenroy. Curvis, we'll have to find clearer ground. The forest is really making Glenroy go nuts.'

Glenroy didn't offer any objection.

'OK,' Curvis agreed. 'Glenroy, you sure you'll be alright? It's only an hour or so till daylight. Carlton, give him something to eat.'

Glenroy nodded, grateful that no one had laughed at his plight.

Five minutes later they were eating the food that Elvin and Sonia had pillaged. They ate in silence fish-eyeing each other. Carlton stared at the image in the tree trunk. I wish I could scream like that, he thought. And let it all out. Be honest like Glenroy. But I can't. I just can't. They don't think I'm scared of anything. I'm s'posed to be the strongest. They'll think I'm *nothing* if I scream.

A Perfect Rage

Sonia smiled into her mirror, happy with her hair, which she had just formed into a neat, bunched ponytail. Mellor likes it that way, she thought. She checked her watch and realised she'd better make a move.

At the base of the stairs, Sonia's housemother waited impatiently. She examined Sonia's blouse. 'About time an' all, my lady. You've been late enough times this term and if I find out you know the whereabouts of those boys, then you might as well use beans to try and pay for that skirt you wanted to buy on Saturday.'

'But I'm getting it out of my allowance. It's not your money.'

'You show me a little manners and prove that you're worth the council spending good money on you. And I'm not having you larking about with that Mellor boy; it gives *my* house a bad name.'

'He's my boyfriend!' insisted Sonia.

'He *was* your boyfriend. What's more, my lady, you can forget about that hair grease and shampoo that you asked for. None of my staff know where you can get the stuff anyways. You'll have to carry on using the Vaseline. It's better than nothing.'

'But this girl at school told me I need *proper* oil for my hair. The ends keep breaking and it's too—'

'*Don't* raise your voice to me, Sonia! Haven't I warned you about that? Vaseline is good enough for the other coloured children. I don't hear them complaining. The council shouldn't have to pay for luxuries like coloured hair oil.'

'But…'

'Now, go on with you!'

Before passing her housemother, Sonia stopped and glared at her. She picked up her school bag near the front door. 'Go on with you!' the housemother repeated.

Sonia went outside and the recently cut grass caused her to sneeze. The hot morning sun only added to the fury inside her head. She walked up the incline towards the community centre and spotted Brenda leaning against a lamp post. Sonia quickened her pace. Brenda was dressed in the same uniform and her big frame suggested she was too old to wear it. 'Did you see 'em?' Brenda asked eagerly.

'Yeah, all four,' Sonia answered. They began to walk. 'They've got the bags of food, but we got a scare when a policeman came down in a car. He got out but they were gone over the fence. Me and Elvin had to hide in the shed. We were shitting brick houses.'

'Did you get a chance to talk with Carlton?' Brenda wanted to know.

'Nah, he was chatting with Elvin. They were a bit secretive. They all looked a bit rough. They had marks, scratches and stains all over their faces. I reckon they must be hiding in the hills. Carlton looked a bit wild. Elvin wouldn't tell me what they were talking about.'

'I hope he's alright,' Brenda sighed. 'If they're up in the hills then that's a good thing. Everyone else reckons they went up to London.'

'London? No way. If they went to London they wouldn't have come back here asking for grub.'

'Auntie Cilla still asking questions?' asked Brenda.

'Yeah, all the bleeding time. Especially as I got in fifteen minutes late last night. It's getting on my nerves. My social worker's coming down tomorrow. All because Auntie Cilla reckons I'll be more honest with him.'

'You can't tell social workers anything,' said Brenda. 'You can't trust 'em.'

'Too right! Fuck 'em and the Jesus sandals they wear! She and him can go and fuck themselves.'

'Did you see Mellor last night?' asked Brenda.

'Yeah, he sneaked out about seven. He's losing it. All that questioning is getting to him. He wants to run away and join Carlton and them. He wants me to leg it with him. He wanted me to find out where they are. I've never seen him cry before. I felt all uncomfortable. He kept on saying I'm all he's got.'

Brenda placed a supportive hand on Sonia's shoulder. 'You two won't be in this place forever.'

Sonia started weeping. 'I … I just know they're gonna move him. I just know.'

'If I know Mellor at all, he'll find a way to keep in touch. He always does.'

'I … I let him do it last night. He seemed so hurt. Crying an' all. It hurt. But in a funny way I felt like I was mothering him a bit. It was a weird feeling. Afterwards he was saying sorry. I don't even care if I get pregnant cos if I do, they'll have to move me to somewhere better than here. And they can't stop him seeing me cos he's the dad.'

Brenda tried to raise a smile. 'Who knows? In ten years' time you might be married to Mellor and I'll be married to Carlton. We'll visit each other and go on holidays together.'

Sonia laughed.

9.00 a.m.

Following their breakfast of apples, oranges, Madeira cake and bourbon biscuits, Curvis led his friends to a brook in the west side of the forest. Curvis didn't know the water's source but it ran down off the hills from the south. It was safe to wash here as the clay banks, steeply rising above their heads, shielded them from view on one side and the pines on the other. Stripping to their Y-fronts they swabbed away a day's sweat and grime and took the opportunity to fill their bottles. The water was cold and tasted much better than the stuff they drank from the café's tap.

By mid-afternoon, they had trekked to a field near Spurleigh, where they played two-a-side football, using one of Glenroy's tennis balls. Curvis and Glenroy were little more than spectators as they watched Bullet and Glenroy tackle each other ferociously for possession. When they felt too hot to continue, they threw golf balls to each other. Carlton thought up a gauntlet run where one of them, twenty yards way, had to sprint in front of the others, trying to evade golf and tennis balls; Bullet proved himself to be an excellent marksman, not missing once with any of his throws. He nicknamed himself the Spurleigh Golf Ball Whirly. 'If you don't run straight then you have to stand still and we get free throws,' Carlton ruled.

Curvis suggested that they should target no higher than the shoulders. Glenroy sustained the most hits but he took it in good humour.

They spent the early evening lying on their backs, tired from their exertions. At Glenroy's request, they played 'I spy'. The game died when Curvis spied something beginning with 'H' that flew in the sky. After half an hour of frantic guessing, Curvis finally revealed it was a hobby bird.

'It should've been B,' Glenroy protested. 'It's a bloody bird! Don't know why you have to give them fancy names.'

By nine forty-five p.m., they were hungry but they had eaten all the food they had brought with them. Carlton had a plan. While explaining his idea, he led them out of the forest and into a quiet street. They sat down on a low wall outside a row of shops. They watched the traffic go by. The sun dipped behind the hills that overlooked the town, and the forest to the east was now cloaked in grey; the Seven Sisters barrow hills appeared like a pale ribbon fading in the distance. Carlton dug a five-pound note out of his pocket. 'So you all know what to do?' he asked quietly. He searched all eyes and received nods of understanding. 'Just act normal,' he added. 'Like you're waiting for me to get the fish and chips.'

Carlton led the way into the takeaway, making sure his five-pound note was visible in his hand. Behind the counter was a man of about twenty-five-years old, who Carlton guessed had never served more than one black person in his life. He watched the boys curiously and spotted the cash in Carlton's grasp. He was turning over chips in a heated, transparent container, ready to place them on yesterday's newspapers.

Carlton produced his most innocent smile and looked the shop assistant in the eye. Glenroy paced back and forth behind him as Curvis stood by the door, pretending to watch the traffic. Bullet stood beside Carlton, noticing the tattoo on the man's right forearm – a dragon. Carlton tilted his head and squinted as he studied the price list on the wall. He placed his five-pound note on the counter, keeping his fingers pressed upon it. He spoke in his best Surrey English. 'Can I have steak and kidney pie and chips four times, please?'

'Wrapped up or open?'

'Wrapped.'

Bullet edged nearer to the exit. Glenroy had already stepped outside and Curvis, still standing by the entrance, was humming. Carlton still had his fingers on the note as the shop assistant presented the takeaway meal, wrapped up in newspapers and placed inside a large brown paper bag. Carlton snatched the food, swiped the five-pound note and pushed it into his pocket, then bolted through the exit. Curvis and Bullet had already flown. Carlton soon passed Glenroy. 'We done it!' he exclaimed. 'We done it! Did you see the look on the man's face?'

'Fucking thieving niggers!' the assistant yelled after them.

The boys raced across the road, leaped over a fence and ran uphill across a field. Without looking back, they jogged on for another five minutes until they were out of sight. They stopped to catch their breath. They mopped away sweat, finally resting near the edge of a wood. Daylight had died and darkness spread rapidly over the sky. As they enjoyed their view of the town below, Carlton served their supper.

'Hey, Carlton, did you ask the man to put salt and vinegar on it,' laughed Bullet.

His three friends fell about in hysterics. They finished their food in five minutes.

It was close to midnight when they reached their base. Exhausted, they laid the blankets down. By now, they had their own designated sleeping positions. Carlton sat against a pine, chewing a blade of grass. He didn't want to come back to *this* place. He had wanted to say something during the day when Curvis suggested that they should spend one more night here and he'd scout for another camp in the morning. I'm not sure if I can take another night, he thought. How can I tell the others without losing face? I wanna go back and tell Auntie Josephine about Thomas. I want to confront *him*. Don't wanna wait.

Bullet took out his penknife and searched for a suitable stick or twig to carve. Glenroy played with his tennis ball, juggling it from hand to hand, quietly singing a hymn to himself. '*Onward Christian soldiers marching off to war…*' Curvis looked up to the stars, not believing their caper back at Spurleigh.

Glenroy lost control of his ball and it bobbed down to the hollow. Curvis tried to locate the ball with his torch. Glenroy went off in search.

'Look for the thing in the morning,' said Carlton. 'You'll be searching all night.'

'Nah, I wanna find it now,' replied Glenroy, bending shrubs and kicking away a small cluster of bushes.

'Are you stupid or something?' Carlton mocked. 'Leave the ball till morning!'

'Curvis, lend me the torch.' Glenroy asked defiantly.

'Don't give him it,' laughed Carlton. 'Let him look for the ball in the dark.'

'Shut up, Carlton. You're just pissed off cos you didn't bring a ball yourself. Stop picking on me.'

'If you weren't so stupid, I wouldn't pick on you.'

'Shut your mouth!' returned Glenroy.

'Come and make me, you idiot!' challenged Carlton.

'I don't make shit!'

'Can't we ever get some peace?' pleaded Curvis.

Carlton watched Glenroy climb the hill to confront him. He knew he offered no threat. 'Who are you calling shit? You fucking spastic.'

Bullet tried to intervene. 'Come on, you two.'

'You can talk!' Carlton snapped at Bullet. 'You're always arguing with that idiot. He's as mental as his mum!'

Glenroy was shocked into stillness, his mouth agape. He stared at Carlton, his eyes filling with tears. He shook his head as if trying to rid Carlton's words from his mind. Carlton dropped his head and gazed at his feet. Curvis shone his torch at Glenroy. He started towards him to check if he was okay. Bullet's eyes flicked from friend to friend.

'LEAST MY MUM AIN'T NO WHORE,' yelled Glenroy.

The regret washing over Carlton turned into a boiling fury. His eyes narrowed and his face wrenched with violence. He took in a huge breath, as if he was summoning every bad experience he had ever had. His mother's image flashed in his brain. Before Curvis could separate them, Carlton launched himself at Glenroy, wading into him with a flurry of blows, using all his limbs. Curvis dropped the torch and leaped on Carlton's back, trying to restrain him. Bullet joined the melee, attempting to parry Carlton's blows. Glenroy dropped to the ground. The torch rolled down the mound and rested in the hollow, its beam exposing the tennis ball. Carlton's fury could not be quelled. Bullet was struck by a wayward elbow. Curvis strangled Carlton. 'Stop it! Stop it!' he implored.

'You fucking big-mouth cunt!' raged Carlton, now kicking his helpless victim. 'Why don't you fuck off and play with your girl ghost! You mental divo! She can fucking put up with ya. No one else will!'

Glenroy rolled himself into a ball.

'Leave him, Carlton! Leave him!'

Bullet bear-hugged Carlton, trying to haul him away. Curvis viced his neck. Gripped by frenzy, Carlton lashed out with his feet. 'Uncle Thomas is *right*. You're as mad as your nutcase mum!'

Bullet and Curvis summoned all their strength. They finally managed to wrestle Carlton to the ground, their sweat mingling with each other's and their bodies covered in dusty green. Chests heaved up and down. Heartbeats sprinted.

'Calm down,' Curvis panted. 'Calm down. He doesn't realise what he's saying.'

Carlton glared at the writhing Glenroy, doubled up in pain. Glenroy returned the stare and suddenly something terrified him. The nightmare he had suffered the night before became all too real in his mind. He shook violently. Something told him to run. Run as hard as he could. He scampered off, running aimlessly into the woods, his sense of self-worth shattered, his nightmare becoming a reality inside his mind.

Still breathing hard, Curvis and Bullet wondered where they had found the strength to restrain Carlton; he was still in Curvis's stranglehold. They looked around. They realised that Glenroy was gone. 'Oh, shit!' Curvis looked at Carlton. 'Are you gonna calm down now?'

Carlton closed his eyes. He nodded. 'Yeah.'

Curvis released Carlton. Bullet blew hard and wiped the sweat off his face. Carlton stood up, tears welling in his eyes. He trudged off and sat against a tree. He rested his chin on his collarbone. Curvis found his torch. Bullet looked for his. They glanced at each other, realising everything had gone horribly wrong. Curvis tried to think rationally. 'We'll have to find Glenroy,' he said to Bullet. 'Carlton, you'll be alright? We're gonna find Glenroy.'

Carlton didn't look up. 'Tell ... tell him I'm sorry.'

Curvis and Bullet carefully stepped their way down the mound, cracking pine cones under their feet. They shone their torches this way and that. 'Glenroy! Glenroy!'

Glenroy, who had sustained cuts and bruises to his face, and a dizziness that denied him co-ordination, plunged deep into the thickest part of the forest. Blinded by the sweat dripping off his eyebrows, he collided into trees, tripped over shrubs and felt the leaves lashing his face. He came to a complete halt and tried to listen for something, something that was normal, something that he could recognise. He only heard the terrible cry of a beast, the beast of his nightmares.

His breathing accelerated. He lifted his head to catch more air. His whole body trembled and convulsed. He tried to focus but all he saw was blackness. A blackness that was encroaching, a blackness that was in pursuit of him. 'Help me, Jesus,' he cried weakly. 'Lord help me.'

Tears ran down his cheeks. His mouth was open. He could smell his own blood. Fear charged inside his stomach. The sound of the beast ricocheted in his ears. He could sense a presence. He covered his ears with his palms, only to hear an echoing voice in the distance. 'Glenroy ... Glenroy.'

To Glenroy, it sounded like a young girl's voice. 'Glenroy ... Glenroy.'

The voice seemed to be getting closer. 'Glenroy ... Glenroy.'

His eyeballs darted around like a ball bearing in a glass tumbler. His heart wanted to escape his chest. The sweat encasing his body turned icy cold. He ran as hard as he could, launching himself into the forest, not looking behind, and not caring if his face smashed into a tree trunk or his legs were speared by thorns. Exhausted, he sat down, pushing his knees tight to his chest. He rubbed his eyes and attempted to focus.

'Glenroy ... Glenroy.'

To him it was Gemmele, running around in a glowing white nightdress. She had nothing on her blackened feet. Her eyes were red and her teeth were long and cruelly sharp. Her ears dripped with a goo-like liquid and her bloodied neck was crudely stitched in a macabre, jagged arch. Boils on her face wept blood and she had no hair, only horns. She was gesturing to him, smiling. He slammed his eyes shut and muttered the first prayer that came into his head. '*Our Father Who art in Heaven. Hallowed be Thy name...*' He shivered, not daring to move. Sweat poured off him. Then, he opened his eyes slowly. Gemmele was gone. He noticed his legs and feet were bleeding, but didn't realise that blood also soaked his forehead, mixing with the sweat that fell onto his eyelashes. He felt his supper rising through his chest and pausing just below his throat. He stood up and started to walk, swabbing his face. His brain had regained its co-ordination. He began to jog.

With fear giving him a reservoir of energy, he ran for twenty-five minutes, only pausing when his lungs were about to burst. He leaped over bushes, slid down hillocks and passed through vegetation. He came to a road. A road he knew. Not thinking of his friends, he ran downhill, heading back to Pinewood Oaks.

'Glenroy! Glenroy!' called Bullet, shining his torch around. 'There's no sign of him! What're we gonna do?'

'I haven't seen him either,' responded Curvis. 'Let's double back and check the other side of the camp.'

'Alright!' shouted Bullet. 'But I'm getting lost myself.'

'Stay where you are and shine your torch upwards. I'll meet you in a sec.'

Bullet stood motionless and did what he was told, showering light on the black fingers of the canopy. He heard the rustling of bushes. Curvis emerged. His eyes betrayed his panic.

'What're we gonna do?' Bullet asked again.

'I dunno,' replied Curvis. 'I just don't know.'

Curvis didn't want to admit it, but he knew that if Glenroy failed to return back to the camp soon, they would all have to return and report him missing. There was no way around it. 'Fucking Carlton and his temper!' Curvis raged, his frustration alarming Bullet. 'If he had told us about his mum then none of this would've happened.'

'I've never seen Carlton like that before,' remarked Bullet. 'It's like something took over him. He tried to beat Glenroy up bad. It's *this* place. Carlton wouldn't have done it in Pinewood Oaks. This place freaked him out. And it's made Glenroy go *nutty*. Did you see his face? What do we do? You shouldn't have taken us here. I'm leaving in the morning.'

'Will you calm down! I can't change it now, can I? We've just got to find him.'

'He could be anywhere by now. Say he gets lost? What're we gonna say? I *can't* believe you talked me into this. From now on, *I'm* gonna start giving orders and you better listen!'

Curvis thought for a moment. 'Alright, alright,' he nodded. 'But we still got to find him. Let's check back at the camp. He might've gone back there.'

Bullet agreed.

Twenty minutes later, they returned to their adopted part of the forest. They spoke little to each other on the way, only too aware of their fate back at Pinewood Oaks. They spotted a brooding Carlton, still sitting against a tree, peering unblinking into the dark. Tears smudged his cheeks.

'Has Glenroy been back?' asked Curvis.

Carlton shook his head and covered his face with his palms.

Curvis could not keep his anger in check any more. 'What did you have to go mad for? For fuck's sake, Carlton! You know what he's like, saying stupid things he doesn't mean. But he's *one* of us!'

Carlton buried his head in his arms. 'It wasn't stupid,' he mumbled. He paused for a few seconds before he spoke again. 'It's true … my mum's a slut.'

Bullet and Curvis stared at each other. In the awkward silence, Carlton moved his arms away from his face. Curvis noticed the chewed remains of a blade of grass dangling from his mouth. Carlton looked at Bullet and Curvis in turn. 'Glenroy must've gone back,' he said in a near whisper. 'And at first light, I'm going back too. Apart from saying sorry to Glenroy, there's something I've gotta do.' There was a deep menace in his last words.

'What d'you mean there's something you've gotta do?' Curvis wanted to know. 'This ain't a fucking John Wayne film.'

'You'll find out,' Carlton replied, his eyes unblinking.

Bullet searched for his penknife, found it and dug the ground with it. 'You never know, Glenroy might come back in the night.'

'No, he won't,' said Carlton. 'We can't hope for that. I fucked everything up … sorry.'

'You two go back,' Curvis suddenly cut in. 'I'm gonna stay up here for a day or so yet.'

'Don't be so fucking stupid!' reprimanded Bullet. 'It's *over*! You're coming back even if I have to drag you by your balls!'

Curvis thought about it. 'Sorry,' he said. 'Not thinking straight. Four of us mighty are we…'

'Yep,' Bullet nodded. 'We gotta stay together.'

'This was my idea in the first place,' said Curvis. 'I shouldn't have dragged you lot into it.'

Carlton stared intently into the bush. 'I dunno if I can face him,' he said.

'Glenroy will get over it,' said Bullet. 'He's had it the shittiest over the years, what with him living in Uncle Thomas's house.'

'And because of that,' Carlton said, 'there's no way I'm letting Glenroy take all the flak.' He eye-drilled Curvis. 'And you're coming even if I have to kick your arse all the way back!'

Curvis nodded, the light from his torch exposing his watery eyes.

'Alright,' Bullet said. 'We'll have one more look for him and if we don't find him, we'll leave first thing in the morning.'

Curvis bowed his head. He stood up and restarted his search, tears running freely down his taut cheeks. Bullet and Carlton watched him until he was out of sight. 'He's right, you know,' Carlton remarked. 'It might've been better if he had legged it on his own.'

'Yep,' Bullet nodded. 'It would've taken the SAS to find him.'

Bullet and Carlton set off together. They did not veer too far away from the camp, fearing they could easily get lost themselves. They looked behind trees, navigated bushes and shone light in hollows. Every now and then they could see the beam of Curvis's torch bisecting the woodland; it was a comfort to them. They searched for almost an hour. Hope evaporated by the minute.

Returning to the camp, Bullet turned to Carlton. 'I know we have to go back, but I tell you what, I've had the best days of my life up here, even though it got fucked up in the end. I … I want you to know that.'

Carlton managed a half smile. 'Yeah, freedom felt good.'

'Where's Curvis?' Bullet asked. 'I haven't seen his torch shining for five minutes.'

'He won't get lost,' said Carlton. 'This place *is* his home. It's where he and Stanton had good times. He still misses his brother. I didn't know how much till we came up here.'

Bullet sat down against a tree, stretched out his legs and looked at Carlton. 'What's that something you've gotta do?'

Carlton took his time answering. He finally met Bullet's stare. 'Fuck up Uncle Thomas,' he said calmly. '*Do* him good … I don't want any of you getting involved. This is between me and him.'

Achilles' Possession of Carlton

The clouds had thickened and the air was moist, waiting for a breeze that never came. The green of the leaves and grass in the Pinewood Hills was now a duller hue, and the morning dew took its time evaporating, covering the ground in a light, silvery film. The humid conditions enhanced the balmy smell of the pines. Two hours before, Curvis had risen from a disturbed sleep to search in vain for Glenroy or any signs of his tracks. He found nothing. As he reached the summit of the mound he saw Carlton and Bullet sitting on the blankets, eating chocolate biscuits and speaking quietly to one another.

'No sign of him,' reported Curvis. 'Not even a footprint – the ground's too hard. I hope he's gone back cos if he hasn't … I dunno what to think.'

Carlton licked his dry lips. 'He must've gone back,' he said. 'Stop worrying – when we go back, we'll see him then.' He stole glances at the image Bullet had carved in the tree.

'For how long will we see him, though?' asked Curvis. 'They'll probably move us. Forget probably, they'll *definitely* move us.'

Bullet wanted to change the subject. 'Should we bring back the blankets?' he asked.

'I don't really give a shit,' replied Curvis.

Bullet decided to leave the blankets where they were. 'I'll carry Glenroy's stuff and his drawings.'

'*I'll* take 'em,' Carlton insisted. He looked up to the threatening sky. 'I've been thinking all night what Auntie Josephine is gonna do when she sees me. I don't wanna see her with a whole bag of social workers and all those cunts from the council around me. And Mr fucking Williams. I wanna see her on my own … To do my explaining.'

'I definitely wanna see my social worker when I see Uncle Rodney,' chuckled Bullet. 'He's gonna do his nut, spanner and washers.'

'I don't give a shit about what they say or do to me,' said Curvis. 'I just wanna get it over and done with. I just hope they don't move any of us.'

'So,' said Bullet, searching his friends' eyes. 'Everyone ready?'

'Yeah,' replied Carlton. 'Might as well go now. If we're lucky we might get a hot lunch.'

Curvis took one last look at the camp. He shook his head at the sight of the sweet wrappers, orange peel and discarded crisp packets that littered the ground. He stooped to check the contents of his bag and squeezed in the remainder of his soiled clothing. He closed his eyes and zipped it up.

Bullet gazed skywards and wondered when the storm would break. Carlton folded a pair of grass-stained jeans and placed them carefully inside his holdall.

'Come on, guys,' Curvis whispered. 'Let's face the shit.'

They picked up their bags and started for home.

Forty minutes later, they emerged into the Pinewood Hills road where they saw the bemused faces of four people waiting for a green bus. They turned left and ambled down the hill. Carlton walked close to the kerb and felt a rush of wind as a truck raced by. He glanced at the darkening heavens and felt his heartbeat resonate through to his throat. They passed the William Blake comprehensive school. Pupils played in the playground. They could hear laughter and banter. They knew that the majority of them would return home to a family and a normal life.

At the bottom of the hill they turned right. The Pinewood Oaks water tower came into view. They walked in silence, exchanging fearful glances. Pedestrians were going about their normal business. The buses were full of children going to school and adults commuting to work. As they reached the seven-foot-high perimeter wall that encircled Pinewood Oaks, they slowed their pace. Bullet took the lead and Curvis followed closely behind. Carlton peered into the distance. 'Say someone sees us by the Lodge?' he asked.

'Just ignore them and carry on walking,' replied Bullet.

Bullet glanced over his shoulder at Carlton. He sensed something uneasy. Something violent. 'You alright, Carlton?'

Carlton didn't meet Bullet's eyes, his attention distant.

The entrance to Pinewood Oaks came upon them quicker than they would have liked. They stopped and looked immediately ahead at the Lodge. They spied an old man talking on the phone behind a counter. The man looked up and spotted the runaways. He quickly replaced the phone and re-dialled.

'It's Taylor,' Bullet said. 'He's bound to ring up everybody and tell 'em he saw us. *Cunt!*'

'You'd think Taylor would've retired from working in the Lodge by now,' laughed Curvis. 'He can barely lift up the fucking phone.'

They started once more, walking abreast on the pavement. Sweat poured off Carlton's forehead. His licked his lips again. He stared directly ahead and flexed his fingers. Bullet watched him but didn't know what to say. Curvis walked with his eyes fixed on the asphalt.

Across the fields, Bullet spotted the odd figure in their school uniform. Fifty yards down the road, he watched a six-year-old girl play with a tennis ball outside a cottage. The girl heard something. She turned around and saw a dark blue van motoring quickly towards her. She picked up her ball and got off the road.

Bullet stopped. Curvis did likewise. He lifted his head. Carlton sidestepped to the grass.

'This is it,' said Bullet. '*Stay* together.'

The van accelerated. Carlton sprinted into the field, leaving his bags behind. Rooted to the spot, Bullet hyperventilated as Curvis glared ahead, awaiting his fate. The van screeched to a halt just a few feet in front of Curvis and Bullet. Carlton ran with Olympic speed across the sloping field. Three men emerged from the van. The driver remained in his seat. He looked at the two runaways with disgust.

A man wearing a Mickey Mouse T-shirt and faded blue denims

stepped up to the boys. Curvis recognised him. He was one of Mr Williams's assistants. 'Get in the fucking van!' he ordered.

The two other men watched Carlton disappear into the bushes three hundred yards away. 'What about the other nigger?' one of them asked.

'We'll get him later.'

Without protest, Curvis and Bullet got into the van. They sat down together on a double seat. They dropped their heads. One of the men picked up Carlton's bags. He joined his two colleagues, sitting opposite the runaways. 'We'd knew you'd come back,' one of them said. 'You've led us on a right merry-go-round.'

The driver performed a jerky three-point turn. He steered the van towards the main office. The girl who was playing with the tennis ball looked on from the pavement. Curvis and Bullet wondered if they were returning to their respective cottages, or somewhere else.

Sprinting as hard as his legs would allow, Carlton watched the van race past the community centre from the fringes of the piggery. He didn't have time to ponder Bullet and Curvis's fate. Darting into the bushes, he hared along a mud path. Two hundred yards later and near to exhaustion, he stopped, bent down and placed his hands on his knees. The image of Thomas molesting him had developed into a short film in his mind. Fury charged through his body. His adrenaline called up new reservoirs of strength, giving him the power to run.

He looked up and saw the flat roofs of the nursery. Not even checking to see if the blue van might be motoring up the hill, the sight of his home spurred him on. He only slowed down when he arrived at the path that led to his front door. Someone was watching him from a window. A nursery teacher, preparing for her day, looked on from a classroom. She had never seen him like this before. She ran to the phone.

His eyes spoke of primal revenge. He tried to open his front door. It was locked. He smashed the letter box twice. He pounded his fists on the door. Next door, Thomas watched from an upstairs window.

The front door opened. Wearing a pair of oven gloves, Josephine stared at Carlton. She didn't recognise the hateful face in front of her. She struggled to find words. 'Do … do you know how … how bloody worried I've been about you?' she stressed. 'Mr Williams has just called … He'll be on his way soon. Carlton? What … what *were* you thinking?'

Carlton seized Josephine's arms. 'Just *listen* to me! *Listen!* I haven't got a lot of time. I didn't run away cos of you. And that cunt next door is a nonce. I *swear* to God he's gonna pay. Now you know. So get out of my fucking way!'

Carlton pushed Josephine with such force that her head smashed into a wall. She fell to the ground. Female staff appeared in the hallway – one had a saucepan and dishcloth in her hand. Josephine tried to haul herself up. A colleague ran to assist her.

'Is Glenroy home?' Carlton asked, strangely calm.

Josephine finally got to her feet. She could hardly dare to look at her charge. She tried to meet his eyes.

'IS GLENROY HOME!' he raged.

Someone dialled a phone. Carlton's head snapped towards the person dialling. Two other staff members backed away.

'No,' Josephine answered. 'He … he was very disturbed. He was babbling. We had to get a doctor out. He wasn't making any sense. I'm sorry, Carlton. I know he's your best friend.'

'Where *is* he?'

'Ho … hospital,' Josephine stuttered. 'He's been taken in. It's just temporary.'

'What hospital? Where!'

Josephine took a deep breath. She closed her eyes. Tears were falling down her cheeks. 'A mental hospital,' she said. 'He's been sectioned. They came for him an hour ago.'

Carlton's face tautened. His eyes blazed. He turned around, grabbed the front door and slammed it behind him with all the strength he had, the frame resonating in his wake. He marched to Uncle Thomas's front door. Josephine scurried after him. 'Carlton!

Carlton!' Carlton ignored her. He banged his fists on the door. He tried the door handle. It wasn't secure. He stepped inside. He jumped the three steps leading to the hallway. Pairs of feet trotted up the stairs. Three teachers were running towards the cottage from the nursery. The first spit of rain fell. Carlton sprang down the three steps and slammed the door shut. He heard someone shouting from outside. He paid it no mind. 'Thomas! Thomas, you cunt!' Carlton tightened his fists until his fingers reddened.

Thomas emerged from his study. He held a biro in his left hand. His other hand trembled. The pen dropped. For a long moment Carlton and Thomas stared at each other. 'Carlton. Now calm down. I know I should've apologised. Don't do anything stupid. You're already in a lot of trouble.'

Josephine stumbled into the house. Her face was swollen. Her eyes were full of panic.

Carlton spoke quietly, his voice barely a whisper. 'I'm gonna kill you.' Thomas backed away. Josephine scampered up the three steps that led to the hallway. She bear-hugged Carlton around the waist. Carlton lost his footing, falling backwards. He landed on his side. He shoved Josephine off him. Thomas saw his opportunity. He made for the front door. Carlton sprang to his feet. He set off in pursuit. Josephine was left at the foot of the staircase. 'Carlton! Carlton!'

The rain fell steadily. Thomas slipped and fell over near the nursery fence. A siren could be heard in the distance. The blue van was on its way for Carlton.

Carlton cornered his prey. Thomas raised his arms to protect his face. 'Carlton, please calm down,' he pleaded.

There was a junior cricket bat propped against the nursery fence about ten feet away. Carlton spotted it. He ran to pick it up. 'How many!' he screamed. 'How fucking many! You sick bastard! Enjoy it, did ya? Who are you buying sweets for? Bought anyone a bike lately? Enjoy this, you fucking nonce!'

Thomas attempted to leap over the fence. Before his right foot could land on top of the barrier, Carlton swung the bat in a full arc.

He smashed the side of Thomas's head. Instantly, his mouth oozed blood. Thomas lost his balance. As he fell, he seemed to be moving in slow motion. Carlton struck him again. And again.

Someone ran up to Carlton and tried to wrench the weapon from his grasp. In his rage, he didn't even recognise Josephine. He cracked her square on the chin, the sound resonating in the nursery grounds. She fell to the grass as if shot by a mortar. Carlton turned around, his eyes blazed. He beheld a whimpering Thomas, unable to move. He heard an indistinct voice in his head. *'Do it! Do it!'* He struck Thomas once, employing the full power of his shoulders. He followed through like an ace baseball player. Again and again. A trail of blood trickled over Thomas's beard, collecting in a pool that stained the grass. Thomas lay perfectly still.

Suddenly, Carlton felt many hands grab him. They wrestled him to the ground. He put up no resistance. He dropped the bloodied and concaved cricket bat. His head cracked on the ground. His forehead seeped red, mixing with the drops of Thomas's blood that covered his hands, arms and face. He glared at Thomas's lifeless body. He squinted at his crotch and wished he had saved a few blows for that region. Carlton didn't hear the approaching sirens. He kept his eyes trained on Thomas's dead body. He let out a scream of pain as his right arm broke. His vision became blurred. His five senses suddenly left him. A moment before he blacked out, his brain conjured up the image of Thomas molesting him inside the swimming pool cubicle.

'Jesus Christ!' someone exclaimed. 'Has someone called an ambulance?'

'It's on its way,' a woman replied. 'I don't think they'll be able to do anything for him though.'

Josephine was given first aid by her staff. She watched Carlton being carried away by three men. They flung him inside the blue van, awaiting the arrival of the police.

'Where's Thomas's wife?' someone asked.

'She took one of the kids to school,' a female voice replied.

'Oh Christ!'

Within the next number of minutes, three ambulances and two police cars arrived. Three officers escorted Carlton to the hospital in an ambulance. Josephine refused to travel in one. Thomas's body was placed on a stretcher. A dark blanket covered his face. Other officers proceeded to seal off the whole area and tried to keep onlookers at bay. Staff were instructed to touch nothing. The bloodstained, dented cricket bat lay on the grass near the nursery fence, awaiting expert examination.

Bullet and Curvis were locked in a room with no windows. They sat on wooden chairs. There wasn't enough space to swing a pillow. It stank of muggy, stale air. Book shelves, filing cabinets and boxes of council-headed paper surrounded them. Three male staff silently kept watch over them.

'Did you hear the sirens?' Curvis whispered to Bullet.

'Yeah. I hope Carlton hasn't done something stupid.'

'*No* talking!' ordered one of the guards. His name was Henry. 'You can save all that for when your social workers arrive. You've a lot of explaining to do.'

Curvis spoke slowly. 'Who the fuck are you, telling us not to talk! Last time I looked it's a free fucking world! Or it's meant to be.'

Bullet looked at Curvis and shook his head. He pleaded with his eyes. Ignoring Bullet, Curvis stood up. 'What're you doing?' whispered Bullet.

Curvis didn't reply. He watched Henry take a stride towards him. 'So we got a cocky one,' he said. 'D'you think I'm gonna stand here and take all your lip?'

'What're you gonna do about it?' challenged Curvis. 'You *cunts* are s'posed to be our guardians! You're s'posed to do what's best for us! That's a joke! They should put you on *Morecambe and Wise*.'

Bullet tugged Curvis's T-shirt. '*Sit down and sssshhhh!*'

Curvis didn't even look at his friend.

'You better shut your fucking mouth before I close it!'

Curvis laughed. 'That's real fucking manly of you,' he grinned. 'I'm sure that in the child carers' guide book, it says *must beat up kids if they tell the truth!* Well, *come* on then. You gonna shut my mouth? How *hard* are you?'

Curvis pointed to his top lip. 'Come on! Let's see how hard you are ... You fucking *Sesame Street* reject!'

Bullet could hardly look. The other two guards stared at each other. Henry stepped closer to Curvis, their faces only an inch apart. Curvis refused to flinch. Henry ran his eyes over Curvis's lean body. He spat in Curvis's face.

Curvis refused to wipe the saliva away. He stood his ground. The spit ran down his right cheek, creeping over the corner of his mouth. He could taste it. Behind Curvis, Bullet couldn't move, unable to say anything.

'Is that all you can do?' challenged Curvis. 'Some hard nut you are, you son of an ugly whore! Spitting like a girl. Do you fight like one as well? You're about as hard as soft dog shit! D'you always pick on boys? D'you *fuck* 'em an' all?'

Bullet shuddered, his mouth agape. Henry couldn't take any more. He swung his right fist, smashing Curvis's left cheekbone, knocking him to the ground. Bullet moved quickly to tend to him. '*What* the fuck you doing. You wanna get us killed?'

Curvis managed to stand again. He staggered towards his assailant, the right side of his face reddened and swelling visibly. 'Feel better, do you?' he mocked. 'Will you tell your friends down the pub what you done today? You're a real fucking hero! Let's give you a Victoria Cross! Fuck me! You hit one of the kids you're s'posed to look after.'

Henry hit Curvis with a right and a left, then another right, an uppercut that lifted Curvis off the floor. He kicked Curvis in the head. Tears dripping over his lips, Bullet dashed to Curvis's aid, standing in between Henry and Curvis. The other two guards stepped in.

Painfully hauling himself up from the floor, Curvis stood again. His nose gushed blood. The force of the uppercut slammed his teeth against his tongue. He tasted his own blood and felt a wonky tooth in his mouth. He spat it out on the floor. His left eye was bloodshot. Yet, he advanced again. He did not see Henry before him, instead, he saw his own father. He wanted to distract his father from killing his mother, offering himself as a sacrifice. The vision was crystal clear. He could smell the beer on his father's breath. He could almost feel the whiskers on his chin. His mother's screams blitzed his ears, and as Bullet tried to hold him back, Curvis thought it was his brother, Stanton, restraining him. 'Why don't you try me?' he provoked once more. 'You fucking bully! Is that all you can do? Hit people smaller than you? Why don't you fuck off and leave us alone. We'll be alright without you! Go on! Fuck a dog or something! You animal! You're not a man, you're just a piss-sniffing, crotch-licking…'

Henry launched himself on Curvis. Bullet jumped to his friend's defence, sustaining blows to his body. 'Can't punch *that* hard,' Curvis yelled. 'You fucking wanker! You think you're hard? You fucking animal!'

The two other guards finally restrained Henry. Bullet shielded Curvis. Curvis's nose was broken in at least two places. One of his eyes was just about shut and his lips were misshapen. The blood pouring from his mouth forced him to dangle out his split tongue. 'Enerly,' he stuttered. 'You'll al flucking walanker.'

A guard yanked Henry out of the room and closed the door behind him. Bullet wiped away the blood from Curvis's face. He cradled his head and wept over him. The other guard tried hard not to look.

An hour later, feeling groggy and disorientated, Curvis heard a knock on the door. He turned his head and saw two suited men clutching briefcases. They studied Curvis's battered face. 'They were all fighting and all sorts before we caught 'em,' said a guard.

Bullet heard the remark but didn't have the spirit to contest it. Tears still fell down his cheeks. He wiped Curvis's face with his fingers.

'Ah! The Cavaly,' Curvis whimpered. 'Where youl takling us? Plison?'

The two men didn't acknowledge the runaways. One of them turned to a guard. 'Get them down to the car.'

Holding one of Curvis's arms around his shoulders and helping him to his feet, Bullet was led out of the building and into a waiting car. Incessant rain was bouncing off the windscreen. Standing on the pavement, holding a black umbrella, his eyes unforgiving, was Rodney. Bullet did not see him through his tears.

Ever so gently he laid Curvis down in the back seat. He felt the car pick up speed and was jolted as the vehicle negotiated the road ramps. 'Four of us mighty are we,' he whispered.

Disfigured, Curvis managed an ugly smile. 'I wasn't scared, Bullet. I'm *not* lying. I wasn't scared. I didn't run … I'm gonna be alright.'

PART 4

Till Shiloh
8 July 1985

A lean, coffee-coloured man with dreadlocks stared studiously across the grassland before him. He glanced at his digital watch and saw it was just before ten thirty a.m. He heard, amid the loud hum of the snarling traffic, the high-pitched tone of a skylark. He turned around and watched the vehicles inch by. Away to his right, the congestion on the A40 flyover had not relented since the rush hour.

Wearing black jeans that were now greying and a simple blue shirt over his black vest, the man scanned the drivers of the vehicles, expecting to recognise someone any moment. He gazed beyond the road and winced as he ran his eyes over the harsh, brown exterior of Wormwood Scrubs prison.

It was a warm day. The sun attempted to steal a look through the stubborn cloud cover. The man could smell the over-cooking engines and petrol fumes in the air. 'I hate London,' he whispered to himself.

His diamond-shaped face was underlined by a goatish beard and his eyes seemed too alert to belong to a city dweller. He concentrated on the drivers again. Dangling from his right hand was a plastic bag that contained a paperback and a broadsheet newspaper.

A car slowed down. The rasta ambled over to it. In the back seat, a young woman tended to a child. She had straw-coloured hair and a freckled, pale face. Her chestnut-coloured eyes were round and kind. The man smiled and nodded in acknowledgement as the driver, his brown hair crudely cropped, stepped out of the vehicle.

'You wanna cut off those locks, Curvis,' Bullet hailed. 'You look like a nutter.'

The friends embraced for a long moment, patting each other on the back.

'So you made it then,' said Bullet.

'As if I would miss this day,' replied Curvis. 'I would've hitchhiked from John O'Groats!'

'And you would've stopped at the nearest forest and probably stayed there for the next fifty years,' Bullet chuckled.

'Fuck you,' grinned Curvis.

'Fuck you too.'

Curvis said hello to Bullet's wife. He smiled at the baby. 'How's my little godson?' he cooed.

The baby gazed at Curvis's locks, wondering what to make of them. Curvis turned to Bullet again.

'So what was Live Aid like?' Bullet asked. 'I saw some of it on the telly.'

'Brilliant, especially U2.' Curvis laughed. 'My only problem was everyone thought I was selling weed!'

Linda, Bullet's wife, joined in with the laughter. 'So what time is Carlton being released?' she asked.

'In about twenty minutes,' replied Curvis.

Linda sensed the excitement in their eyes. Since Bullet had been demobbed from the army, she had become the silent watcher as her husband and Curvis reminisced late into the night about adventures involving home-made trolleys, secret camps, forests and hills. She felt a little jealous that Curvis knew more about her husband than she did.

Curvis climbed into the passenger seat. Bullet pushed the car into gear and made the short journey up a side road to a small car park in front of the prison gates. He switched the engine off. Linda took this as a cue to ask Curvis: 'So how's Stanton?'

'Not too bad,' Curvis answered cheerfully, not letting anything deflate him on *this* day. 'He's a lot better than he was. Now and again he gets dizzy spells – it's all the meds they gave him. But he's started to do things for himself.'

Bullet and his wife shared a glance. Curvis continued: 'He'll be alright. I'll make sure of that.'

'You think Carlton will be alright?' wondered Bullet. 'I spoke to him two weeks ago and he seemed okay. But I think he's a bit scared of coming out. I hope he takes to it.'

Curvis made a funny face at the baby. 'All of us are gonna have to help him to adjust. He's still pissed. Who wouldn't be? After all, the judge didn't believe what Carlton said about Thomas. And I'll never know why Elvin didn't testify. We'll have to keep a close watch on him. But Carlton's mentally strong. He had to be, to survive in that place.'

'What're we gonna say when he asks about Glenroy?' asked Linda.

There was silence. Bullet and Curvis watched the baby play with Linda's right index finger.

'Tell him the truth,' Curvis answered finally. 'We haven't found him. What more can we do? I know he's told us we could've done more, but we've done our best. He'll just have to help us. We'll find him.'

Linda nodded. 'Yeah, we will. The system can't hide him forever.'

They looked out of the car window and started to count down the minutes.

'So, what was it like in Northern Ireland when you left,' asked Curvis.

'It was rough,' replied Bullet. 'It was hard to take that most of the people over there hate the boots you walk in cos you have an English accent. I'm glad to be out of it. To be honest I don't get it. They're both Christian, aren't they? If it was left to me, I'd leave 'em to it. Fuck it! I mean, even a small kid would walk up to you as a dare from older kids and spit in your face. I used to wonder what the fuck I was doing over there. And on the other side, Protestants were glad to see us, offering to buy us drinks and introducing their daughters to us. And if you take up their offers, the Catholics look down on you even more. All the shit's not worth it.'

Curvis shook his head. 'The biggest cause of war is religion. Always religion.'

Bullet stared through the windscreen. 'There's so much hate over there. You can just feel it walking the streets, going shopping, going for a drink. They're just like two tit-for-tat gangs killing each other.'

'Seems like you've had enough,' said Curvis. 'You're out now and you can do what you like.'

'I've served nine years and seen the world,' replied Bullet. 'The army has been good to me. It bought me a house, taught me how to strip any engine, and I made some good mates. I couldn't believe how many guys from children's homes I met. We had each other's backs.'

Linda took a milk bottle out of her bag. She lifted the baby onto her lap and the tot began feeding. Bullet watched the prison gates. 'So what about you?' he asked. 'You can't travel around so much now you have to look after Stanton.'

Curvis thought about it. 'Yeah, well. Stanton looked after me when I was a kid. You're right, I miss the travelling around. I loved working in the Lake District doing stuff for the Outward Bound Centre. Wales was good an' all – I helped the scouts up there building log cabins and stuff. Funny that. But I get by. Just the other day I was doing a private landscape job on this big house. Hopefully, when I make enough money, we'll move to the country somewhere.'

'Where would you go?' asked Bullet.

'I dunno,' replied Curvis. 'Somewhere quiet with a lot of green. Maybe the New Forest. I done some work for a rich family down there; they treated me really good. They had a big stone house and they wanted me to do up their front and back gardens – there was enough space for two five-a-side pitches.'

'It's a pity you couldn't have taken Stanton down there with you,' said Linda.

'I told the people I worked for about Stanton and they used to give me the fare to go up and see him. But I felt guilty, you know. There was me enjoying life while my brother is banged up. Glenroy gets to me the same way, even though I don't know where he is.'

'Me too,' nodded Bullet. 'Sometimes I ask myself why did life work out for me? I feel *too* lucky. It's fucked up.'

'You two got nothing to feel guilty about,' Linda cut in. 'Carlton and Glenroy wouldn't want you to feel guilty.'

Ten minutes later, Carlton emerged from the prison gates. Bullet watched him for a long moment, unable to move. He even forgot to climb out of his car to greet him. A rush of emotion overwhelmed him, and without realising it, he shed tears. Curvis leaped out of the vehicle. 'Over here! Carlton, over here!'

Carlton was wearing a tatty denim jacket. His blue, faded denims were struggling to contain his muscular thighs. His thick moustache and beard added five years to his age. A sports bag was draped over his square shoulders. As he stepped out from the shadows of the prison gates, he looked up to the heavens, tasting his freedom. He spotted a bird, fluttering to rest on the prison roof, and smiled. A car horn prompted him to snap his head to the right, realising he hadn't heard a sound like it for so long. I'm *out*, he thought.

Bullet climbed out of the car and sat on the bonnet. Curvis ran to greet his old friend. They hugged each other warmly; Curvis couldn't stop crying. 'Whassamatter with you?' Carlton grinned. 'Don't go all fucking soppy on me! You only saw me three weeks ago.'

They walked together towards Bullet's car almost bouncing with joy. Carlton spotted Bullet. 'You fucking nutter!' Carlton hailed, spreading his arms and enveloping Bullet in a bear hug, lifting him off his feet.

Linda sobbed and the baby didn't quite know what to make of it all. Carlton glanced at the infant. 'I didn't know you were capable. Have you bought him a little uniform yet? Has he joined the cadets? Can he march?'

As Bullet grabbed Carlton's bag and placed it in the boot, Carlton climbed into the back seat beside Linda. He offered to hold the child. 'Linda, how could you let Bullet call him Monty? He didn't tie you up and torture you with a dripping tap, did he?'

Linda burst out laughing. 'It was his choice – but I call him Monny.'

'I can't believe it,' said Carlton, peering through the window at the prison walls. 'I thought I'd never get out.'

Two minutes later, Bullet drove towards the Shepherd's Bush round-about. 'So where're we gonna go? Carlton's gotta have a few beers.'

'Down my way, innit,' replied Curvis. 'Croydon. There's a decent pub just up the road from my flat.'

Carlton shook his head. 'Look, er, it's a nice thought, but I don't wanna spend my first day in a pub.'

'How about we go to an off-licence and buy a few cans,' offered Bullet.

'Yeah, that'll be better,' Carlton nodded.

'We'll pick up the drinks and head for my place,' said Curvis.

'Who won the tennis?' Carlton suddenly asked. 'Did Becker win? Cos of some fight in my block, we lost privileges.'

'Becker won,' answered Curvis. 'He's only seventeen. He wouldn't have won if McEnroe was there.'

'They let us see the Barry McGuigan fight last month,' said Carlton. 'Inside, one Paddy calls him the Nuclear Leprechaun.'

'Nuclear what?' asked Bullet.

'Nuclear Leprechaun,' repeated Carlton. 'Leprechaun's Irish for midget, innit.'

'Yeah, he's good,' said Bullet. 'But that Pedroza bloke looked like he was pushing forty.'

Half an hour later, Bullet motored alongside Streatham Common. Carlton appreciated the clear blue sky. He then looked at the expanse of grass. It reminded him of something from his past. 'Hey, Bullet,' he called. 'Stop the car for a sec.'

Bullet braked and pulled over, his two left-hand wheels riding the pavement. Carlton climbed out of the car while his friends exchanged curious glances. Carlton ambled onto the grass and unleashed an extravagant yawn, stretching his arms wide. 'YES!' he suddenly roared. 'YES!' He stooped down and plucked a blade of grass. He studied it and smiled before inserting it into his mouth. Returning to the car he found his friends laughing. He grinned wide. 'I feel free now.'

'Get in the car, you nutter!' Bullet mocked.

On the journey to Curvis's home, they passed a secondary school where kids enjoyed a break in the playground. The yelping and screaming made Carlton realise he hadn't heard children playing for nine years. A sudden sadness and loss swept over him. He turned his head away and momentarily covered his face with his palms.

'You alright, Carlton?' Linda asked.

'I don't know,' replied Carlton. 'Ask me again in a little while.'

Twenty-five minutes later, after Curvis and Bullet had bought canned lagers, crisps, peanuts, cigarettes, tobacco, cigarette papers and chocolate bars from an off-licence, they pulled up beside Curvis's four-storey block of flats in a small council estate in south Croydon.

Curvis led the way to his third-floor flat, leaving Bullet to get Carlton's bag. Linda winded Monty before carrying him out of the car. Arriving at his unpainted front door, Curvis turned to his friends. 'Stanton's probably asleep – he sleeps a lot.'

Curvis turned his key in the latch and stepped aside to usher in his friends. The walls of the short hallway were painted a turquoise colour. Curvis had fitted beige-coloured ceramic tiles on the floor. Leading off to the right was the kitchen, where there was just enough room to walk around the four-seater pine dining table. Curvis turned right at the end of the hallway and led his friends to the lounge, where the biggest feature was a rubber plant, its top leaves kissing the Artexed ceiling. The walls were painted in a calm sea-blue. Between the sofas was a rectangular smoked-glass coffee table, supporting another green plant. A portable television set was placed on a wooden table in a corner of the room, where on either side of it, Curvis had placed two more plants, their stems coiling around two sticks of bamboo.

Carlton studied the room. 'You're taking this jungle thing a bit too far, Curvis. What next? Stagbeetles?'

'Maybe a leopard?' Bullet chuckled.

Linda took one sofa, laying Monty to sleep. Carlton sat on the other as Bullet set up the beers on the table. 'Carlton,' called Curvis. 'Grab a can then. D'you wanna glass?'

'Nah, I wanna drink out of a can. Makes a change from drinking out of paper cups for so long.'

Everyone picked up and opened their cans. Curvis offered a toast. 'To Carlton, and the muscles that grow on the big bastard. Cheers!'

'CHEERS!'

Curvis went to fetch something from the kitchen. Carlton watched Monty struggle to find sleep. Bullet grabbed a handful of peanuts. 'Couple of years ago,' Carlton started, 'I was sharing a cell with this guy who wouldn't accept any drink at mealtimes. He never trusted anybody, not even other prisoners.'

Linda rocked Monty to sleep. Everyone had eyes for the baby. 'Weird he was,' Carlton resumed. 'He was inside for beating up his mum. His mum's about seventy and this bloke's nearly fifty.'

'Sounds like a nutcase to me,' said Linda.

'Yeah,' Carlton answered. 'Fuck knows why the screws put him with me. One and a half years he was in my cell. When he got out he started to write me letters, telling me I was his only mate.'

'Didn't you make any friends inside?' asked Bullet.

Carlton thought about it. 'Not really. Not real friends. You talk to people and get on, but I never got too close. I just kept myself to myself most of the time. If someone wanted to try it on, then I'd fuck 'em up. Doing the solitary was worth it cos when you come out, no one fucks with you.'

Linda winced.

'There was one guy I kinda liked,' Carlton went on. 'I felt sorry for him. His name was Hilton Daniels and he came from up north. At first I couldn't understand a word he said. His mum was a smack addict and she would do anything to get her fix – she was a lost cause. She wanted Hilton to nick stuff so she could buy smack and in the process, Hilton got addicted too. When he came to the Scrubs, he was going through cold turkey. The screws didn't give a shit, taking the piss out of him and beating the fuck out of him when they felt like it. I'm telling ya, I've never seen a man sweat or spew up so much. He stank.'

Curvis returned and sat down on the carpeted floor, his back against the arm rest of a sofa. He opened a bag of crisps. Carlton continued: 'When I first moved to the Scrubs, I had a fight on my second afternoon. This guy thought he ruled the place and started to pick on me, trying to nick my tobacco. At games, me and this guy had a roll. I fucked him up good and proper. Got solitary again. But it didn't bother me cos I've done it all before – got all the badges. Funny enough, when I came out, me and this guy got on. We used to share our roll-ups. He got out but now he's back inside. He can't handle life outside. It fucks him up. Prison is like a home from home for him.'

Swigging from his can, Carlton was oblivious to the concerned glances his friends exchanged. 'After a few months in the Scrubs, it wasn't that bad,' he resumed. 'Every Friday afternoon, we were led to a building in the middle of the grounds. They showed us films. Some guys used to have a wank if there was anything sexy on. All it would take was a woman in a bra combing her hair in front of a mirror. You had to be careful what chair you sat on.'

'Gross!' said Linda.

'I think I'd stand,' remarked Bullet.

'Bullet, thanks for asking me if I wanted some Rizlas,' said Carlton. 'You won't believe how precious those bits of paper are inside.'

Carlton lit a roll-up, pulled hard and reclined in the sofa. He sighed pleasurably. 'Most of the time we had to use brown paper that we got from recreation. Some guys could roll up tobacco in anything. One guy could use shit paper. He was an expert at it. No one picked on him cos he could roll you up tobacco in anything. Very useful.'

Just then, a shuffling figure emerged from the hallway. Carlton was just about to recall another incident when he diverted his eyes to the lumbering, giant figure of Stanton. Standing six-feet-five with the build of an A-list celebrity minder, Stanton slowly scanned the room, attempting to recognise the guests.

Stanton had a round, bald patch on the top of his head; the hair around it was thick and uncombed. Thick sleep matter stuck in the corners of his vacant, hound-dog eyes, which blinked more than normal. His mouth was agape, his breathing audible. He moved in slow motion. His gaze located his brother. 'Alright, bru', bruv. Who's? Who's these people here? What? What're they doing here?'

Curvis stood up and walked towards Stanton, placing a reassuring hand on his left shoulder. 'You know Bullet and Carlton. Remember? From Pinewood Oaks? Bullet was here the other day.'

Bullet, Carlton and Linda could almost hear the slow whirring of Stanton's mind, trying desperately to remember. Bullet wanted to nudge his memory. 'Stanton! You know me. You should do, cos you gave me a right beating a long time ago. I was well cheeky back then.'

Stanton squinted and thought about it. His eyes flickered into life and he nodded. A slight smile rippled from his eyes as he searched Bullet's features.

'You've grown a bit!' Carlton chuckled. 'I thought I would've caught up with you by now.'

Stanton laughed freely, the deep sound emanating from his stomach. He turned to his brother. 'Yeah, bruv. I know 'em. If they wanna start on you, bruv, let me know. I'll do 'em in for you.'

Stanton shuffled towards the sofa, staring at Bullet and Carlton. Linda made space for him, picking up Monty and placing him on her lap.

'What d'you want to eat?' Curvis asked his brother. 'Egg on toast?'

'Yeah, bruv. Make it two eggs, not three.'

Curvis returned to the kitchen, leaving his friends watching Monty being rocked to sleep once more. There was silence for a few seconds.

'I wish Elvin came to visit me before he killed himself,' said Carlton. 'I might've stopped him from doing it. When I heard about it, I felt sick. I couldn't eat for a couple of days. I didn't talk to no one for ages.'

'Me too,' said Bullet. 'I couldn't understand why he didn't call one of us if he was feeling like shit. I still can't believe it. His wife's in a right state. I couldn't tell her anything. Elvin didn't want her to know. It took him four years to finally tell her he spent his childhood in a children's home.'

'It's for the best,' nodded Carlton. 'It's enough for her that she lost him. No point spreading distress on her toast by telling her about Thomas and what that cunt did to him.'

Linda shuddered. She glanced at Bullet, hoping he might change the topic. Carlton glanced at Stanton, who was trying to remember who the hell Elvin was. 'You know,' Carlton began, 'sometimes I wish I never killed Thomas. If he'd lived I might've had a stronger case. People might've believed me. In a way, I did the nonce a favour. It still gets to me that all the other staff in his house said he done nothing wrong. And it's a good thing I don't know where his wife lives. She must know, cos he wasn't fucking her, he was trying to fuck kids.'

Linda winced again. Bullet stared at the floor. Carlton went on. 'I wouldn't hesitate to kick her face in. She must've known!'

'Hopefully, one day,' Bullet said, 'all the shit that happened in Pinewood Oaks will come out. I've heard stories that Thomas wasn't the only one. That guy he was friends with – the one who drove that blue Mini with the blacked-out windows. Julian's his name. He used to take kids up the top field for football practice. I've heard some sick things about him. There must've been some perv club or something.'

'Yeah, I remember him,' nodded Carlton, picking up another can of beer. 'He looked like a hippy with his long hair and beard, and he was always taking the little kids in his car, packing them all in. It gives me the shits just to think about it. Back then, we didn't have a clue what he was up to.'

Curvis returned carrying a tray of toast, fried eggs and a mug of hot chocolate. He placed the food on Stanton's lap, his locks nearly falling into the breakfast. He then parked himself on the arm of a sofa. Carlton watched him. 'Do you know where Mellor is?' Carlton asked.

'Last time I heard, he was selling drugs,' Curvis replied. 'He moved to Liverpool where he's got two kids with a girl up there.

Sonia went to visit him. He's got a big-time car and was wearing some pricey suit.'

'So what's Sonia doing with herself?' Bullet asked.

'Training to be a social worker,' Curvis replied. 'Can you believe it? Her son, who she had with Mellor, is seven now. I think she still has a soft spot for Mellor, but she's got her head screwed on.'

'Mellor lost a good thing there,' remarked Carlton.

Curvis watched his brother eat his breakfast. Egg yolk dripped down Stanton's chin. He turned to Carlton. 'So you'll be alright at Bullet's house?'

'Yeah, until I sort myself out. I learned about picture framing inside. I'll have a look around to see if I can put it to use.'

'As long as he doesn't snore and ride a bike in our front room, he can stay as long as he likes,' laughed Bullet. 'I hope you don't mind living in Sutton. Nothing ever happens there.'

'Course I won't mind,' replied Carlton, placing his beer can on the table. He lit another cigarette. 'It's got a park with football pitches, hasn't it? And now its summer, I wanna get into a cricket team. Take out my anger on a few wanky suburban batsmen. I really missed sport inside, especially as I was in isolation so much, and I don't wanna see a gym with weights again. I'm fucked off with doing weights.'

'Maybe you can take Monty out for walks in the park,' suggested Linda.

'Yeah, I'll be up for that,' Carlton smiled. 'I'll teach him how to bowl bouncers and be the best sportsman ever. And I'll make sure he doesn't join the army. Fuck all that marching up and down and polishing shoes bollocks. Any Action Men that Monty gets are going up in a firework on November fifth!'

Curvis laughed and even Bullet couldn't resist a smile. Carlton turned to Curvis. 'So you've finally given up crapping in the bushes and tramping around the countryside? I could never understand why you went off to Wales, Cornwall and places like that where black people are as rare as a giraffe. I bet the white people who saw ya are still recovering from the experience.'

Even Linda joined in the laughter. Carlton continued. 'There was one guy in my block who sniffed some kind of paint. Sad bastard he was. I mean, of all the things you can get addicted to. Paint! Poor bastard wasn't allowed to go to art classes – screws wouldn't let him. Sad thing about it was that he was a bit tasty with his drawings.' He paused and thought of Glenroy. 'One day he paid for half a cup of turps with his tobacco. We called him Nasal Angelo.'

Bullet almost fell to the floor and Curvis laughed harder than he had in a long time. Stanton grinned a ridiculous grin.

Pulling hard on his roll-up, Carlton waited until everybody had composed themselves. He eyed Curvis. 'So what are we gonna do about looking for Glenroy? That's the elephant in the room here and he's doing a huge crap.'

Curvis felt the merriment being sucked out of him as he exchanged worried glances with Bullet. Stanton still grinned as Linda gazed at Monty, not wanting to take part in this conversation.

'I've managed to get some mental hospital addresses,' Curvis finally answered. 'Linda's got some as well. They're all in the Surrey area. We thought we'd start there first.'

'You should've started years ago,' Carlton raised his voice. 'Let me know when you're going to check them out. At the time I made a vow that I'd see him again and say sorry. I mean to keep it.'

'We'll find him,' nodded Bullet. 'As four mighty are we…'

On hearing Bullet's chant, Carlton's eyes misted over. Guilt crept up on him. He tried to suppress it but it was a pointless struggle. He dropped his head and stared at the floor. 'I have to say thanks to you lot,' he said in a quiet voice. 'You kept me going when I was going through all sorts of shit. And one of you was always visiting me when you had the chance.' Tears fell freely. 'Even Elvin saw me when I was in Wandsworth. Bless his soul. You lot kept me alive, man.'

Carlton covered his face with his right palm, his sobbing just about audible. Curvis crossed the room and squeezed Carlton's left shoulder. 'You would've done the same for any of us, and even more.'

Bullet gazed at Carlton and fought back his own tears. As Carlton lifted his hand away from his face, Bullet caught him with a look and clenched his right fist. 'I wouldn't have survived what you went through,' he said. 'But you did cos you're the strongest.'

Carlton tightened both fists.

Curvis stood up. 'I'm taking Stanton to the Pinewood Hills tomorrow,' he announced. 'Get some fresh air and get out of London for a bit. Why don't you come with us? It'll bring back some memories. Who knows? Maybe we'll let loose some scout canoes and stone a greenhouse!'

'How are you getting there?' asked Bullet.

'This guy I'm doing work for, I can borrow his car – he don't mind cos he reckons I'm doing up his garden a treat. I'll just say I need the car to get some supplies.'

'Yeah, I'm up for that,' responded Carlton. 'As long as Curvis doesn't set up camp and have us all living up there and tramping around the hills on some sort of hippy yomp.'

Bullet looked at Linda. He waited for her reply. 'Why not?' she said. 'Monty could do with some fresh air too. It'll be a good day out. I'll make some sandwiches and stuff.'

'So no going to the chippy to get our lunch there?' Carlton joked.

Bullet and Curvis chuckled. Carlton downed the last drop of his beer and stood up. 'I don't want you lot to think I'm ungrateful, but to be honest, I can't wait to drop down on a decent bed.'

'It's all made up,' smiled Linda. 'There's a little portable TV in your room as well, and Bullet left some sports magazines on your bed.'

'And you still kept that Michael Holding poster?' Carlton asked. 'The great Whispering Death.'

'Of course!' Bullet replied. 'You think I'd be here now if I lost it? I still reckon Jeff Thompson bowled faster than him though. A hundred miles per hour!'

'And Whispering Death bowls at a hundred and five miles per hour!'

'Oh, God!' Curvis shook his head. 'You two haven't changed.'

Linda picked up a sleeping Monty and held him against her shoulder. Bullet and Carlton stood up and said their goodbyes. Curvis glanced skywards from the balcony as he watched his friends leave, and said: 'We'll see ya tomorrow, Mum.'

The next day

Bullet had to drive with his sun visor down to shield his eyes from the glare; the afternoon heat was nudging ninety degrees. On a country road, five miles out of Pinewood, he followed Curvis's borrowed Citroën. Carlton, his passenger window wound down, and the head wind cooling his face, stared out into the fields, remembering the past. As they passed sheep and cows grazing in the meadows, Carlton concluded that the landscape hadn't changed much. Linda was in the back seat with a restless Monty. Bullet spotted a road sign for Spurleigh – three miles on the next right turn. Curvis palmed his horn in acknowledgement and Carlton smiled, recalling fondly their day out at the open-air swimming pool.

Curvis, who had Stanton in his passenger seat, pointed out landmarks to his brother in an attempt to jog his memory. Stanton only became animated when they overtook a country bus. They climbed uphill, passing large detached houses with individual names on their gates. The Hollies, Brambles, Ash Cottage, Laburnum Meadows. Curvis knew them all, and recollected travelling to his uncle's place on the top deck of a green bus, reading these very names and wondering why they didn't have numbers.

Fifteen minutes later, Curvis drove along a dirt track that wriggled its way into the Pinewood Hills. The trees didn't seem as colossal as before but the scent of the pines and the baked earth invited childhood adventures. Curvis inhaled deeply and closed his eyes for a second. Stanton looked all around, sensing something familiar.

The dried-mud track sharply inclined, cutting into the forest for one and a half miles. It came to a sudden halt at a natural plateau, where the now-named Seven Sisters Café stood. Panting outside the café, gulping cold drinks and wearing tight Lycra shorts and brightly coloured T-shirts, were a group of cyclists. Carlton watched them through the window. He wondered what had happened to the bike that Curvis had made for him for the Pinewood Oaks cycle race.

Curvis pulled up in a small, gravel car park that hadn't been there nine years ago. Bullet parked beside him and took the picnic bags out of the boot. Climbing out of the car and holding a fidgety Monty in her arms, Linda circled on the spot, taking in the spectacular scenery. Looking south-west, she marvelled at the different shades of green fields, bisected by the twinkling Crown Ash river that sliced through the lowest depths of the valley, offering life to the tall reeds and bushes that lined its route. It looped around the southern tip of Spurleigh where a straight row of oaks stood tall and magnificent beyond the hills. Bales of hay specked the green ocean and the isolated farmhouses appeared as if someone had painted them in. 'Wow!' she gasped.

Cows and sheep looked like Christmas cracker toys, and a lonesome tractor, its driver invisible, left in its wake a strip of parched brown field. The still, black windmill, standing in a glade and surrounded by woodland, looked like a dark, misshapen crucifix. Linda thought of Elvin and Carlton and the suffering they had had to endure. She peered due west and saw the best sight of them all: appearing like a golden Loch Ness monster, and with the barrow stones returning the sun's glare with interest, the Seven Sister hills dipped and rose as far as Linda could see, disappearing into an unguessable distance. The leaves in the trees caught the sunlight, reflecting a lucid green. Linda could just make out the faraway outlines of the North Downs that shielded the Sussex border, underlining the brilliant blue sky, and crowned by a ripple of heat. 'It's beautiful here, innit.'

'Yeah,' Curvis answered, smiling at Linda's wonder. He collected an ice box full of soft drinks from the boot of his car. 'The scenery around here always made me calm. But at night it gives you the shits.'

'You can say that again,' said Carlton. Bullet nodded in agreement. 'It ... it *changes*.'

Curvis felt a primal urge to return to the base camp that he had located nine years ago, but thought it would be too far a trek for Linda and Monty. Instead, he led his friends to a nearby glade surrounded by pines and bramble. Bullet laid down a blanket. They enjoyed late afternoon tea underneath a blazing sun, washing it down with Coca-Cola and lemonade.

Curvis had spotted the perfect glide of a hobby bird and followed its flight. He could hear the tuneful songs in the trees from warblers and skylarks, and he wished he could warn them of the peril above. His eyes returned to ground level and he pointed out to Linda the routes that he and his friends had taken nine years ago, while Stanton challenged Carlton to an arm wrestle. Stanton won, leaving Carlton to curse under his breath. Bullet played with Monty, tickling his stomach, trying to teach him to say 'daddy'.

An hour later, when the sun dipped beneath the branches, and despite the Pinewood Oaks children's home having been closed for over a year, the friends decided to visit their former home. As Curvis turned into the complex, he noticed that the Lodge was now vacant and signposts indicated that demolition was about to commence. Oddly, he felt a sudden sadness. Behind him, Bullet and Carlton sensed a similar poignancy. Curvis drove slowly. The deserted fields and unoccupied cottages and buildings troubled him. The sounds of shrieking children, gardeners mowing their lawns, barks of house-mothers and housefathers, screams of foul play during a football game, and the cry of tin-tam-tommy coming from the piggery, was no more than a fading memory. Beside him, Stanton pointed out locations and trees. He grinned as the environment refreshed his memory.

Curvis turned right as he came to the community centre. He almost expected a child to emerge from the bushes and pelt his car with acorns. But there was no one around.

Bullet tailed Curvis into the valley of the piggery. Carlton felt a pang of guilt as they approached the cottage where he had spent his childhood. Auntie Josephine gatecrashed his mind. I have to try and get in touch, he promised himself.

The nursery was still there, its flat roof scorched by the sun. Curvis picked up speed. They veered left into a bend, approaching the swimming pool complex and the top field. A hundred yards away, Curvis could make out the branches and leaves of the sycamore tree, standing in splendid isolation, their rendezvous point nine years ago. He smiled and decided to stop there.

Everybody climbed out – they noticed that the gnats hadn't departed like everyone else. On their left was the southern tip of the orchard – it was overgrown and thicker than they remembered. To their right was the top field. Carlton recalled cricket matches with the onlooking mayor sitting on his throne being fed endless cups of tea and cream cakes.

Just twenty yards from the hedges stood the sycamore tree, its stature imperious and its leaves a browny-green – skylarks swooped in and out. The trunk was as straight as a Buckingham Palace guard, the inconsistent grooves in the bark visible from fifty yards away. Suddenly, Carlton ran for it. Bullet and Curvis quickly followed him. They caught up with him beneath the sycamore leaves.

'What is it?' asked Bullet.

'It's stupid, really,' replied Carlton.

'What's stupid?' asked Curvis, watching Stanton running freely into the field, singing an *Oliver Twist* song. Linda, with Monty hanging on her shoulder, walked quickly to catch up.

'For some crazy reason,' Carlton finally answered. 'I thought I might see Glenroy. Right here.' He dropped his head and stared at the grass. A lone tear appeared on his cheek.

'We'll find him,' Curvis promised. 'Whatever it takes, we'll find him.'

Bullet nodded.

Curvis lifted his head and closed his eyes as his gaze met the sun.

He visualised his mother. Her face was unblemished, so pretty. She was smiling. He now knew that to truly enjoy the most perfect happiness, you had to experience the lowest pits of pain. He had never been so convinced that a guardian angel had been watching over himself, Stanton and his friends. He sensed his mother's blessing on his search for Glenroy. 'Thank you, Mum,' he whispered. 'Thank you.'

Acknowledgements

A Brixtonbard salute to all members of SOSA (Shirley Oaks Survivors Association) and a massive thanks and lasting gratitude to those of you who helped to lift me up when I was flat on my back.

A shout out to those journalists and whistleblowers who kept the lost, unbelieved stories of child abuse in the news despite appalling establishment bias. And lastly, those we have lost in the struggle will never be forgotten.

Alex Wheatle,
South London, November 2017

'Oh children weep no more
Oh my sycamore tree, saw the freedom tree...'

Bob Marley